Freak
Show

JAMES St. JAMES

Freak Show

DUTTON CHILDREN'S BOOKS

DUTTON CHILDREN'S BOOKS
A division of Penguin Young Readers Group

Published by the Penguin Group

Penguin Group (USA) Inc., 375 Hudson Street, New York, New York 10014, U.S.A. • Penguin Group (Canada), 10 Alcorn Avenue, Toronto, Ontario, Canada M4V 3B2 (a division of Pearson Penguin Canada Inc.) • Penguin Books Ltd, 80 Strand, London WC2R 0RL, England • Penguin Ireland, 25 St Stephen's Green, Dublin 2, Ireland (a division of Penguin Books Ltd) • Penguin Group (Australia), 250 Camberwell Road, Camberwell, Victoria 3124, Australia (a division of Pearson Australia Group Pty Ltd) • Penguin Books India Pvt Ltd, 11 Community Centre, Panchsheel Park, New Delhi - 110 017, India • Penguin Group (NZ), 67 Apollo Drive, Mairangi Bay, Auckland 1311, New Zealand (a division of Pearson New Zealand Ltd) • Penguin Books (South Africa) (Pty) Ltd, 24 Sturdee Avenue, Rosebank, Johannesburg 2196, South Africa • Penguin Books Ltd, Registered Offices: 80 Strand, London WC2R 0RL, England

The publisher does not have any control over and does not assume any responsibility for author or third-party websites of their content.

Excerpt from "Evergreen: Love theme from *A Star Is Born*," words by Paul Williams; music by Barbra Streisand. © 1976 Warner Brothers Publications, Inc. All rights reserved.
Excerpt from "Annie's Song," words and music by John Denver. © 1974 Cherry Lane Music Company. All rights reserved.
Excerpt from "(Love Is) Thicker Than Water," words and music by Andy Gibb and Barry Gibb. © 1979 Andy Gibb Music, Brothers Gibb, B. V. All rights reserved.
All paraphrased excerpts appear on page 68.

Library of Congress Cataloging-in-Publication Data
St. James, James.
Freak show / James St. James. — 1st ed.
p. cm.
Summary: Having faced teasing that turned into a brutal attack, Christianity expressed as persecution, and the loss of his only real friend when he could no longer keep his crush under wraps, seventeen-year-old Billy Bloom, a drag queen, decides the only way to become fabulous again is to run for Homecoming Queen at his elite, private school near Fort Lauderdale, Florida.
ISBN: 978-0-525-47799-0 (hardcover) [1. Female impersonators—Fiction. 2. Homosexuality—Fiction. 3. Prejudices—Fiction. 4. High schools—Fiction. 5. Schools—Fiction. 6. Fort Lauderdale (Fla.)—Fiction.] I. Title.
PZ7.S14238Fre 2007
[Fic]—dc22   2006029716

Published in the United States by Dutton Books,
a member of Penguin Group (USA) Inc.
345 Hudson Street, New York, New York 10014
www.penguin.com/youngreaders

Designed by Jason Henry

Printed in USA ∘ First Edition
3 5 7 9 10 2 6 4

Oh! Oh! Wait! Wait! I need to thank people. You HAVE TO THANK PEOPLE!!!!!!!! Of course, everyone at Dutton, Mark McVeigh (my Yoda), Elece Blumberg, and Christian Füenfhausen.

Everybody at World of Wonder, the WOW REPORT, and WOWTV, especially Randy Barbato, Fenton Bailey, Stephen Saban, Tom Wolf, Moye Ishimoto, Steven Corfe, Thairin, Chris, Nicole Flowers, Jim Galasso, and Kristin Rasmussin.

I need to give a big shout out to my posse of online freaks: Alex Allendorf, Christian Ellerman, Suze Rat, Dani Darko, Molly SweetDoxy, Skillz, Melissa Chauvin, and everybody connected with the James boards, and omg I can't forget Bret Clemmant! You all give me such bliss.

Oh! Oh! I need to thank Austin Young for the fab photos, and Eva Posey for holding the light juuuuuuust riiiiiiiight THERE!

ALSO: THESE PEOPLE SHOULD CALL ME: John Witherspooon, Doris Kloster, Gabriel Rotello, Julie Vychulbaum, Maryann Hagerty, Xeon, and Pepe.

Freak
Show

Introduction

HERE WE GO!

Being fabulous, *being relentlessly fabulous*, is damned hard, hard work, I can tell you that much. It requires more than just, you know, platform boots and an ironic tee to cut it in today's marketplace. Yes, fashion is important, and Belgian fashion is MAJORLY important, but it requires more.

Dedication, yes! Perseverance, yes! And a keen eye for details. . . .

For those of you who choose this path—who crave the glamour and attention—and dare to scale those mountains to reach those lyrical heights, I salute you.

I understand, of course. It is a noble pursuit. I plan to dedicate my life to it. I, too, pray that I will someday experience that magical moment when the hair, the outfit, and the party all come together in one glorious explosion of energy. When suddenly it's just you and Diddy and the Queen of England alone in the VVIP room, oh, I don't know, comparing ring tones and whatnot. I have goose bumps just thinking about it. Don't you?

But there is a dark side. One mismatched accessory and your whole night—NAY, your whole *life*—can fall apart.

That, Momma says, is when the runner stumbles.

I can only imagine the holy horror.

Perhaps your belt is too wide or your shoes are too pointy. Maybe your breath smells of goat cheese, or you got a twitchy batch of Botox, and your eyes are vibrating. That's when the waitress at (insert hot restaurant here) will sneer at your failed attempt to be hip and pronounce your look "very November." Suddenly, you've been exposed to everyone as the nerd in biology class who got pelted with spit wads every goddamned day.

It's not a pretty picture.

That's why I'm here.

I'm going to teach you how to be fabulous. It's true.

Now pretend we're going to a big event. Something real ra-sha-sha.

I always find the hardest part about getting ready for a big imaginary event is simply finding the energy it takes to face the mirror. I suggest a few hours of bed rest before starting ANYTHING (preferably with a big bowl of mashed potatoes and the latest issue of *Soap Opera Weekly*). Two hours in bed is ideal. Two hours UNDER the bed is even better. Don't even think about what you're going to wear during this rest period. For now, you must clear your mind of everything.

Now get up—*slowly*—and go to the full-length mirror. Take off all your clothes and look at yourself—*Really look at yourself.*

Now go have a good cry. God is cruel, I know, I know.

That was to let you know what you're up against: reality.

Your goal is to do away with reality. Reality is for poor people. It's for ugly people with no imagination and no hope.

Reality is for everybody else.

You're ready.

Free your mind of doubt.

Here we go.

THE APPLICATION OF THE MAQUILLAGE:

Your face? White! Yes—Look-At-Me White. White like Elmer's

glue! White like an electric snowball! Think Bozo the Clown! Edward Scissorhands! So strong is my conviction, I will not dilute it with warm beiges and soft ivories. If you don't look like a frozen corpse or the underbelly of a trout, then you've done it wrong.

The foundation must be thick and oily—the worse it is for your skin, the better it will look. Pile on pound after pound of it. Slather it on with a spatula—it should be two or three inches deep. *I want to see bird tracks in there by morning.*

Now the powder. White, too, of course. Baby powder will do the job. It's very absorbent, *and you know what a sweaty pig you are.*

Close your eyes and let the spirit lift you up and take you away. Feel the rhythm of the powder puff. *Darling, you're doing fine.* Now, BEAT THAT FACE, GODDAMNIT! Be generous! Be liberal! Throw it in the air and run through the cloud! Put it in a flour sifter and grind it onto your face. More! More!

Your face is a canvas now, blank except for two eyes and two nostrils.

Now for the liquid eyeliner. Start at the inner corner and let it sweep majestically across your lid. *Again,* to lengthen and thicken it. Lift it higher, take it to your temples. Think Maria Callas! Martha Graham! Divine! Don't know who they are? We have a lot of work to do, darling. But no mind! Tonight you could be a *go-go geisha, a glittering Vegas showgirl,* or perhaps a *fashion model from Mars.* Let it rip!

Fake eyelashes? Of course! Three or fourteen pairs. Sometimes, darling, *more* is more. Now here's something new! Fake eyebrows! Start a new trend—cut them out of felt or fake fur. Make them sparkle with glitter.

Oh, you're cookin' now, baby.

Your lips—a slash! A gash of red, blood red—raw like a wound. There's no time for lip liners; that's for sissies. Just do it now.

On the cheeks? Around the eyes? Perhaps a little color?

Technicolor, darling!

And perfume—lots of it. Bathe in it. Make it loud. Make it cheap. Let them know you're there!

Tonight you're a temptress, a siren. You are the lusty Lorelei, luring sailors to their watery graves. Tonight you are a renegade mermaid, a rock 'n' roll fish-mistress with a patent leather fish tail and tangle of Sargasso-green seaweed hair. Anything goes! The sky's the limit!

See how easy it is?

Now. Look at yourself. You . . . are . . . FABULOUS!

If only we had someplace to go!

I

THE SLIPPERY SLOPE OF DESPAIR

Monday:
  There are days that start off just fine. God is in his place and all is right with the world. The sun is shining, the birds are singing, and your hair is feathering just so. You look like Paris Hilton at the MVAs or Farrah Fawcett in her prehag days.
  A little blush.
  A little gloss.
  And you're good to go.

Then it happens. Something goes wrong. Maybe an eyelash won't go on right. Or your mascara clumps. You turn on the TV and you see Star Jones clutching a bloated stick figure, asking you to help fight world hunger, and you start to cry. Your whole world crumbles. Suddenly, you find yourself thinking about ozone depletion, chiggers, and dead babies. You break out in a rash. Your hair goes limp.
  And before you know it, you're hiding under the sink. Oh, it always happens.
  Just like that.

On those really depressing days when nothing seems to go right and the world is caving in on me, I climb into the cupboard underneath the sink and drift into a peaceful daydream. I dream that I'm Mary Hart.

Now there's a happy girl, I think. If I were Mary Hart, my life would be complete. I could dress in crisp white linen suits, hang out on the red carpet, date movie stars and billionaires, and still successfully juggle a career, a home life, and the occasional spot on Letterman.

Sometimes I make believe that I'm married to Alex Trebek and the two of us hold court on the Jeopardy! set. We are to the twenty-first century what Marilyn Monroe and Arthur Miller were to the twentieth. I lend the show an air of elegance, and Alex introduces me to the wonderful world of seventeenth-century literature, famous phrases, and White House trivia. Sometimes I go off and make movies. Other times I just stand around over subway grates. Either way, I'm happy, pretty, and loved—and that's all that matters.

Have I mentioned yet? I may be a little manic. You know: up and down. On the ceiling, under the bed. Shit happens. Of course, some days are darker than others.

Like today. I knew it from the moment I woke up.

You know that feeling—that terrible, awful feeling—that things just . . . aren't . . . right? That supercreepy feeling that something, somewhere, is horribly, horribly wrong?

Is there a dragon in the doorway? An elephant in the living room that no one will talk about? Are there accidental shadows on your walls at night—and what could that even mean?

Try and ask. Try and find out. But while the experts hem and haw, the monsters grapple and claw, and in the heat of the night, you are still alone with your fears.

What to do? What to do?

It's back under the sink for me, where, with any luck, I can stay hidden all day.

⌒◯

KNOCK KNOCK

Oh, dear.

I've been discovered.

It's the maid, Flossie. "Billy, get out of the cupboard. You don't want to be late for your first day of school. And wash off that mascara before your father sees you and has kittens. OUT. NOW."

I scowled loudly and stomped off to my room. I heard her yell after me: "And lose the purple blush. This ain't no disco, kid. It's Fort Lauderdale. You're in the red states now." And oh, how she chuckled at that.

II

So there you have it. TA-DA! The big reveal: I'm a guy, technically speaking. Didn't see that coming, huh? Well, of course you did. You read the jacket sleeve. And even if you didn't, my rather unrestrained approach to makeup might have tipped you off.

So let me just float you the vital stats and we can get on with it.

Name: Billy Bloom.

Seventeen years old. Fabulous beyond fabulous. Total future icon. Gifted, yes, but just short of genius. Mad verbal skills, though. I watch a lot of *Gilmore Girls*.

What else? I'm a sultry redhead with sissy-soft features and a voice like a mink foghorn, I don't know what that could mean either. Just keep it moving, kid. I'm just a wee slip of a thing—118 pounds—and about as sporty as a soufflé. Weak as a kitten. Check out these scrawny chicken wings. Even Mary-Kate Olsen makes fun of them. As a young drag-queen-in-training, my looks are perfect for size four Chanel suits and turquoise eye shadow, but not so perfect for blending with the locals, if the locals are, you know, of the *mulleted persuasion*. . . .

Which brings me to . . .

FLORIDA. The reddest of the red states.

Florida—where 98 percent of the population are ugly, and the other 2 percent are out of your league.

Florida—Satan's strip mall, where even the crustiest crack whore is a registered Republican, and Gloria Estefan is inexplicably the biggest star in the world.

There it is. Here I am. Every once in a while I just have to stop and let the cold, hard truth wash over me again. I'M IN HELL!

(I'm from Darien, Connecticut, you see, birthplace of Chloë Sevigny, so you can IMAGINE my anguish.)

What am I doing here?

I wish I knew.

From what I can piece together, my mother just didn't want me anymore. Threw me out like an old shoe. Said she couldn't take it another day. Said she was at the end of her rope.

Whatever THAT'S all about. Drama much?

She sat me down and started crying, and said it was Dad's turn to deal with me. Time for him to STEP UP, goddamn it. She washes her hands of the whole situation.

Again, I can't imagine what situation she was going on about, but it must have been real to her, though, because two days later I was here in Lauderdale.

That was a month ago, and I've seen my dad exactly twice since moving in. Big house, different lives, you know. So much for stepping up to the paternal plate. It's just as well. He's a growly old goat, and he scares the crap out of me.

So there you are—*la la la*.

I spend the hot, glassy afternoons alone, exploring the house and gardens, looking for fresh places to hide, and cooking up new looks to rock the fashion world.

III

GETTING DRESSED FOR THE BIG DAY

Although my sexuality is still largely theoretical at this point, I hope that I don't actually LOOK gay—you know, all pursed and twittery with big, bulgy, "gay" eyes. It's a new school after all. I need to test the waters first before I break out the tiaras and leg warmers. I've given this a lot of thought, as you can imagine.

OKAY, HERE IT IS. MY OUTFIT:

Don't worry.

It's totally masculine.

Swarthy, even.

Nobody will suspect a thing.

I'm going with a whole retro-new wave/Vivienne Westwood/pirate look. Fab, right? What's straighter than a pirate? Ruffled lace shirt, unbuttoned down to THERE. High-waisted blue pants, practically sprayed on. Nothing gay about that, right? Only rednecks and Eurotrash dare to wear pants that tight and vulgar.

A thrift store military jacket in Prussian blue, a crimson sash, some rags tied in my hair. . . .

Then what? Pearls?

Eye patch?

Cap'n Crunch hat?

Trusty sword?

Gold teeth?

No, no, no. It's all too much. Well, maybe one gold tooth. So, I guess you'd say I was doing more of a "post-pirate" look. I'm a pirate who's getting out of the life. But slowly, you know. I'm lubbin' the land but missing my parrot. Yarg.

MY FACE: I'm going for that "no-makeup look" that straight boys do. The idea, see, is to look "rested" instead of painted. I KNOW. What's the purpose? But this is not an Adam Ant–Johnny Depp pirate. This is a farmer-friendly pirate.

So, no purple blush and just the remnants of mascara. And that's it. Okay, and maybe just a whisper of Soiled Oatmeal eye shadow (NOBODY WILL EVEN NOTICE) and possibly a little glop of gloss. Not even a glop. More like a glip (Wet 'N Wild Sheer Puppy Snot).

DONE! PERFECT!

I want the look to say: I'm not gay; I just flew in from Williamsburg. Where I had sex with girls! Many of them! The kind with boobs! So please don't punch me!

That's what I'm going for, anyway.

IV

A NONFAN'S REACTION

"No, no, no, you did not," Flossie muttered when she saw me. "What is wrong with you, boy?"

"Flossie," I said as nicely as I could, "I think I know a little bit more about fashion than you. This is vintage Westwood. It cost a pretty penny on eBay. Any teenager, in any state, will immediately recognize how cool this is."

"If you say so. Mmm-mmm."

"Are you going to drive or play Fashion Police?"

V

AND WE'RE OFF

Apparently this superprestigious, ultraexclusive school is forty-five minutes away! and located in the middle of a SWAMP! Huh? What? They didn't mention THAT in the bloody brochures. Who would build a school in a swamp? And why hasn't anyone mentioned this little fact to me until now? It's just another sign that this is all wrong. Everywhere I turn, there are little pop-up omens warning me to stop, drop, and get the hell back in my cupboard. High up on this list of bad signs is THAT IT'S BUILT ON A SWAMP. You know a school is suspect if it HAS ITS OWN ALLIGATOR-WRESTLING TEAM. Really, how top drawer can it be? Also, I'm going out on a limb here, but any school that has to issue QUICKSAND WHISTLES? NO GOOD. It's just these *little ominous signs*. Like, you know there might be trouble when the school mascot is AN ESCAPED CONVICT. See, it's a SWAMP. And when chemistry class consists of a COUPLE OF KIDS KEEPING AN EYE ON THE STILL, well, that's no good, either. What kind of place are they sending me to, anyway? Who's idea was this?

"I get it. The Everglades is a swamp. Are you finished yet, Carrot-top?" Flossie said. "We're almost there."

Oh, dear lord.

It was worse than I thought.

As we pulled up, I actually witnessed a Swamp Thing leap from the slime, snatch a student off the sidewalk, and carry her, kicking and screaming, into the bog.

Tough school.

"See," said Flossie, "it's perfectly fine. Go on. I'll see you at three."

Yes, yes. Just another country club school. Could be anywhere. Except for the mutant mosquitoes carrying off jackrabbits. And I still say: Any school that crowns a MALARIA QUEEN just feels wrong.

Sigh.

And so it begins.

One foot in front of the other.

VI

WELCOME TO THE TERROR DOME

1414 Sparkleberry Lane (I couldn't make that up).

And there's the sign: Dwight D. Eisenhower Academy—Home of the Fighting Manatees.

It appears I'm in the right place.

So.

Here we go.

First day of school.

At a NEW SCHOOL.

Starting as a senior.

Christ on a cracker, I am screwed.

One step. Two steps.

Three steps. Four.

I made it all the way to the edge of the well-tended lawn before I lost my nerve. I hid behind a tree and watched as the spectacle unfolded. What I saw was horrible and hypnotic. Worse than I ever imagined. There. In the pristine courtyard. A seething, surging, wreathing, writhing army of upper-crusties . . .

Crème de la Caucasians . . .

Nothing but nothing but Stepford teens in full preen. In your choice of blond or blonder.

Welcome to the WASP nest. . . .

Yes, it was Preppies on Parade: Hi, Muffy! Hi, Buffy! Hey, Binky! Hey, Biff! There's Moose McLettersweater! And his best girl, Abby Add-a-pearl!

Look at them all—impossibly confident, impossibly beautiful, flawless to a fault! All of them perfectly dressed in crisp tennis whites and jaunty golf-wear. They're so beautiful. Look at their perfect skin, their perfect smiles. No zits. No body fat. No split ends or less-than-pert noses. I love them. I hate them. They terrify me. Can I please be one of them?

Are they real? Do they actually walk in slow motion? And are they really always in soft focus? Does the sun actually reflect starbursts in their hair?

Obsenely rich and frighteningly good-looking. Truly a case of God giving with both hands.

But where were all the nonblonds? The non-Nazi types? They can't ALL be Children of the Corn!

Where were the brooding malcontents? How come nobody was wearing black? Where were the stoners and the Goths? Where were the wiggers and the sluts? The K-Feds and the Brit-Brits?

Where were all the saggers, the mopheads, the club kids, fashion fags, robo-trannies, go-go goths, Hello Kiddies, sk8r boys, pixie chicks, hood rats, boho babes, betty bots, electroclashers, giant monster fag hags, Paris-ites, and angry/lesbian/ovo-lacto-vegans? Where is the great and terrible cross-section of teen culture that makes school such wicked good fun?

Well, there must be some sort of special theme today. It must be MAL-IBU STACY DAY or BRING A PROTESTANT TO CLASS DAY.

Or maybe I was mistaken. Maybe the sun was playing tricks with my eyes. I mean, they can't ALL be leggy blond superteens.

I probably JUST MISSED all the culturally diverse kids. Yeah, that's it. It's probably 90 percent Blapanese or Inuit, and they're all on the other side of the building, celebrating Cinco de September third, or something. In full tribal feathers. And maybe a lot of these students are from those superexclusive, PRIVATE countries where you have to be a member to know where it even is. And those types don't look foreign, so you'd never know.

Anyway.

I'm sure this place is just fine.

I don't need to panic.

(Smile.) (Whistle.) (Carry on.)

VII

PRELUDE TO A SLAUGHTER

Oh! Hey! That's interesting! Is that a—? And that! Look! And what's that over there?

I can't get over it! My new school! Why, it's a WHOLE NEW SCHOOL! How exciting!

Just think! New friends! New experiences!

Anything is possible. The world is my oyster.

I'll have to join all the after-school clubs here, of course. Get my fingers in lots of pies. That's how you really meet people. Oh, I hope they have a wig club! And a Jackie O club! And maybe a Salute to Sondheim club! Oh, you gotta have one of those. I should check out the local Gay-Straight Alliance over lunch. I'm sure they'll be a great help to me while I get my gay legs here. You know, back in Darien, I was Mistress of the Robes at my school's GSA. *Good times, good times.*

I should look into maybe getting a trendspotting column in the school newspaper. Or maybe an etiquette column! Everybody loves etiquette! Oh! Oh! And maybe they'll let me set up a What Not to Wear booth in the lunchroom! Oh my God! I've got it! What about Moulin Rouge Mondays and Studio 54 Fridays? Can you imagine? SQUEAL! I'll be a hero.

Now, as for the general decor.

Well, no, no, no. This will not do at all. There's nothing here but poster board and crepe paper. Those are not tools for interior design. So it's a total teardown. Yes, yes. First of all, I'll need to form a committee and get a budget. Then I'll need a theme. Something exotic but familiar.

Chichi but homey. I see fabric draped about, lots of giant throw pillows, purple velvet walls. Sort of a turn-of-the-century–opium den feel . . .

And these gloomy gray lockers—GONE. We'll paint them pink. Yes, pink! Make them loud. Make them gaudy. Pink I tell you! Pink! Like Donatella Versace's uterus!

And we'll put DJs and go-go dancers in the bathroom!

And a Kabbalah corner, for spiritual guidance.

And a crepe bar, everybody loves making crepes!

So.

It's a challenge. Yes. A fixer-upper.

It looks as if I have a purpose. I love having a purpose.

It's up to me to bring a little gay glamour to Eisenhower High. Really "nelly" up the joint.

Room 213 . . . 214 . . . 215 should be next . . .

Well, there it is. There's my class.

There's the door.

Biology with Mr. Reamer. Right there.

I just need to adjust my sash . . .

Fluff my ruffles. . . .

I should have brought the eye patch . . .

Given them a REAL pirate show. Too late now.

Oh! Oh! Here we go! I can't believe it! It's almost showtime now!

Remember: Project big!

And enjoy myself.

Pretend it's a party for me . . .

READY FOR MY GRAND ENTRANCE . . .

DEEP BREATH.

3 . . . 2 . . . 1 . . .

AND . . .

VIII

AND . . .

I threw open the door with a bang and swept into the biology room with a flourish and a bow.

Big smile.

Hold for effect.

AND . . . ACTION!

"Ah, biology," I cried, and threw my hands in the air. "The science of LIFE! Up from the primordial goo and all that! Here we stand, on the threshold of such great knowledge. Don't you feel it? Isn't it TOO exciting? Couldn't you just SQUEAL? *Aude saper,* my friends. That's Latin: 'Dare to be wise'!"

And every head snapped to attention.

Every mouth opened in a perfect O of disbelief.

A captive audience! YAY!

I paused for dramatic effect, then lowered my voice to a quiver.

"Our first day together. I will remember this moment for as long as I live. The sweet, sweet smell of swamp roses, the haunting cry of the swamp loons, the way the swamp light hits all of your faces . . . Truly we are the CHILDREN OF THE SWAMP. Brought together by this magical place. Taking our first steps of this journey together . . . Decoding the very secrets of life, side by side . . . Here's to a memorable year! And sharing it together! HEAR! HEAR!"

AND . . . SCENE!

Then . . . nothing.

Not a smile. Not a nod.

Just glassy, uncomprehending stares.

What to do? What to do?

Well, keep pushing on, of course.

More! More!

Some audiences are just harder than others. Win them over with the old meet and greet. Work the room. Sparkle, Billy, sparkle! This is your moment to shine! Yes, yes, that's it. NOW GO!

I pushed my way into the hub of it, grabbing random hands, introducing myself, making small talk.

"I'm Billy Bloom! How perfectly marvelous to meet you all! How do you do, darling. Divine blouse, yes yes. Pardon me. Oh, hello, how are you? Lovely weather we're having. Hello, hello. Another year, can you believe it? So nice to meet you. Oh, MY DEAR, who does your hair? Well, it's just the most, to say the least. Kiss, kiss."

And on.

Like so.

Why, you would have thought I was backstage opening night at Liza's the way I shrieked and screamed and cried and carried on. I mingled like a maniac. I triple air-kissed complete strangers. I gushed over perfectly hideous outfits. I was a rocket. A cyclone. A force of nature. Next to me, Tara Reid was a grumpy wallflower. I was on fire!

And yet.

Nothing.

Just the same blank stares. I mean, what? Do I have a pubic hair in my teeth? A string of snot swinging from my nose? What is it with these preppie pod-people? Have they never seen a woman of style and distinction before? Do they have a problem with pirates in this neck of the Everglades? Where's that Southern hospitality when you need it?

I was a bit rattled, I don't mind saying. Completely thrown off my game. But still I pushed on.

To no one in particular: "What a lovely school. I'm so glad to be here. . . ." But it rang false, and my words trailed off.

And still the same roaring silence.
Still the same gaping, unresponsive faces.
AS IF TIME HAD STOPPED.

Not knowing what else to say, I made some windy "yes, yes" and "well, well" noises—and dabbed my forehead with a handkerchief. Tough crowd. And I was losing ground.

Okay, okay. Stay calm. Think clearly. Strategize. It was time to pull back. Yes, yes. Retreat and refocus. Zero in on just one person. "With Caesar goes Rome," and all that. I needed an ally. An "in."

Who would be my first friend? I quickly surveyed the cat clique of cheerleaders, alpha debs, Bible belles, and Southern beauty queens. Eeeesh. I wouldn't share my lip gloss with any ONE of them. Then I moved on to the sea of chisel-chinned quarterbacks, WASPy golden boys, Aberzombies, and rumpled teenage fogies. Cute, yes. But not the usual kind of people on my friendship recruiting list. Too well scrubbed. Too Young Republican. What would we talk about? Who's wearing whose promise ring? Not my style. But this was no time for pickiness. My very survival was at stake.

Now, if I were a hungry lioness and this were a class of wildebeests, I would separate the weakest from the crowd and wear him down. And that would be . . .

That one.

That tragic boy—over there, him!—he has been red-tagged for further inspection. Hmm . . . Oh my. Yes. He's a pig of a boy, all right, and a runty one at that. I will devour him.

I mean just look at him: ugly as a boil, face like a frying pan. His face is flat! FLAT! A level surface! And that's exactly why parents shouldn't let children play with anvils! Why, you could pound horseshoes on that face! You could fold shirts on that face! Clearly, he doesn't belong here. He's not one of them. He is the only ugly person I've seen so far. I bet he buys his clothes at the grocery store. Does he smell like he looks? And obviously he gets his hair cut by drunken epileptics. And would you look at those teeth! I've only ever seen teeth like that on hillbillies and demons. And demons wouldn't be caught dead in those shoes.

So. He's absolutely perfect. He'll be my first friend.

I walked boldly over and shook his hand.

"How do you do? I'm Billy Bloom. You can call me Bill or Billy or Bloom or Bloomie. You can call me Silly Billy for all I care. Just call me. Ba-dum-dum." He actually flinched when I spoke, like I caused him physical pain, like I had shoved an oyster fork up his ass instead of introducing myself. I really had an effect on this boy. There was genuine terror in his piggy blue eyes.

So I just started rambling with absolutely no idea what I was talking about. I just wanted to keep the conversation going. Not give him a chance to bolt. I just opened my mouth and hoped words came out.

"You know, I've been thinking of changing my name," I began, when, in reality, it had never crossed my mind. But I was off and running, and who knows where I was headed. "I mean, Billy Bloom is a good name, and all, but I didn't choose it. It was thrust upon me. And I think I want something with a little more ZING to it—something with PIZZAZZ. It needs to be something that will look good up in lights, of course, but also at book signings, on giant cardboard checks, purloined love letters, death warrants, clemency papers; but most importantly, it has to look good on the *Jeopardy!* screens, because NOBODY has a good signature on *Jeopardy!* Anyway, I've narrowed it down to two. . . ." (When I hadn't. But that wouldn't stop me now.) "I'm torn between either Pagan La Rue or Pippin Polyglop—which do you think?"

And I stared deep into his eyes.

He squirmed like a lamb on a meat hook, and said nothing. So I just continued staring into his eyes. I was all up on his grill, as the urban folk say.

"WHICH DO YOU THINK?" I thundered at him, thinking maybe he was mute. "PAGAN LA RUE OR PIPPIN POLYGLOP?"

"Mumble, mumble," he finally said. Good enough. He can talk. But I wasn't finished with him yet. I wasn't backing down.

"And what's YOUR name?" I asked, sweetly batting my eyes. "I mean, now you know THREE of my names, and I don't even know ONE of yours!"

"Uh . . . Bernie," he yelped. He looked at the floor, then looked at the door and contemplated a run.

I smiled a supernova and mentally increased my gravitational pull. There would be no escape.

"Bernie? Well, I'll call you BERNARD. Yes, yes. It's much more distinguished, don't you think? So, BERNARD, what a lovely shirt you're wearing. WHO designed it?"

"Um . . . Camel filter . . . ," he trailed off.

"Oh, how utterly charming!" I cried, and clapped my hands. And then I touched his arm for emphasis.

Well, he LEAPED back as if burned by holy water. He looked up at me and hissed: "Touch me again, faggot, and I'll kick the crap out of you!" And then scurried out of reach.

Wait. What?

Where did that ugliness come from?

Did I lose him that quickly? Was that the same person I was just talking to?

None of this was making any sense. I thought I was making progress.

Oh, but there WAS progress made. Just not in my favor.

It was like the crack of a bat.

POW.

He leaped back, and that was how it started.

He leaped back, and it was the toppling of the first domino.

His angry reaction was exactly the galvanizing force the other students needed, the opening salvo, so to speak. Things happened very quickly then. In every direction and in every part of the room. Plans were organized, weapons chosen, and distances measured.

But first.

Back up. Rewind. If you look closely, in the minutes leading up to the leap there had been an oh-so-subtle change in the climate of the room. Like marionettes coming to life, the students were shaking off their dopey-eyed daze and clearing the cobwebs of confusion. Was it a dream? They rubbed their eyes. *Had there really been a gay pirate in the room, a stranger, air-kissing them, even the boys, and telling them they looked "too divine"? And what the hell was all that about swamp roses? There was some minor shaking and shuffling. A little low mumbling.*

As I spoke to Bernie I noticed the slight increase in the background activity but thought little of it.

Then he leaped back. "Touch me again, faggot, and I'll kick the crap out of you!"

POW!

In unison, every head pivoted back to me. Snap and lock.

And that will unnerve you.

When, suddenly, every redneck eye in the room is squinting at you, you just know it can't be good.

And it went downhill from there.

In unison they shouted: "Holy shit!" and "It's a fucking fag!"

With that, they broke into a series of loud monkey hoots and back slapping and table banging and wall thumping and jumping up and down and onto and off chairs. And not just the guys. Girls, too. Oh yeah. Evil cheerleaders flying through the air, shrieking and leaping like rampaging apes. BANG! BANG! HOOT! HA! WHOO!

They all laughed and laughed and laughed some more. They laughed until I hurt.

Then, individually, each person in the room shouted how they couldn't believe what a fag I was.

"I know!"

"I know!"

"What a fag!"

"Yeah!"

"I know!"

"I can't believe what a fag he is!"

And then, after each person in the class had expressed, for the record, their level of surprise that I was a fag, then speculated on the enormity of my fagginess, they all agreed to agree to a general consensus, saying that I WAS, in effect, the biggest fag that any of them had ever seen before, and FURTHERMORE, it was to be collectively agreed upon that I was probably the biggest faggot they WOULD LIKELY EVER see. And so it was unanimous.

And lo, this brought them great joy. . . .

That was when they began pounding on the desks with their fists—slowly, and in unison now, like jungle drums. Then they quietly began chanting my name: "BILL-EE . . . BILL-EE . . . BILL-EE. . . ." Some of them began lisping "THILLLY BILLY . . . THILLY BILLY . . ." because apparently that was a source of endless entertainment. As their pounding got faster, their chanting grew louder.

Then . . .

It was Goons Gone Wild!

A bumpkin bugout!

As the Junior Klansmen took turns running up right into my face, one at a time, and screaming "YOU'RE A FAGGOT!" into my ear, they sometimes gave me a little punch. Sometimes they spit in my eye.

Yes, suddenly, everywhere I looked, everywhere I turned, I saw nothing but faces, hate-filled faces swarming and looming, wild and out of control, like bubbles boiling in a pot.

From my point of view, it was life out of balance, a mad hallucination, some kind of fevered dream. I couldn't escape the feeling of being upside down, underwater, out of body, anywhere but there.

There was the fetid taste of fear, like tin, like copper, on my tongue, and inside my head, a ringing, a buzzing, like the emptying of a hive . . .

I was teetering on the very brink of sanity, people! For the love of God, please: STOPITSTOPITSTOPIT!!!

This went on for several eternities.

ASTOUNDING FACT: Everything that just transpired—from the moment I made my grand entrance, to the last charging of the fag—all of that occurred in just the FOUR MINUTES AND THIRTY SECONDS before the bell rang and the teacher came into the room.

I can only imagine there was a rip in the space-time continuum that day because those four minutes felt like forty years. And it's still going on, I think, in another dimension right now. It never stops. Evil never dies.

But at exactly nine o'clock, Mr. Reamer strolled into the middle of my nightmare and said, "Welcome, everyone, to the beginning of the school year."

And I realized, for me it was already over.

The teacher entered, and order was restored.

"I'm Mr. Reamer," he said. "Please find a seat, and we'll get started."

As a former musical chairs champion (three years running!), I was able to quickly snatch my seat of choice in the mad scramble that followed—front and center, directly in front of the teacher's desk. Perfectly safe. Always in his field of vision. Always in his shadow of protection. Quick thinking, old boy!

Now: Picture, if you will, four rows of desks. Eight seats per row.

The varsity football team took the back row, forming a solid wall of class domination.

With militaristic precision, the cheerleaders fell into a V formation (with me as the center point).

I was flanked on either side by a couple of nasty-looking alpha debs.

And directly behind me: Bernie/Bernard.

With a sinking heart I realized that instead of being perfectly safe, I was at maximum vulnerability—both my sides and back were open to attack, leaving a full 360 degrees of body exposed. I was accessible to every student in the room.

I had picked the killing chair. There might as well be a bull's-eye on my back.

Mr. Reamer had everybody call out their names so he could create a seating chart.

I listened closely, and for the first time heard the names of my would-be assassins.

ROLL CALL
    Flip Kelly

Bib Oberman

Betsy Kittenplan

Lynnette Franz

Tiff Tarbell

LittleAnne Swafford

Baba Deschler

The Takaberry twins (Dilbert and Dooley)

Bernie Balch

Sesame Blixon

Eustace B. Teeter

Bo-Bo Peterson

Dottie Babcock

Vera LaBree

Payton Manners

Buster Bennet

Sissy Russett

Violet Beauchamp

Buddy "Brute" McGlute

Louis-Don Pettigrew

Reed Runyon

What, are we at Hogwarts? Those aren't real names! They're Archie Comics' characters! What sort of Bizarro world have I fallen into?

I mean, how scary can these people be with names like Baba and Bib and Bo-Bo?

And this Mr. Reamer is a piece of work. He LISPS.
    Loudly.
    Proudly.
    And isn't it typical how HE has a genuine speech impediment, and yet these Bubba Gumps have the nerve to attribute the silly panhomo-

sexual cliché to ME. And I speak with a fluent heterosexual accent, thank you.

He lisps, and has a funny name. And yet, I'm the freak. You know, there's something else about him that's odd. Something about his hair. . . . What is it?

That was when the first spit wad hit.

It hit my neck, slid down my back. Cold. Wet. Disgusting. A tiny wad of evil. It was my first encounter with one, but sadly, far, far from my last. I ended up learning more about the various styles and varieties of said balls than anyone should know.

HOW TO MAKE A SPIT WAD (DUH)

Thoroughly chew a three by three section of paper into paste, roll into tight ball, allow to harden, then top with excess phlegm or snot (optional). The resulting pellet can be spit directly from mouth at short distance, but for pinpoint precision and maximum sting, it's best to use a straw. FOR THE ADVANCED: Fashioning slingshots from rubber bands gives the wad an extra sting and is more suitable to stealth shooting.

ALTERNATELY: To inflict more collatoral damage, pellet should be still soft and gooey. That way when they hit, they will splatter and dry, resulting in time-consuming mess.

FUN FACT: The red ring of a spit wad welt strongly resembles ring-worm! It's true! And multiple welts can pass for measles from afar!

Thip thip thop.
    Thip thip thop.

The steady rain of artillery continued for the rest of the hour.
    Sometimes one at a time, more often in unison, like a firing squad.

Sometimes they struck up a rhythm. More often it was just chaos.

But one thing remained constant. Each shot was always announced with that lisping, little girl voice. From every corner of the room.

"Billy! Thilly Billy!" PLOP!

"Over here, Billy!" PLOP!

"Oh, ithn't biology fabulouth, Billy?" KERPLOP!

"Tho exthiting! Do you feel it?" SPLAT!

"NOW do you feel it?" POW! POP! SPLAT!

"What about this?" KLUMP! (That was a presucked cough drop landing in my hair.)

Behind me Bernie kept up a low and steady muttering in my ear: "Fucking fag, you fucking fag, you're just a fag, aren't you? I'll kick your ass. You better watch out; I'll kick your faggot ass . . . ," and he punctuated each "fag" with a kick to the back of my chair. "Fucking fag, watch your back; I'm going to get you. . . ."

And not once did Mr. Reamer step in to help. Not once did he tell the back row to settle down—no fag-bashing in class, please. Not once did he reprimand them for throwing sticky cough drops onto my hair, a protractor at my calf, and a slew of booger balls—BOOGER BALLS!— rubbed into my vintage ruffle shirt.

But then, why would he?

Anyone? Anyone?

Because they are football players, of course. Because football players are gods, and provide great publicity, and give the school clout. Because the ordinary rules of behavior do not apply to them. They are given a leniency that diplomats crave, and get away with everything short of chain-saw rapes and ritual beheadings. And even then, the odds for acquittal and an apology are in their favor.

No teacher would dare risk being the reason the school lost a game, and thus incur the wrath of an entire community. Teachers who rock the boat have been forced to leave town, so great and unrelenting is the hatred directed toward them.

Only the coach could discipline them. Only he had power over them. So if there was a problem, a MAJOR, LIFE AND DEATH type of problem, it was easier just to go to the coach and then wait for nothing to change. "But I did all I could," at least you could tell yourself, while the little monsters ran amok in your class.

All that was true, yes, but on top of that, it was obvious that Mr. Reamer was a big fan, as well.

That would explain Mr. Reamer's love for the back row. Directing all his jokes and comments to them, and basically playing to them like he was freakin' Cedric the Entertainer.

He was positively giddy with them. Like he was a best bud, a dawg, and a bro. Why? Was there some sort of weird straight-guy flirtation going on? Especially with the one they call Flip—if I didn't know better, I'd swear he was hitting on him.

"Right, Flip?" he'd say after each sentence. And: "Flip gets it, don't you, Flip?" "Bet Flip won't have a problem identifying mitochondria cells, will you, Flip?"

And Flip would sort of "Aw, gee" and "Heck, yeah."

So that's how it was going to play out.

Not once would he publicly acknowledge the flying wads of paper or the ritualized humiliation right in front of him. I watched him as he flicked errant spit wad after errant spit wad from his desk without so much as a frown. A few wads are to be expected, of course. Boys will be boys. Faggots will be brutalized. Blah blah blah.

As the bruises darkened, the welts reddened, and the swelling worsened, I left my body.

I just closed my eyes and let my soul pour out my ears. I was off to a better place, a safer place, a place where the Charlie Manson All-Stars couldn't touch me and I could ponder my situation in peace.

I remembered an apt allegory.
  Or perhaps it's a metaphor.
  It's a little long and seems off-point, but stick with it.
  It's this:

Have you ever seen the movie Poltergeist? *Do you remember when the nerdy ghost buster is alone in the kitchen, rooting through the refrigerator? He comes across an old chicken wing and begins to gnaw on it. Delicious at first, until . . . what's this? What's wrong? Suddenly the wing is covered with maggots. Horrified (to say the least!), he drops it, and it begins writhing and undulating across the counter. By itself. The meat is now ambulatory. And bubbling. It stops, it pops, and then explodes. So does the nerd. He vomits into the sink.*

* But wait. The scary part is still coming.*

* He washes his face and looks into the mirror. He looks like hell. There is a little something, there, on his cheek. He tries to wipe it off. A flick, a fleck, a rip, a tear, and suddenly it's a wound, a gash—**a hole in his face**!*

* There is a nauseous feeling in the pit of your stomach as you watch this. He's digging deeper; it's getting wider; he's gone too far. Much too far. **He's ripping at his face**! Ripping off pieces of meat. **Ripping off chunks of flesh and muscle and tissue.***

* Do you know that feeling? Do you know it all too well? When what starts off as a minor problem, a tiny fleck of a problem, suddenly snowballs into a life-altering tragedy? Because you wouldn't leave well enough alone. Because you had to be you, had to do it your way, had to ignore common sense. And when you hit the point of no return—when you know what you've done but can't stop it, because it won't stop, the hole is too deep, the damage is too great—when you finally realize that you have ripped your face off, you must simultaneously confront the horrible truth*

that you have been the cause of your own undoing. And when you are mired in the pain and self-pity and self-loathing, do you think of this scene? I do.

I was back. Three minutes left of class.

In the final moments I could hear everybody furiously texting their friends in other classes, punching out the story of my big gay appearance and extraordinarily faggy behavior. THILLY BILLY'S BIG ADVENTURE.

And those friends, in turn, began texting THEIR friends:
"OMG, QUICK GET TO RM 216!"
"DID U HEAR?"

Word was spreading quickly.
HOMO ALERT! HOMO ALERT!
After class! In the hall! Hurry! Hurry!
Come see the pirate faggot, watch him flounce down the hall!
You won't believe your eyes!

The crowd was small at first, but it grew. By the second. By the foot. More! And more! Kids everywhere! Suddenly a swarm, like red ants, angry redneck ants.

People pushed to catch a glimpse of the new boy in the mascara and lip gloss and too-tight satin pants that now seemed gayer than gay. Students jumped and jostled and jockeyed for position. They hung from lockers and clung to poles, straining to see for themselves the homo in the pirate outfit.

A flick, a fleck, a rip, a tear . . . getting bigger, growing wider. . . .

IX.V

LET'S LISTEN

"There he is."

"Look at that freak."

"What is it?"

"That's disgusting!"

"Shit, man, it's a guy!"

"What the fuck!"

"Gross!"

"He should be shot."

"Look, Joey, it's your girlfriend."

"Isn't that the guy from *Access Hollywood*?"

"Holy shit!"

"Get out of the way, faggot."

"Look at that."

"We're being attacked by butt pirates!"

"What the fuck are you supposed to be?"

"Don't touch him—he probably has AIDS."

"Faggot."

"Homo."

"Cocksucker."

"Weirdo."

"Is that MASCARA?"

"I don't get it."

"Why do you dress like that?"

"Where do you find an outfit like that?"

"Just ignore it—maybe it will go away."

"What does his mother think?"

"Not from around here, I'm guessing."

"Since when is this a school for homos?"

"Are the Queer Eyes filming here?"

"People like you make me wanna puke."

"I don't get it."

"Why do you dress like that?"

"Where do you find an outfit like that?"

"That's so tired."

"Hey, watch this: Wanna suck my dick, faggot?"

"Fuck you."

"Fuck off."

"Die, faggot."

"Can I take your picture?"

"I must be tripping."

"You're joking, right?"

"Quit looking at me."

"What are you looking at faggot?"

"Let's get out of here."

X

ANOTHER HOUR, ANOTHER HUMILIATION

Next class: American lit.

Only a slight improvement.

Terror Level: Downgraded to Orange. Mild-to-moderate fag bashing expected.

The breakdown: No football players, thank God. In fact, almost no boys at all. Just the Ladies Who Lynch.

The marauding cheerleaders were here, looking like grim assassins

(Are they at least cheery on the field?), as well as a sizable presence of the Muffy Mafia (DEATH WEARS DUCK BOOTS!), and a small-but-poisonous clutch of DebuTAUNTERS.

The biggest turnout, however, seemed to be of Bible Belles, those overly scrubbed Christian girls whose headbands are purposely a bit tight ("Pain is the cleanser! Pain is the cleanser!"), and who obviously picked this class for its Puritan studies. Well, of course. Hester Prynne, Cotton Mather, "Sinners at the Hands of an Angry God"—nothing like a bit of hellfire to chase away those impure thoughts. But don't be fooled by the crosses around their necks; these girls are the coldest of all the cold-blooded killers here today. The worst of the bunch. Because when they're being hateful, they're being hateful for God.

That means there would be no foot-in-the-back attacks or barrage of booger balls here. Instead, this Estrogen Block intends to systematically wear me down with an aggressive campaign of withering looks, hissing whispers, and echoes of "ew."

Ah, but I was an hour wiser now.

There would be no shrieking, double–day-Glo fag attack this time. No wild-eyed theatrical outbursts to give them ammunition. I've learned my lesson. Save the ra-sha-sha "Life is a banquet" crap for a more swish-indulgent crowd. . . . From now on, I keep my mouth SHUT.

I chose a quiet corner desk and tried to become one with the potted ferns. Now, if I only dress in brick-patterned clothing for the rest of the year . . .

It started almost immediately.

I could see much squirming and making of faces and pointing at me and shrieking in disgust.

"Well, it's just so grooooooooooooooooss!"

"I knooooooooooooooow!"

"Would you ever?"

"Ewwwwwwwwwww!"

"Mumble mumble . . . anal sex . . ."

ALL: "EWWWWWWWWWWWWW!"

"Mumble mumble . . . poo . . ."

ALL: "GROOOOOOOOOOSSS!"

A pretty blond cheerleader, the first I've seen smiling, came over to me, shyly. "I'm Tiff," she said.

"I'm Billy," I said warily.

"We were all just wondering"—*giggle, giggle*—"do you eat poo?" And every girl SHRIEKED with laughter as Tiff raced back to her seat, clearly having accomplished her dare.

I was too shocked to answer, but I blushed as though I had just been caught eating some, in fact, *at that very moment.*

They ROARED and repeated and replayed the scenario over and over. "She asked HIM!" "She asked if he eats poo!" "He didn't say no!" "Tiff, you are so BAD!" "You are BAD, Tiff Tarbell!" "Oh my Gaaaaaad!"

I should have told them off. I should have said something witty or wicked or clever or assertive. I should have done something. Anything. Instead, I did nothing.

I sometimes think I'm too delicate for this world.

And then just to make sure I didn't confuse our little conversation as a genuine overture toward friendship, Tiff called me a fag as she walked to the pencil sharpener.

Sweet.

❦

Oh, I am learning to dislike these cheerleaders (or as I think of them, Future Former Cheerleaders). I know they're just stupid swamp girls with dirty minds and hate-filled hearts, and they aren't worth the effort, but GODDAMN, do I dislike them.

I closed my eyes and quietly seethed.

Cheer now, Miss Perkybottom, I thought, *with your pom-poms and panties on parade.*

Cheer now Miss Life-of-every-party, Miss Girl-with-the-most-cake.

Because I have seen the ghost of your Christmas future, and it's in a housedress, watching Passions *with a cat named Touchdown. You are in for quite a comedown, my leggy tormenters.*

For you I see:

Early marriage, early motherhood.

Lost dreams, and a lost midriff.

Boobs drooping with your spirits.

Yes, yes. It's all saddlebags and sweat pants, for all you pretty girls.

Yes, yes, I hope all you mad cows are enjoying yourselves, because time will take my vengeance for me. . . .

XI

AND SO ON

And so on.

The rest of the day passed like molasses.

There was another class. Then another.

Each one a separate hell.

For instance: by the end of lunch, I didn't even feel the hot, steady thud of the Tater-Tots that carpet-bombed my back. But as I got up to leave, I estimated about seventy of them on the ground. *Shocking how little adult supervision there really is in high school, huh?*

NOTE TO SELF: Lunch in the library tomorrow.

Each class was basically different configurations of the same rooty-tooty, rich-and-snooty kids. A few footballers, a few cheerleaders, a few beauty queens, but in less potent combinations than what I saw in biology class, so they were increasingly unfocused, and their anger was diffused.

Still, when the final bell rang, I thought to myself: Well, that didn't go well AT ALL.

It was like *Pleasantville*. But not pleasant AT ALL.

Oh, and in case you were wondering? There is no Gay-Straight Alliance at the Eisenhower Academy. No surprise there. When I went to the front office to inquire, I was informed by a snooty office lady that there has never been a homosexual student in this school, so the issue never came up.

(*ROLLS EYES.*)

XII

Flossie was outside waiting for me when the final bell rang.

"How did it go?" she asked when I got in the car.

"Fine," I bluffed.

"I told you to change." She called my bluff, and flicked a few paper wads from my hair.

Sigh. "I don't know what I was thinking."

"How bad?"

"I gave them the full Liza. The whole Minnelli. The varsity football team might never recover. Even the fat girls hate me."

Flossie laughed, because really, when it comes right down to it, she hates me, too. Oh, yeah. Truly. Deeply. Just loathes me.

◌◌

We drove in silence the rest of the way home. Never thought I would call it home, and never thought I'd be so excited to see it again.

But there you are, and there it was.

Yes, there! In the distance!

The house! The house!

My home!

A few words ought to be said about it. Yes, it's time to tell you about the house now.

Tucked away in the tony South Summit part of town, at the end of a hidden cul-de-sac, on a little peninsula that juts out like a finger in the water. Yes, there! On the banks of the New River Canal, HOME! And its Gothic glamour never fails to surprise me.

It's an estate, but of course we never call it that. That would be vulgar. No whimsical name for it, either. No "Riverbloom" or "Bloom's Glory." No, no, no. It's always just "The House," even though it actually consists of two houses and a gardener's cottage. "The Compound" might be more apt, but no, that, too, would be trying too hard. Just THE HOUSE.

The first house past the gates is the spooky old guesthouse, long since abandoned. It's built in the classic "haunted plantation" style—pillars, porticoes, gingerbread balconies, and verandas—you know: the works. It used to be the main house, back when my grandparents were alive. Back then, see, WE lived in the guesthouse, but as we continued to live there even after both grandparents died, and because we kept adding on various breakfast rooms and game rooms and Florida rooms and sundecks and so on and so forth, eventually IT became known as the main house, and the old main house was relegated to guesthouse status. Got that?

Our house, THE house, is farther down the drive, right around the bend, just up ahead. It rises forth like a mad LEGO experiment spun horribly out of control, or a giant human Habitrail. It's a holy hodge-podge of conflicting periods and styles and colors. There's a little bit of everything: Italian gazebos! Faux-Japanese gardens! An African tree house! There are imposing Corinthian columns up front, a couple of turrets up above, and over there, a great glassed patio.

Inside, it is a home without a center. To the first-time visitor it can seem like a mindless and frustrating maze. Rooms lead into other rooms that lead into forgotten little half-rooms, which might suddenly open up onto a hallway that goes nowhere. It's a dizzying, disorienting place, and if you ever visit, leave bread crumbs.

There are several different "upstairs" areas. One is on the north side, where my father's master bedroom is, as well as his gym, and the various guest rooms and other little dens and studies and blah blah blah. On the west side, there is another second floor, but that one is mostly just used for storage now, or as hiding places for visiting boogeymen. The last upstairs area is located in the south tower. That's my bedroom.

It's accessible only through a nondescript doorway in the back of the house, which is pretty far off the beaten track. You really have to go looking for it. Even if you do, odds are, you'll get lost, or disoriented, or dehydrated, and miss the door altogether.

My room is my womb. A Look Factory! An International Style Laboratory, My Fortress of Attitude! It's the secret lair where I cook up my new revolutionary styles to unleash on the world. . . .

Littered about: dozens of half-finished and forgotten experiments, loose ends, ideas that sounded good in theory but sucked out loud when stitched together.

On the bed: odds and ends and bits and bows and cuffs and capes and clogs and cocktail rings and helicopter hats and whore hose. Look—a basket of strudel-flutes. What do you suppose they are?

Costumes, my God, I've got your costumes right here! A quick inventory: I have a cocktail olive, a glittery green artichoke, a banana, a gay cockroach, a patent-leather mermaid, a couple of different chicken outfits, a can of Coke, as well as all the fixin's for milkmaids, hula girls, geishas, and an eight-armed Vishnu.

Back in Connecticut, I would wear these costumes to the weekly surrealist parties my friends and I would give (where we feasted on barbecued baseballs, porcelain potato salad, and black button stew served on broken shards of glass). And—hoo doggy!—do I miss those days. Funny how a whole world can just slip down the drain, *plip plop*, like it never happened at all. My old friends don't even return e-mails anymore.
(CHOKE.)
ANYWAY. Where were we? Oh yes, these costumes.
I doubt I'll be getting much wear out of them here, but see, I'm stockpiling them for when I move to Manhattan and become an instant cult icon. I plan on wearing them all day, every day, as a matter of course. To the grocery store. The gym. The Department of Motor Vehicles. And why not? Who's going to stop me? You?
By then, my fashion influence will be so great that it will kick-start a national craze for foam vegetable outfits. But by the time Old Navy co-opts it, with Morgan Fairchild in a beaded kumquat outfit for the commercial, I will be way beyond that, of course. I'll be into the post-apocalyptic ragpicker look or whatever the well-dressed Martian microbes are wearing that year.
But whatever the inspiration, rest assured, I will be blazing my own fashion trail.
Skroddle ho!

XIII

Once home, I scarfed down fourteen of Flossie's pecan scotchies and promptly fell back down the rabbit hole. I closed the shades, double-locked the door, and crawled into the cupboard beneath the sink. I stayed there for almost three days (okay, possibly an hour), drifting in and out of reality. I've never felt so low. I remember Flossie tossing in another pecan scotchie during a particularly bad stretch. *She cares so much.*

Everything is different.

Everything has changed.

I didn't know people were like that. I just didn't know.

I saw a whole new world today. It's horrible. Hateful. Danger is every-where. Everyone is out to get me.

I feel like I'm made of glass. I'm afraid you can see right through me. And if I go back, if I have to face that kind of shame again, I just might shatter into a million pieces.

Suddenly, I'm scared of everything. Everything.

THE SLIPPERY SLOPE OF DESPAIR.

I'm afraid of rednecks and hate-mongers and cheerleaders and certain doom. I worry about alligators, bad clams, and booger pudding. ALSO: malaria, cannibals, and antiheroes. I'm afraid of those eerie Oompah Loompahs—who are they really, and where did they come from?

Can I go on?

Lord help me, I'm scared of pickles and pinworms. Earwigs and earth-quakes. Spinning meat. Land sharks . . . sea cucumbers . . . cooties, killer bees, and hissing cockroaches—I MEAN, MY GOD, just look around you. . . . Secret rooms, unwatched candles, Clay Aiken. . . .

Wait, wait, there's more: I hate mutating moles, angry black nose hairs, unintentional dreadlocks. . . .

I'm terrified of most kinds of coffee (but Tanzania peaberry, in particular), ambiguous street signs, bats in my toilet. Snuggles, the fabric softener bear. . . .

Mostly, though, I'm scared of Bernie Balch and the Hitler Youth Brigade in the back row of biology. I'm scared it's only going to escalate from here. I'm scared that by not standing up for myself today, I've set a precedent. And I'm scared because I've never been more alone.

I'm scared because I've never been hated by EVERYONE before. I mean, EVERYONE can't be wrong. Can they? They must all see the same thing.

I think about the orphaned children who survived the great Afghani earthquake a few years ago. They were sent, of all places, to San Francisco. And after the last big earthquake there, those poor kids have become convinced that God is after them. Trying to kill them.

And who's to say he isn't?

Imagine: hiding from God.

I need to get out. To get away.

I want to leave Florida. Maybe go to Africa. Find me some crazy little bushman in the Kalahari Desert. Wouldn't that be bliss? Wouldn't that be wonderful? We'll lead a simple life. We'll drink the morning dew off leaves and toast to our love. We'll frolic with the gazelles and make out under the stars.

One thing's for sure: I'm never going back to that torture chamber again.

No way.

XIV

And now . . .

Oh, manic me!

Up and down, up and down.

The Bi-Polar Express.

BAM! Suddenly, I was tired of my mewling, tired of feeling powerless, and tired of being traumatized. I burst out of the cupboard and took my place at the makeup table. Ah! The healing power of creation.

POUND! POUND! POUND! went the beat onto my face.

SLAP AND SLATHER! Yes!

More goop! More glop!

Thicker! Harder! Darker! More!

Hide the terror! Hide the desperation! Hide the panic!

Tonight's goal? To erase Billy Bloom completely.

Let someone else take over for a while.

Here we go.

XV

Tonight I am many people. You would be surprised.

Tonight I am Kali, Goddess of Destruction.

Who dares to stand before me? Who dares to feast upon my great and terrible beauty? Insolent dung beetle! Stinking canker! I am carnage made flesh! The very manifestation of rage! I am unending annihila-

tion! Your ignorance of my catastrophic power angers me. You are nothing but pus and spew, rot and spoil! I am indestructible and infinite, ceaseless and measureless. I will vivisect you! I will lay you open, slice you into quarters, then feed your moldering carrion to the pigeons in the McDonald's parking lot!

But first, can I tell you what I'm wearing?

I look really hot. My face is a molten shade of vermilion, buffed to a high gloss. My eyes are golden, and so are my lips. I have five pairs of number 201 eyelashes on each eye. I'm wearing a lovely set of horns, all curly and ramlike. I just had them glittered gold recently, and I think they look rather stunning. Especially jutting out from a waist-length black wig. Oh, and I'm wearing a stretchy gold cat suit from, I'm guessing, the seventies.

Anyway, where were we?

Oh, yeah. You clot! You blot! You less than senseless thing! What are you looking at? You are a worthless, foaming curd and a polluted tumor! I am numinous and all encompassing! Glory to Shiva!

Yes, yes, tonight I am many people.

Tonight I am also a Vengeance Demon called to this dimension for the simple reason that if people won't punish THEMSELVES for their trespasses, then SOMEONE needs to do it for them. Otherwise the balance of the universe is thrown off-kilter, and eventually it will wobble off its axis. Last time that happened, Tony Danza got a talk show, Paris Hilton became a star, and Philip left Days of Our Lives. Those were three signs of the coming Apocalypse IN ONE WEEK. So we don't want THAT to happen again.

Just so you know, Vengeance Demons and Destruction Gods look a lot alike. But the vengeance demon opts for a skullcap of silver scales instead of the wig and horns, and he sports a silver cape to facilitate balance during interdimensional flights.

Anyway. Hm. Hm. (Clears throat.)

Obviously, we have a situation on our hands. That's why I was brought here. Regarding . . . (Shuffles through notes.) *Yes, yes. Bernie Balch.*

As a vengeance demon, my advice is to cover him with hundreds of blisters—painful, oozing, abscessed blisters—then roll him, naked, down a gravel road for a couple hundred years.

That's Option A.

Option B is a little harsher. Okay—first you give him a TOTALLY FLAT FACE. Like a pounded veal cutlet. I mean FLAT. So his head is like a meat-loaf pan. Then. . . .

Hmmm?

Oh.

Huh?

I'll be damned.

That's the first time THAT'S ever happened.

Then, at the risk of sounding like a bleeding-heart demon, this boy is clearly suffering already. I'm not sure I can do much more.

With that, I was gone.

ALSO HERE TONIGHT:

Who's this?

Look at me. Gaze upon my face. Do you not recognize me? I am Eve. I am the Fall of Man. (Not the UPN star.) Take. Eat. I bring you your downfall now in delicious turnover form.

Look at me now: I am Mary Magdalene, the only hooker in heaven. It pays to be connected.

I am Lilith; I am Delilah; I am Bathsheba; I am Salome dancing the dance of the seven veils. I am wicked and wanton, and I make my own destiny.

Who else might I be? I am every woman who has been picked on, beaten, or betrayed, who then rose up to smite her oppressor. I am Aileen

Wuornos, but a prettier version, one that looks more like Charlize Theron,
and who likes men, and wears nicer clothes.

I am every woman of power. I am Cleopatra, who totally ruled a third
of the world in slutty, kohl-rimmed eyes, and drank pearls dissolved in
wine for my complexion.

I am Lindsay Wagner, TV's Bionic Woman, and I can hear you,
bitch. I will crush you in slow-motion.

I am all the women whose wicked glamour is both terrifying and
inspiring, whose rotting souls and taste for evil only make them MORE
glamorous, MORE bewitching, and MORE compelling.

I am the White Witch from The Lion, The Witch and the Ward-
robe.

I am Cruella de Ville.

I am the Wicked Stepmother in Snow White.

I am Alexis Morell Carrington Colby Colby Dexter Rowan.

I am Nicole Richie.

And . . . um . . . that's it. I'm really tired.

XVI

OH! OH! I FORGOT! ONE LAST NOTE ABOUT THE HOUSE!
VERY IMPORTANT! CRUCIAL TO THE PLOT! Strangely enough,
as sprawling as the house is, every single room manages to overlook the
river—an enviable thing, of course. Except when it isn't.

The problem? You are always being watched, see. It's life in a fishbowl.

And the worst offender? The bane of my existence? My arch nemesis? THE BLOODY JUNGLE QUEEN! GRRRRRRRRR!

The *Jungle Queen*, of course, is an old-fashioned, Mississippi-style paddleboat that tours the intercoastal rivers filled with approximately two hundred sunburned Yankee tourists.

Back and forth it goes. Back and forth. Six times a day. Each and every day. Rain or shine. Hell or high water.

And the captain always announces us, always blows the horn, and the passengers are always relentless in their enthusiasm. "On your left is the historic home of the Bloom family, one of the city's founding families, who made their fortune in BLAH BLAH BLAH . . ." And then like clockwork, two hundred tourists in flamingo sunglasses and flip-flops begin snap-snap-snapping pictures of me picking my nose in my underwear. It never fails.

BLOOM FAMILY LAW: When that happens, when you have been spotted, whatever you are doing, you must stop and acknowledge the passing guests. Sit up, smile, and wave as if it were the most thrilling part of your day. NO MATTER WHAT. Smile and wave, smile and wave, SMILE and WAVE and stand still while two hundred people take your picture without fail. They are guests in our home, after all. It's only polite.

This can lead to some awkward moments and racy photos, as you might well imagine.

Especially at night when I'm . . . *oh, say* . . . A NAKED GODDESS OF DESTRUCTION who is perhaps in the process of TAPING DOWN MY NETHER REGION! . . . Or taking the chicken cutlet from my bra! . . . or shaking my naked red booty to Hilary Duff!

SNAP! SNAP! SNAP!

People in glass houses, huh?

XVII

★ MORNING, SECOND DAY OF SCHOOL

I am lying under the bed and praying for a terrorist attack on the Everglades, please. Or maybe a natural disaster—any kind—earthquake, tidal wave. Either. Both. Just make it quick. Before nine A.M.

You don't understand: I can't go back there. I won't. I'll hide under here all year if I have to. I'll grow old under this bed. I am NOT coming out.

"Billy!" Flossie yelled up. "Get out from under the bed now, and come down to breakfast!" Then in a rare moment of compassion, she added, "Who knows? Maybe today will be different."

And, WHOA.

You don't know.

From Flossie that's ENORMOUS. She's usually rather stingy in the support department. So if SHE has faith . . .

Then maybe there IS hope, after all!

Maybe today WILL be different!

Maybe it was just the outfit!

Sure! Maybe Vivienne Westwood just doesn't play well in the South. Maybe if I was a bit more "region-appropriate."

Of course!

Something less ironic. Less swashbuckling. With color! Yes! They seem to like color here.

I can do this!

I crawled out from under and threw open my closet doors.

Okay! Yes, yes! Here we go!

SO THE WATCHWORDS FOR TODAY ARE *PREPPY* AND *CON-SERVATIVE*.

And the objective? To blend in. Yes. Blend! Blend, bitch, like you've never blended before. Blend like a daiquiri, like powder and base combined, blend like honey-mustard, or "greige." Blend it like Bleckham, baby!

If you can't beat 'em, join 'em. YES!

Become your enemy!

Ask yourself: "What would Thurston Howell wear?"

I want the look to say: "I am one of you." And: "Yesterday was just a misunderstanding. I don't even LIKE pirates. I'm really ALL ABOUT fifties country-club culture. It's true!"

So I'm thinking: give 'em the old Nantucket Fuckit! YES!

PREPPY 3000—NOW IRONY FREE!

Hair: side-parted, like so . . . feathered in a WHOOOSH . . . sprayed stiff, like Biff. . . .

And to wear: pink-and-green clamdiggers in a cabbage-rose chintz by Lilly Pulitzer (*doesn't get more country club than that!*); pink espadrilles; two polo shirts, one a flamingo pink, the other a lizard green—collars UP; a belt with little pink whales on it; a daffodil-colored cardigan draped over my shoulders, like so! And a tennis racket for effect.

(I tell you, this closet is magical.)

I glimpsed into the mirror and MY GOD! I was one of them! It was TOO PERFECT! Why, I could just fag bash myself!

So, yes.

Today I will be part of the parade, not part of the pavement.

Why, they'll probably apologize for their mistake and ask me to join them for lunch.

AND BY THE POWER OF GRAYSKULL, I WILL BE ACCEPTED!

Flossie just shook her head when she saw it, and asked if I was absolutely sure. *(Flossie giveth, and Flossie taketh away.)*
   "Oh yes, I know what I'm doing."
   And we left for school.

∽◯

Needless to say, there were no apologies, no luncheon invitations, and I was part of the pavement, not part of the parade. Apparently, my pink and green was the wrong pink and green. I don't get it, either. When I walked through the door, cocky as can be, they hooted and stomped like I was in full Bree Van De Kamp drag.
   And I was so sure of myself!
   I JUST DON'T GET IT!

These howling hayseeds! These stinking savages! Who the hell are THEY to single ME out? Do they have fish chum for brains? Look around! There are others who should be singled out before me. Look at Bernie!

How does he fit in? How is it that this BULLDOG of a boy who looks as if he ran face-first into a Mack truck—how is HE rude to ME? How dare that creepy Clampett turn on me! I was nice to him! I offered him friendship! Told him his shirt was nice! And . . . um . . . it WASN'T!

Isn't there a Department of Arbitrary Social Hierarchy I can appeal to?

And anyway, isn't there someone else here MORE WORTHY of your homo-hysteria? YES! Look around! I'm talking about Mr. Reamer!

HELLO! His name is REAMER, for God's sake! You don't see anything funny in THAT? Or haven't you noticed? And then there's that lisp! A lisping reamer! Do I have to draw you a map, people? And if that isn't enough, I figured out what was odd about his hair. It's a perm! He perms his goddamn hair! Oh! Oh! Grow up! Of course he does! He looks like Richard freaking Simmons!

And I'm the one you have a problem with?

TRUE CONFESSION: What troubles me the most about the Backseat Boys—well, besides the fact that they're all raging, psychotic thugs—is that they ARE ALL SO BEAUTIFUL.

Yes!

God help me!

Each and every one of the boys in back is a total humpmuffin. Well, except for Flatsy McFlatface, of course. But the others! . . . My God! Why is evil always so damn sexy?

And while they are all slobber-worthy, there is one boy who's in another league altogether. A boy whose wild, supernatural beauty is for the ages. That one, there, quick, with the white blond hair, and the flushed red cheeks, and the petal white skin—well, he's just TOO BEAUTIFUL! Like Malibu Ken brought to life, but BETTER! He makes all the other beautiful boys look like Tom Arnold.

Seriously, it HURTS to look at him. It actually hurts HERE (*Thump!*) to look at him. I just want to chew on his lips. And lick him a little bit.

Oh, I'm such a masochist!

I think that's the one they call Flip Kelly. The one that everyone acts all ga-ga around.

XVIII

RECAP

I just can't do it. I can't go on recounting every incident of abuse, every day. It's too painful. Too emotionally scarring. So here, instead, is just a quick overview to keep you updated.

FIRST WEEK'S TALLY OF BALLISTIC WEAPONRY:

Rubber bands, erasers, paper clips, pennies, pencils, pens, Gummi bears, M&M's, Tic Tacs, Yu-Gi-Oh pogs, maxi pads, mini pads, scrunchies, ketchup in a condom, cough drops, thumbtacks, a dead frog, birdseed pellets, food pellets, dirt clods, large and small rocks, swamp berries, golf balls, tennis balls, chewing tobacco, dog shit, bird shit, hamster shit, fish tank algae, and more booger balls than I care to count.

FOOD ITEMS FOUND IN HAIR AND, OCCASIONALLY, MY UNDERPANTS:

Tater Tots, peas, banana–fish-stick mash, peanut-butter-covered tofu balls, milk–meat-loaf–lima-bean paste.

(This is not counting the gym socks in my mouth or the dead lizard up my nose.)

INJURIES SUSTAINED:

23 punches to the upper arm in EXACTLY the same place
6 donkey punches to the stomach
1 old-fashioned foot stomping
1 protractor stabbing, right calf
1 purple grid pattern on my right temple — the result of cleated golf shoes.
1 palm-frond whipping

MOST HUMILIATING INCIDENT:

Well, there was a chair leg that almost took my virginity, courtesy of the Takaberry twins . . . any number of wedgies, including the one that actually ripped the Underoos OFF MY BODY. . . . But the most humiliating was being forced by Bib Oberman to say "I'm a thilly faggot who loves it when you hit me" twenty times in front of the cheerleaders. As Bib hit me, of course. Twenty times. I just hate him so much. But he's really hot, though. Have I mentioned that? I hate him, but he's hot. It's SO CONFUSING.

MEANEST GUY:

Bernie Balch has only a slight lead over Bib Oberman. But that's sort of like saying Darth Vader is slightly meaner than Ming the Merciless. Or a great white shark is just slightly nastier than a polar bear. Why quibble when you're the one being eaten alive?

MEANEST GIRL:

Hands down, Tiff Tarbell—her sunny good looks and coal black heart make her the Klaus Barbie doll of my darkest dreams. Why, when she smiles and goes in for the kill, it's like being disemboweled by Jessica Simpson! YOU JUST NEVER EXPECT IT. Of course, that Lynnette Franz is a real piece of work, too. But she has that sharp and snarly look about her, anyway, so that you expect her to be a bit nastier.

XIX

POOR ME

I take the bus now.

Trusty number 12—The Eisenhower Express.

Flossie put down her foot—*KER-CLOMP!*—and told my dad: "Never again!" She said that driving me forty-five minutes there and back, every damn day, was just too much. By the time she got back to the house, there wasn't time to lick the butter off a knife before she had to turn around and drive back to get me. Gave her a headache, she said. *KER-CLOMP!*

So now I'm a bus monkey. Yep. Ridin' the big banana. Old Yeller.

Four sad-sack losers and me, and that's it. We are the only five kids IN SCHOOL who do not have cars of our own.

Pretty pathetic, huh?

You'd think that would be a common bond that might bring us together. That we might even start our own little "Breakfast Club." But, oh no. There is nothing even remotely fun about this ride. And why is that? Because even THESE geeks won't have anything to do with me. Yes, I am rejected by the school rejects. Even among the friendless, I am friendless.

So every day I sit and stare out the window at the passing landscape. It's not much to look at. Nothing but palm trees, meth labs, monster trucks, and boiled-peanut stands . . . then, IHOP after IHOP after IHOP. . . .

Terror mounts with each passing mile. What fresh hell awaits me today? A scream begins to build in my throat around the Bobblewood exit. Then when we pass Ezaline's Laundry and Tacos, I quickly try and think happy thoughts: *birthdays, rainbows, bunny rabbits, Super Hold Aqua Net, tap-dancing grannies, Cinnamon Pop-Tarts, warm summer breezes, meteor rocks falling on the back row of biology, obliterating everyone but Flip Kelly . . .*

The bus stops. I exit. I walk the 148 steps it takes to get to biology class. The first spit wad hits my neck before I even sit down. It slides down my shirt and remains a wet, cold presence for the rest of the class.

AND THE BEAT GOES ON.

XX

NEWS FLASH!

I made a friend!

I know! Me!

A girl. Her name is Blah Blah Blah.

That's what it sounded like, anyway. "My name is Blah Blah Blah," she whispered to me in the hall, and motioned for me to follow her behind the lockers. "Quickly! Quickly!" she hissed. A friend maybe, but not one who would risk being seen with me, yet.

"It's just TERRIBLE how they treat you," she said. "I'm so AWFULLY sorry. It just makes me sick. What HORRIBLE beasts they are." She was in a terrible rush, but we could meet in the library over lunch, where we could talk some more. "Not EVERYONE here is a jerk."

Then she zipped off, making absolutely sure no one had seen her talking to me.

So cloak and dagger!

A secret friend!

Things are looking up!

Later on, when I met up with her in the library, we hid behind the microfiche, and I was able to get a better look at my new friend. Plain, but perky. Blah Blah Blah suits her. Blah Blah Blah she'll remain. But who am I to judge? She's an angel. A savior. I should love her like a sister and clutch her to my bosom. "God bless you," I tell her.

She started whispering up a storm. Whispered like it was going out of style. She whispered as if her life depended on it.

This is what she said:

"This school is a terrible place," she said. "Full of terrible people."

"Oh, really? I hadn't noticed."

"No really," she said. "This school is the last stop for rich kids that no one else will have. Spoiled brats with anger issues and social integration problems. And it's so expensive because they know they can name their price. What are the parents going to do? Homeschool them?

Yes, it's forty-seven miles from Fort Lauderdale, but that's the selling point, see. In fact, 90 percent of the student body commutes from Lauderdale every day. Most of them probably South Summit residents—i.e., the forgotten children of Fort Lauderdale's rich and fatuous. The commonly accepted reason for sending their children so far away is that it gives the parents an extra two hours a day to drink, shop, embezzle, take "lessons," and screw their instructors.

Suddenly it all made sense. Well, except for why I'm here. Obviously, Father didn't know it was for troubled kids when he got me in.

She was the go-to girl for gossip at Eisenhower. She knew everything about every kid here. Her mind was a vast storehouse of campus gossip. She started telling me about the various kids in biology class.

For instance, did I know:

• *Bib Oberman was in a BOY BAND, back in his hometown of Orlando? How HOT is that? They were called DA LUV THUGS, and he went by the name KID KRUSH. (Couldn't you just DIE!)*

• *The Takaberry twins have webbed feet and vestigial tails? YES! Parents were first cousins, they say. Or maybe even half-siblings.*

• *Baba Deschler is MAJORLY addicted to suppositories? Every class break . . .*

• *LittleAnne Swafford wears diapers? Frequently WET diapers?*

• *Lynnette Franz is secretly Jewish? (Well, SHE finds it shameful.)*

• *Sesame Blixon is secretly dating the basketball team? (WAY TO GO, SESAME! Show some self-esteem!)*

• *Betsy Kittenplan is a diet pill addict?*

• *Dottie Babcock is a cutter for Christ? Haven't you wondered about the long sleeves and high collars? In a tropical swamp?*

• *Buddy "Brute" McGlute likes to bring out and play with his little . . . um . . . Buddy during class. If you catch my drift . . .*

• *Reed Runyon is a manorexic?*

• *Vera LaBree, the pious Bible Belle, was found naked in a shopping cart, reeking of cheap gin and lawn boys?*

• *Sissy Russett spent eight months in juvie for shoplifting a Jones New York blazer. (Tan. Ew.) More embarrassing than circumstances of her arrest was the fact that Miss Uppitydoodles was shoplifting JONES NEW YORK. What would drive somebody to such depths?*

• *Tiff Tarbell's father is currently serving five to ten for elder abuse. Years and years of granny-bashing his live-in mother. And doesn't that explain a lot?*

Yes. Yes. Yes. All terribly interesting.

"But what about Flip Kelly?" I asked my gossipy new friend. "What's his story?"

"Flip's story?" she said, and then she laughed and laughed, like that was the funniest thing she'd ever heard. Then her eyes got all wide when she realized I was serious. "You mean, you really don't know? How could such a thing be possible?"

Then she leaned in and whispered Flip's story . . .

FLIP'S STORY

Flip Kelly, so named for the Flying Flip maneuver he made famous.

It was the night of the big game, sophomore year, when the former Mark Kelly executed a spectacular last second save by LEAPING and SPINNING ten feet into the air—up and around, like God's yo-yo— catching the ball in midflip, and using the forward thrust of the somersault to propel himself over the crush of the opposing team and across the goal line, before landing on his feet, yet, triumphant, and with two seconds left in the game.

There was a moment of silence as every person in the stands registered what they had just seen.

People don't do that.

People can't leap and bounce like that.

Giant bionic spider monkeys, maybe.

Genetically altered superfrogs, possibly.

Not sixteen-year-old pretty-boy quarterbacks!

The only possible explanation? Obviously, a miracle had taken place on their football field. God, himself, in the form of Mark Kelly, had come down from heaven and ensured the Manatees victory that night.

There was a twenty-two-minute standing ovation, and that included the fans of the opposing team, and after a few minutes, even the opposing team joined the fanfare, and simply felt blessed to have witnessed such a magical moment.

"Flip" Kelly was born, and he was golden. If ever a boy looked great in limelight, it was Flip.

"Born for greatness," most folks said

There was a parade for him, of course.

October 23 was declared Flip Kelly Day.

He was on all the news channels and interviewed in all the Florida papers. Tough-as-nails female news reporters got all giggly when interviewing him, and gushed in a most unbecoming way.

He was recognized everywhere he went. "Local heartthrob Flip Kelly." "Teen sensation Flip Kelly."

Parents everywhere were a little colder to their children that season. Why couldn't they be more like Flip Kelly?

Every father would trade his no-good son in a heartbeat to be Flip's father.

Every mother wished her daughter would date Flip, marry Flip, have Flip's babies.

At school the girls left their panties in Flip's locker.

And the boys! They were besotted! Like lovesick puppies! Following him around, vying for his attention. "Hey, Flip!" "Over here, Flip!" "Watch this, Flip!" This was as close as most boys were ever going to come to the homo heartland. Secretly, they all would have happily melted into Flip's arms just to be close to him, to be with him, to smell him. "Oh, Flip, Flip, Flip, really I'll do whatever you want me to. . . ."

And when Flip declined the honor of homecoming king, and instead asked that it go to Bib Oberman, the captain of the football team and best friend a guy could have, because, aw shucks, it was Bib who led the team to victory (not him; he was just following orders), well, people were just floored by the grace with which this boy prince wore his crown.

And when Flip went on to tell the crowd that Bib's dog, Diggery-doo, had just been put down yesterday (impacted anal gland), Bib choked back a sob, and Flip went over to him and gave him a big bear hug—right onstage—two boys, almost men, hugging and crying, unashamed. Indeed, everybody cried for the dead Diggery-doo, yes, and for Bib's loss, but really for what a wonderful, heroic, and selfless boy Flip Kelly was. It was a great moment for friendship, sportsmanship, and mankind in general. From that point on, Flip could do wrong.

So while Bib Oberman may have been the actual king of the home-

coming dance, it will always be remembered as the night Flip entered the pantheon of the gods.

XXII

Flip's haunting tale of early promise really struck a nerve. It stayed with me the rest of the day. I couldn't stop thinking about his odd predicament.

That moment defined his life, changed forever who he was and how people would see him. For the rest of his days, he will always be FLIP KELLY: FORMER FOOTBALL HERO. That one spectacular leap, ten feet in the air, locked him on a path. It was the best and worst thing that could have happened to a guy like him.

And he's had to try to live up to it ever since. Prove to everyone it wasn't an accident, it wasn't a fluke. He's had to try and become the person people want him to be.

How odd, to have the most important event of your life happen so early. At age fifteen Flip had already done the greatest thing he would ever do. The entire rest of his life is just one long epilogue. To peak at fifteen, then be almost past your prime at seventeen, and by twenty-five be a washed-up has-been living in the glory days. At thirty-five he'll be a ghost, a shell, a husk of a man.

He'll never escape that one moment of greatness.

We're sort of opposite ends of the same stick, in that respect.

I will never live down those first few minutes of that first class, that first day. I, too, will be forever defined by that one moment. In my case, it wasn't a moment of glory, but of shame. I'll always be Silly Billy, the gay pirate. And I have to fight that for the rest of my time here. It locked me on my path, all right.

So he is my opposite, and my twin.

So unattainable, and yet so connected on such a base level.

No wonder it was love at first sight!

XXIII

STRANGE ENCOUNTER

Later, standing by my locker, wondering if I could successfully drown myself in the water fountain, I felt a tap on my shoulder.

"Hey." It was Flip. He smiled.

I was rendered mute.

"My name's Flip."

I made some gulping noises and clapped like a seal, which is the international sign for "I'M A BIG, GAY IDIOT! KILL ME NOW!"

He didn't seem to notice. Or maybe he's used to it. "Anyway," he continued, "I just wanted to say, don't pay attention to those guys back there. They're boneheads. You're okay, dude."

I made a barking sound—"*ORF*" or "*GORP.*"

He smiled and touched my arm. "Yeah, well, okay. Take care."

And he was gone. I stared at the still shimmering air where he had stood. What the hell was THAT about? What just happened?

FIVE OTHER WAYS THE CONVERSATION MIGHT HAVE GONE:

1. "Oh, hey, Flip. What's up? How 'bout that mitosis lecture today?"

2. "Hi, Flip. Oh no. I barely even notice the boogers. Don't worry, dude. But hey, thanks."

3. "That's sweet of you, Flip. Maybe you'd like to get together later and talk about various proactive solutions I might endeavor to undertake to resolve my dilemma."

4. "Well, aren't you a doll? I'd LOVE to make out with you behind the gym, after school!"

5. "Oh, Flip! Yes, I'll marry you!"

Instead, I chose "ORF?"

D'oh!

XXIV

ALONE IN MY ROOM

You there, Gentle Reader, pour me a Dr Pepper and pull up a chair. I'm going to get ready now—it's up to you to look, listen, and learn. Watching me get ready will be a lesson in the Glory of Glitter, the Majesty of Makeup, and the Royal Romance of Drag.

This is my life, darling—and it's in Technicolor.

Tonight I will take flight. I will soar into the night and burst into flames. I will sparkle and shine with the brilliance of a thousand disco balls.

Tonight he will notice me.

Tonight everyone will notice me.

Tonight my hair will be pink and my skin will be blue. There will be feathers on my face and ruby rhinestones on my lips. I will be swathed in a flowing cloak of iridescent sequins. My eyelashes are going to be so long and heavy that they will obstruct my vision. I will be blind and forced to let a nearly naked Nubian slave boy carry me around.

Tonight I will say witty and wonderful things to all the right people. I will be endlessly entertaining, tossing off quips and epigrams, puns and aphorisms—even as I'm facedown in the vichyssoise. People will gather from all around to hear pithy pearls of wisdom spew from my sparkling lips. They will laugh uproariously at my droll little jokes, and later scribble them onto napkins so they can retell them to their boring little coworkers in their dull little offices.

Tonight he will notice me. Tonight he will see the spell I cast when I walk into a room. He'll realize how much fun it is to be with a drag queen. We'll laugh at the commotion my presence causes. He will be my co-conspirator when the crowd parts, the energy level rises, when all eyes are on me. People are attracted and repulsed by me. Tonight he will be drawn into the circle.

He will be mine. He will love me.

Let the dance begin.

Now where are my tools? Where are my creams, my powders, my potions and lotions? Where are my ointments and emollients? Grab that brush! Give me that goop!

Slop that gunk onto my eyes, wipe that crap on my lips! More!

Feathers, feathers, rhinestones, and glitter!

Tonight I need war paint! I am Jezebel. I am Helen of Troy. I am Venus Rising from the Foam.

Look at that eyebrow! Leonardo da Vinci couldn't have painted it better!

Now I'm ready to conquer the world. Huzzah!

Then again, maybe I'll just stay in and watch The OC.

XXV

Heaven help me, this is it. I've fallen in love.

And I'm a new woman because of it. Suddenly this skittish little drag queen has been transformed into a sultry woman of substance.

From crusty gargoyle to blushing bride. From Queen of the Pig People to Fairy Princess.

And that's a long road to travel.

I've never felt like this before.

Whenever I'm near him, I'm on the verge of some great emotion. I cry easily; I'm quick to laugh. It's like being at a very high altitude—the blood thins; the pulse quickens—sometimes I can't quite breathe right. *What if he thinks I'm stupid? What if I have bad breath? What if, what if, what if . . .*

But then I see him in class; I quickly turn and take a peek. Sometimes he catches me and, miraculously, smiles, and I start to tingle all over. My blood is happy; my bones are happy; in fact, my whole body is happy. My feet start tap-tap-tapping to the mambo beat in my head. My heart, once dry and shriveled from lack of use, is now big and wet and doing flip-flops inside my rib cage.

And now—behold!

I have his picture from last year's yearbook! There he is! Now I can stare at him without fear of being caught.

Just look:

Flip Kelly—pride of the Fighting Manatees! The Most Beautiful Boy in the World!

Superstar/quarterback/all-around golden boy.

Bambi-eyed pretty-boy/surf-punk/he-hunk.

A dewy, chewy, girly-gooey, moist and oozy sex god.

A hot and heaving hump muffin.

The Prince of Pouts. Duke of Drool. Man of a thousand sighs.

Blonder than blond. With the face of God. Or maybe Speed Racer.

He's a double dreamboat deluxe.

"Flip!" Consider the name: pre-ironic, neo-nostalgic, retro–golly gee . . .
impossibly wholesome . . . impossibly good-natured . . . destined for
dreaminess . . .

"Flip!" Sing it. Sigh it. Whisper it. Oh, Flip! Flip!

Have I mentioned yet how beautiful he is?

I'm not sure you get it.

Look! Look!

White-blond hair, like Icelandic royalty.

And such killer bangs.

Bright green eyes, like kryptonite.

And have you ever seen such lips? Like two night crawlers.

And that nibbly little nut of a nose.

And his skin, white, like arsenic.

Truly a legendary beauty. Someday there will be songs about him.

He sits in the back row with the other Fighting Manatees — with them,
but not one of them. That much I know.

He glows with inner goodness. A saint among Satanists. No, he does
not participate in their Billy-bashing games. I know that. Whenever
things get out of hand, and I have no choice but to turn to face my attack-
ers, well, that always seems to be just when *he* looks up, too — surprised
at the commotion. He looks up, smiles sweetly, as if noticing me for the
first time, then goes back to work, unbothered by the great apes that sur-
round him.

Of course, he smiles at everybody — he's not stingy with them. Regular smile slut, he is. But WHAT A SMILE! He is happy to spread the
love, and I'm happy to bask in the glow. Why, it almost makes the protractor stabbings and the spit balls worthwhile!

(Um . . . not really.)

Oh, he's just the most magnificent boy EVER. So handsome. So wonderful.

I love him.

I do.

XXVI

LOVE LETTER, NEVER SENT

Oh my darling! Oh my love!

I woke up this morning with a song in my heart and a tremor in my drawers. I can't contain myself any longer: I love you! I love you! I love you! It's true! I'm a monkey on a moonbeam! A pig with a pennywhistle! Whenever I see that chewy little face of yours with that dazzling Colgate smile, well, my ladybird does backflips. BACKFLIPS, DARLING!

And it's true what they say, you know, Love IS soft as an easy chair, fresh as the morning air. It's higher than a mountain, thicker than water. It's the mountains in springtime, a walk in the rain. It's a storm in the desert, a sleepy blue ocean.

I could go on. I won't.

Point is, I've never felt like this before.

Oh, there have been other boys. I won't lie. Chad Michael Murray. Aaron Carter. Hobie from Baywatch . . .

But none of them hold a candle to you.

Flip, my love, my pouty little poster-boy, my own special chew toy—I love it when you are dressed in your football uniform, handsome as all get-out. Of course I do. Who could resist your classic cover-boy looks? But I love you even more in T-shirts and jeans, on your slobby, Aberzombie days. Sometimes during class I sneak a quick peek at you when I'm sure nobody's looking.

I love the way your shirt is unbuttoned to your sternum, so that I can see the rise and fall of your chest. Would that I were an oxygen molecule (also known as O$_2$, as we discovered today) and lucky enough to be swallowed by you! Oh, to be swimming down, down your throat into your circulatory system, paddling to your lungs. IMAGINE BEING INSIDE FLIP KELLY! Imagine the pure pulmonary bliss! Yes! Oh! And the platelets of LOVE! Happy, happy, I would be happy at last.

Now imagine homeostasis with Flip. (Homeostasis being the state of maintaining constant blood composition.)

Oh, Flip, my love, my honeysuckle hunk, we could be so happy together.

I see something in you. . . .

Something the others don't see.

A softness.

A sweetness. A delicate innocence. Yes!

I see a sensitive little boy who tries to hide his "hugginess" from the other Backseat Boys. BUT NOT FROM ME! NOT FROM ME!

You're really just a little bunny-boy, aren't you? Aren't you?

You're my little pocket-poodle, huh?

So, now you know how I feel. I am quite confident that very soon you will get a special visit from the Bluebird of Bisexuality, and you will realize that I am the one for you, too. And from then on, everything will be picnics and plum pudding. And won't that be heaven?

XXVII

ESCALATION

Can you feel it?
Everywhere. Everywhere.
Hostility mounting. Anger building.

Signs go up around the school: GOD HATES FAGS!
FAGS GO TO HELL!
AIDS IS GOD'S SOLUTION TO HOMOSEXUALITY!

Some are more pointed, as if there's a plan afoot. And that's more worrisome:
HOMO GO HOME!
REPENT OR REGRET!
And: CONVERT THE PERVERT!

In what can't be a coincidence, Dottie Babcock, the high priestess of the God Squad, has begun leading a morning prayer group to rid the school of THE RECENT HOMOSEXUAL SCOURGE that has been threatening the good, decent, Christian values of the Eisenhower student body, of late.
Ladies and Gentlemen, I present to you, your Scourge of One!
BOO!
HERE I COME! I'm coming for your decency! YES, I AM!

It seems rather ironic, to me, when THEY are the ones chasing after ME.
Yes, yes. They hound me. Harass me. Hunt me down.

The Sinister Ministers, I call them.

The Cruci-vixens.

Sisters of No Mercy.

With their eerie perma-smiles (holy molars!), excessive eye contact, and sticky-sweet messages of hate, THEY SCARE THE CRAP OUT OF ME!

"Sinner!" they scream at me the second I step off the bus in the morning.

"Sodomite!" they shout.

I smile and wave and try to say something pleasant: "Not today!" or "Don't I wish?"

Then come the bible quotes.

"First Corinthians chapter six: verses nine through ten:!" one of them will scream. "*Know ye not that the unrighteous shall not inherit the kingdom of God? Be not deceived: neither fornicators, nor idolaters, nor adulterers, nor effeminate, nor abusers of themselves with mankind . . . shall inherit the kingdom of God.*"

I give them a cheery thumbs-up. "Wow! Great! Thanks! I'll be sure to tell all my idolater friends about you guys. Bye, now!"

But they aren't finished with me yet.

They gather oh-so-sweetly around me. They smile and take my hand. (I hiss and snatch it back — "It BURNS!")

"Deuteronomy chapter twenty-two: verse five," another will call out, and the chorus responds: "*A woman shall not wear anything that pertains to a man, nor shall a man put on a woman's garment, for all who do so are an abomination to the LORD your God.*"

"Good to know!" I say. "Thanks so much!"

"Leviticus chapter twenty: verse 13," another calls out, and in unison everyone says, "*If a man also lie with mankind, as he lieth with a woman,*" *both of them have committed an abomination: they shall surely be put to death; their blood shall be upon them."*

And they continue to multiply, and their prayers for me become increasingly hostile until I am, suddenly, literally under siege, surrounded by five, then seven, then twelve determined little soldiers, all angrily praying for me and at me, telling me the horrible fate that awaits me in the next life. And all the while, their smiles never slip.

And this is just what happens BEFORE school begins. . . .

XXVIII

So, yes, tensions are mounting.

In biology the terror continues to escalate.

Look: The jackals are circling ever closer, ever bolder. Their shouts and taunts are louder. The violence is now flagrant, even casual. Bruises are commonplace. As is blood.

Lord help me: I am under attack!

The great Homo Jihad has begun!

It's a Freak Hunt! (Say THAT five times fast!)

Open season on wispy fashion fops and gender-blurring glitteroids!

I try to wear protective gear—extra layers of clothes, you know, in shock-absorbing fabrics—but that can only take you so far. I wrap Ace bandages around some of the frequently favored parts of my body, but that, too, has its limits.

Sometimes during the pummelings I close my eyes and think: If I had only thought to bring my flaming chain saw today! Yes! Or my Orc sword! That would do the trick!

Or maybe if I wore a dapper dinner jacket with retractable meat hooks, THEN they'd treat me with a little respect!

But no, I have no choice but to ease back into it and hope it ends soon.

I really don't think I can take another day of it!

It's too much! And I'm not a well woman!

And yet, here we are, and here we go.

(*Sigh.*)

I KNEW it was going to be one of "those days" when I walked in to the room and found the anus of a fetal pig neatly clipped and taped to my chair—a gift from the Biology II class. ("*Enjoy it with a little corn oil, Butt-munch!*" read the accompanying card.)

Well, that must have taken some effort!

Before I can even sit down, Tiff Tarbell leads the Alpha Debs in an unscheduled Q and A.

"BILL-EEEEE!" she calls out.

And the girls immediately start shouting out their questions.

"Do you have AIDS?"

"Do you know Miss Jay from *America's Next Top Model?*"

"Do you pee sitting down?"

"Do you perform as Cher anywhere?"

"Biiiiiilly? We're all just so curious to know: Are you the man or the woman in bed?"

And the girls all tee-heed over that one, and buried their faces in their hands. They're so delicate, you know.

"Oh, please!" Violet Beauchamp purred wickedly, "Like he could ever be the man! Look at how he sits! No. The real question is: Hey, Billy, are you one of those men who are women who are trapped in men's bodies?"

More shocked giggles.

Lynnette Franz was suddenly excited. "Oh! Oh! I've got one! Are you wearing women's panties right now?" she asked.

Sigh. Life would be better, I decide, if stupid hurt. And as I banged my head on the desk some more, she was screaming to the back row: "Boys! Whoo-oo! Hey, Bo-Bo! Or Buster! Someone go 'pants' Billy! We want to see if he's wearing his mommy's underwear."

"You are a freakin' CREEPY dude!" Buster shouted as he dutifully lunged at me and held me tight (but not too close) while Bo-Bo deftly yanked my pants to my ankles. (*Sigh.*)

Here it was only 9:04, and I'd already hit rock bottom.

Witness the class just HOWLING at my Wild West–themed underwear.

"OH, EVERYBODY, HEY LOOOOOK! BILLY'S GOT BROKE-BACK BOXERS! EVEN HIS UNDERWEAR IS GAY!"

"Sweet cowboys," Bernie lisped, and oh, I just about died of shame!

Mr. Reamer looked up from his desk, where he had been correcting papers, and said, "Pants back on, please, Mr. Bloom! This is not a nudist colony! I'll only say it once." Then went right back to work.

Oh, I give up. That is the last straw.

I tell myself that this, too, shall pass. The school year will end, of course. It always does. I will graduate. Move on. Live. Then die. And someday all this warp and woof will be forgotten forever. Isn't that a nice thought? Because everything comes to an end and is eventually forgotten. Why, sometime in the future, nobody will have ever even heard of Bernie Balch.

Which will be lovely. But for right now . . .

I CAN'T GO BACK.

I CAN'T TAKE ANOTHER DAY.

NOT ONE MORE GODDAMNED DAY.
I'VE REACHED MY BREAKING POINT.
THAT'S IT. THAT'S ALL.
BILLY GO BOOM!
SAYONARA, SUCKERS.
I AM OUT!!!
I MUST END ALL BIOTERRORISM!
 BY ANY MEANS NECESSARY!

MUSTGETOUTMUSTGETOUTMUSTGETOUTMUSTGET
OUTMUSTGETOUTMUSTGETOUTMUSTGETOUTMUST
GETOUTMUSTGETOUTMUSTGETOUTMUSTGETOUT
MUSTGETOUTMUSTGETOUTMUSTGETOUTMUSTGET
OUTMUSTGET

XXIX

I linger after class, determined to get Mr. Reamer alone and plead for mercy. I want to be transferred out of his class, ASAP.

"Um . . . Mr. Reamer? Do you mind if I talk to you for a minute? I don't know how to say this. I've been trying to get up the courage for a few days now. So I'll just come out and say it. I've been thinking about it for a while, and I'd like to be transferred out of your class. ASAP. There's another biology class at the same time, Mr. Feldman's, and I could switch right into it. I thought I could take it, you know, or that it would get easier, or they would get bored, but it's just getting worse. So, if we could just get the paperwork started. . . ."

"Oh? Hm? What kind of problem are you having in my class? I wasn't aware of anything?" He looked in his grade book. "Your grades are fine. . . ."

When I say the CHEESE JUST ABOUT SLID OFF MY CRACKER, I'd be using a dumb southernism, but I was gobsmacked that he would continue the charade when we were alone, mano a mano, so to speak. The scoundrel! Was he really going to sit there and tell me that he hadn't heard or seen ANYTHING? My God, it was like the Springer set in his class.

"What's the problem, then?" he asked again.

Was he going to make me say it? "You know, the . . . um . . . teasing and stuff. . . ."

"Oh? Who's teasing you?" he seemed honestly surprised.

"Everybody! Who ISN'T teasing me? Bernie! Bib! The Takaberrys! Lynnette Franz! All day! Every day!" (Was he toying with me?)

"I hadn't noticed. Well, look. Why don't we wait a week or so before we do anything? Now that I'm aware of the situation, I'll keep my eye on things and jump in whenever I see a problem. I'm sure between us we can work this out."

All this as he was leading me out the door. "We'll talk again in a week or so, and see if it hasn't gotten better. Thanks for letting me know. . . ."

SLAM!

Huh?

Justice denied?

I WASN'T ALLOWED TO LEAVE?

HE WOULDN'T ALLOW ME TO LEAVE?

THAT'S INSANE!

XXX

That's when I had IT.

Yes, IT.

My most scathingly brilliant idea to date.

Oh, it's quite delicious.

Bold. Daring. Decisive.

Sometimes my genius staggers even me. I'm THAT GOOD.

Here it is: a plan fiendish in its simplicity. Hold on to your wigs.

If he won't let me leave, I'll just make him live to regret his decision. Yes, yes, by the time I'm through with him, he'll be begging to transfer me.

Here's what I'll do:

I'm going to create complete and utter chaos.

Pandemonium!

Sure!

Because: It's the pussiest pimple that gets popped! It's the unruly nose hair that gets plucked! You gotta be really unmanageable to get kicked out of anywhere. Remember, it's Courtney Love that gets thrown out of all those four-star hotels and strip clubs, not Mandy Moore.

And so it will be for me.

I will commit an act of very uncivil disobedience, of guerrilla theatrics!

I'm going to go to school IN DRAG.

Why not?

It's who I am.

How much worse can things get?

But not just any drag. Oh no. I am going to create a look that is so rococo-loco, so divinely decadent, so twisted and revolutionary, that those bo-hunks will run screaming from the building and I will haunt their dreams for YEARS!

It will be pure me. But more ME than I've ever showed anyone!

This look will be epic. One hundred years from now, people will still find it too avant-garde! There will be a whole museum built around it.

It's got to be big. Mondo Maximus! Too much isn't nearly enough! Over the top doesn't come close!

I need to just open up me noggin. Let the demons come out and play. See what's way in the back recess. Hell, I haven't got a clue.

How do I even begin such a project?

Well . . . first: clear your mind.

The outfit is already there. It's been waiting your whole life to be found. You know it, too. Trust your instinct. Let your hand guide you. It's a divining rod.

Remember Michelangelo's block of stone? Someone once asked Michelangelo how he decided what to sculpt. He said the statue is already in the block, absolutely perfect. You just have to chop off the part of the block that doesn't belong.

You just cast aside the clothes that aren't part of the outfit. Don't think. Just do.

The next two hours were a blur of activity. Gathering, snipping, altering, adding, pinning, pruning. I was surprisingly efficient. I moved with purpose and confidence. Calling out to my imaginary assistants everything I needed.

"Bedazzler!"

"Glue gun!"

"Cheerios!"

"Spirit gum!"

"Hair dye!"

"Wig head!"

"Food dye!"

"Liquid latex!"

While all around me, mice in little sweaters sang, "Cinder-ellie, Cinder-ellie!" and whistling bluebirds carried garments to me from the dressmaker dummy.

A creature began to rise from the pile. SOMETHING started taking shape. A dress? A look? A statement?

Something strange and new, with its own gravity, own rules, and with possibly a brand-new power.

Big. Getting bigger. Adding layers and panels.

Mostly green, but with flashes of pink and orange and yellow.

Bags of petals and leaves and sequins and beads, all carefully sewn on. Special lights were set up to test the angle of refraction for each sequin. NO! Four millimeters to the left! Half a centimeter down!

Then, crinolines, petticoats, and more and more flowers . . .

Was it a jungle theme? Garden of Eden? Enchanted Forest?

The razor came out and began shredding madly—slashing and tearing in a frenzied rapture—freeing its parts to move individually, to lift and float and turn. No longer a dress. No longer something to wear. Shredding gave it LIFE! Let it BREATHE! Now it was something that lives ON you.

And when mud was added to the bottom of the hem, and clumps of Spanish moss were found . . .

Well, of course, of course!

I should have realized . . . !

It was a swamp bride!

Because the mind always knows.

I've known from the beginning.

The swamp! The swamp!

"The swamp brought us together," I told them that first day.

I said, "Our lives will forever be changed because of it." And now it's true!

MAKEUP

Skin tone is SO important.

So it's green. Look at me. GREEN.

Not a grassy green. Or lime green or pine green. Not forest or avocado or pea.

Melon? Maybe. But more of a *whipped* melon, if you know what I mean.

Mint? Possibly. But not that sweet. Do they have a salty jalapeño mint?

Celery? But celery is so bourgeoisie. Unless . . . is there celery toothpaste? Well, there OUGHT to be.

So, just to be clear, it's not the green of algae, but of the algae's FOAM.

The color I'm thinking of is only found on moon-based extraterrestrials and lagoon-living sea monsters. Why? Because it glows.

What I need is glow-stick green base!

I went ahead and began diluting my green base with my white base, mixing them into just the right shade. It's a science AND an art. And in the bathroom I have some glow-in-the-dark sex lotion. Don't ask. Girl's gotta be prepared. But I'll bet if I mix that in with the base, it will glow nicely!

I started affixing the Cheerios to my face with spirit gum.

Five is about right. Here. Here. Here. Here. And here.

Then comes the long, time-consuming process of covering them with liquid latex, one layer at a time. As you build the rubber up around the O, it begins to look like little volcanoes or tentacles on your face! Once they're covered with makeup, they are seamless! Little green suction cups on your face for that new-to-your-land-dwelling-ways vibe!

Then base. Glowing nicely.

Eyelashes: seven pairs of Mondo Feathery 214s.

Eyebrows: pencil-thin, with a look of surprise and transformation.

Pink glitter lipstick, just because.

THE WIG

The wig is bog-water green mixed with livid, vivid pink, two feet high at least, curled up here and twirled down there and swirled over there, with many rare and fragrant plastic flowers pinned in. All of it has been sculpted into a sexy sort of bulb that EXPLODES with the biggest tiger lily blossom you've ever seen, pushing out from the top. Honestly, it's almost two feet tall on its own!

PUT IT ALL TOGETHER: DRESS, MAKEUP, WIG
And . . .
Oh, wow!
Well, it's not drag. I don't know what it is. But it's a statement. With attitude.
And this is NOT a dress, it's an ecosystem. And I transcend the whole boy-dressing-as-girl paradigm in this . . .

I guess if hard-pressed, I would say I'm a Radioactive Swamp Zombie (with tentacles) Who Becomes One with the Glittering Vegetation That Swirls About Her.

Oh! Hey! This will be my first time outside in drag!
Go me!

I looked in the mirror, slightly in awe of the gravity of my appearance. You can't ignore THIS, by God.

"BEHOLD THE GLORY OF THE SWAMP! Puny humans—look upon me with wonder and awe! You shall soon know the power of my drag! Bow down before me, for I am TONDALAYO POTATO-HEAD!"

I left for the bus.
(And as I walked out I heard the thud of Flossie hitting the floor.)

XXXI

ON CAMPUS

My movements were robot-smooth, my expression otherworldly and serene, frozen in a glowing porcelain mask.

I couldn't see a thing. Between the seven pairs of lashes and the tendrils of wig and vine swinging all about, it was a wonder I could maneuver at all.

But I glided like a parade float, hither and yon. Wherever I went, I simply stopped time. People just froze. Yes, yes, we've been through that before. They don't stay frozen, I know.

But judging from my responses, I might have struck some fear into their hearts. Maybe they saw depths they didn't see before. Or maybe they just knew to stay away from the crazy guy.

"This time he's gone too far!"

"That's just disturbing."

And, *"Dude's creeping me out."*

I floated into biology exactly one minute late, for full effect.

I opened the door. There was a collective gasp, and two screams.

As if on wheels, I glided to my seat, but turned and curtseyed to the class before sitting.

I couldn't quite see, as my vision was getting worse, but I could hear the buzz my entrance had caused.

It was hard to hold my eyelashes up, they were so heavy. And I had been up all night, sewing and beading and such.

(I just closed them for a hot second.)

I woke up to hear, "So everybody continue reading, and I'll be right back," then the slam of a door.

What? I can't quite see what's happening.

Oh dear God.

Does that shut door means that I am alone? In biology? Without a teacher? And just when I'm temporarily blind? In my looniest drag ever? Remind me again why I PURPOSELY turned my worst nightmare into reality?

The murmurs were rising to a roar behind me. Danger pitch. I felt the ugliness, of course, but my lashes prevented me from seeing anything. What was going on? Was I suddenly surrounded by savages? Hadn't these feebleminded goons ever seen a girl with a green face and tentacles before?

There was a sudden surge in the energy level. My teeth began vibrating. The hairs on my arm stood up. Outside, the always-present, eversteady swamp sounds went quiet. Every bug and viper and jackaloupe was leaning forward, tensely, listening and waiting for something bad to happen.

Then something did.

I heard Bernie Balch say, "Get him!" and that's when the walls came tumbling down. That's when I met my Waterloo. The fall of Billy Bloom came with just two words, hissed quietly and confidently, as if planned all along.

Suddenly, I was thrust into a great mash of people, pushing, pulling, falling, and dragging everyone down. Somebody in the crowd—*was it me?*—started screaming, and that set off another avalanche of movement.

I seemed to be surrounded by a solid wall of whooping warriors intent on inflicting some serious bodily damage. I was in the process of falling while, in their unorganized eagerness, they were both pushing and pulling me, up and down. The unintentional result was a welcome bit of bobbing and weaving on my part. And due to the enormity of my gown, and the various tendrils and vines and floating panels of fabric, they were having a hard time getting at me. So far, they had only succeeded in slapping my bustle, yanking my pretty wig, and ripping great chunks off of my pretty new dress.

But they organized quickly. Say hello to the grim army of killing machines. With a giant *WHUMPH* a dozen arms pushed me to the floor, where a dozen boots stomped on my face. *STOMPED ON MY FACE!*

They punched and kicked, and kicked and punched, like they had been built specifically for just that job. Their jabs were neat. Efficient. With a breathtaking economy of movement. Consistent impact force. POW! POW! POW! Quick and painful hammerblows. I was bleeding, but from where? And did they just break a rib? And what was that giant crunch? What would crunch instead of crack? Teeth? Knuckles? Spine?

Funny that I felt so removed, and yet, what was the point?

I just give up.

Flossie would probably have to identify the body. Father would never break up a golf game to claim responsibility for a dead homo swamp zombie. "GET THAT THING OUT!" he would bellow to Flossie if it came to that. "JUST PUT IT IN A BOX AND SHIP IT TO HIS MOTHER."

Such a shame—funerals are what Southerners do best.

I thought of my mother. It would be just horrible for her when the package arrived. She'll assume it's her monthly shipment of Oklahoma Kobe steaks. SURPRISE! Out falls my battered and bloody green body instead, with its tentacled face all smashed up. She'll scream and cry, of course. Well, SOMEBODY needs to cry for me.

Oh, that poor woman, always in a crisis, always at the end of her rope . . . and now her baby was squashed like a bug. And we never got the chance to make up after our big blowup . . .

As the pummeling continued, I curled up into a little ball and started singing "Mama, I'm Coming Home."

Minute bled into minute, and still they kept on, never breaking rhythm. POW. POW. POW. More cracking sounds. Little sobbing grunts, made reflexively as they now targeted my lungs and kidneys.

I closed my eyes and began drifting toward the light.

Good-bye to all that. There were no final thoughts, no profound last-minute revelations. The universe did not decode itself to me, no great mysteries were revealed, my life did not suddenly make perfect sense. If anything, I was leaving more confused and knowing less about humanity than when I started out.

Then, out of nowhere, *swinging on a rope*, I swear to God, was Flip! Flip had come to save me. Just like in my dreams.

"Leave him alone!" he screamed.

And from the Skycam above, we see the shock waves those words caused, rippling out in wider and wider circles, flattening everybody and everything in their path.

And they did. Strangely enough, they DID leave me alone.

"Everybody up against the wall!" Flip shouted, and again, everybody backed up against the wall. This was uncharted territory. Nobody had ever seen Flip this angry before. Or this powerful. And while nobody was quite sure what would happen next, they sure as hell didn't like the turn this had taken.

Flip came over to me, still lying on the floor, and lifted my head up. He felt my pulse, then wiped the blood from my nose and mouth.

"Thank you," I whispered. "You saved my life."

Flip Kelly scooped me up in his arms.

ONE MORE TIME . . .

Flip Kelly scooped me up in his arms.

I looked up. He looked down. "We're getting out of here," he said.

And the music swelled as he carried me out of the biology room, down the halls of the Eisenhower Academy, past crowds of slack-jawed students, and out the doors, into the world.

It was a hell of an exit, to be sure, the stuff of legend. I wish I remembered it, but I was unconscious by that point, and fading fast. . . .

Strange Interlude

COMA THOUGHTS

I

At first I was just blood and guts, tissues and arteries. Not a whole person, just separate body parts that needed attention and time to heal.

There was no pain, no suffering, no trauma at all. My brain just stopped taking my body's messages. Yep! Just up and closed shop! Abandoned ship!

"WRONG NUMBER," it said.

"GONE FISHIN'," it said.

"SEE YA, WOULDN'T WANT TO BE YA."

And kidneys don't think.

Bones don't feel.

So without a conscious mind to acknowledge their problems, the various body parts were on their own. They simply knew they were damaged and set about repairing themselves. Because that's what the body does.

Magnificent thing, the body.

Separate pieces of LIFE — just blood and meat and skin and bones — incredibly strung together, forming a system, a machine, now working together, now helping one another, no longer alone, anticipating each other's needs. Too fantastic!

So I was rebuilding myself. From the bottom up.

Pretty kick-ass, huh?

II

In my head, though, there was only darkness. And silence. And nothing else.

For how long? Who knows. Turns out, my mind stretches to eternity, in all directions. (Jealous?) And as time has no meaning in the void, of course, I could have been in there a minute or a million years.

III

Then one day, a dawning thought. A looming realization.

One day: PING! "I am."

That's it. That's all. "I am."

Not: "I am Billy," or "I am in pain," or "I am Queen of the Maypole."

Just a declaration of of life.

I AM.

So I was alive, yes, and aware of my existence. But completely without a sense of self or identity. What I imagine it's like inside a cow's head.

MOO.

In the Billyverse I was both Nothing and Everything all at once—a nifty Zen mashup that is positively prenatal in its narcissism.

ME ME ME ME.

Wheeeeeee.

Free-falling into my frontal lobe.
Somersaulting into space.
Swimming in the Billyverse.

La la la.

IV

Then another day, another leap.
Suddenly, thinking thoughts! Yes! Tiny thoughts, little thoughts, but thoughts nonetheless! Thoughts containing information!
Puzzle pieces from the waking world!
Simple. Random. Snippets of the past.
Without context, without meaning.
Not quite memories, just bits and pieces of this and that. For example:

Wilmington is the capital of Delaware!
Bounty is the quicker picker-upper!
Discretion is the better part of valor!
An ostrich egg can make eleven-and-a-half omelets!
We are living in a material world, and I am a material girl!
The onion is a lily, botanically speaking!

These mysterious pieces of ME, these missing links, just suddenly appear in the darkness, TA-DA!—standing, spinning, flashing on their own—"Thank you! We'll be here all week!"

V

QUICKLY, NOW. QUICKLY.
NEXT UP: RECOGNITION.

A voice.

Not just any voice.

Why, that's Mother's voice! Yes, of course! I'd recognize that husky coo, that throaty cigarette-whisper, from the grave.

"DARLING!" she cries. "IT'S YOUR MUV!"

And suddenly, there she is.

PLOP!

VI

It's SO TYPICAL that she would precede all other memories. Typical that SHE would be the first thing I would focus on in my coma-sleep.

Details trickle in slowly, then pour forth in a steady stream. I couldn't stop them if I wanted to.

Here we go. Here's mother.

Muv.

Yes, yes. I call her Muv. She calls me Junebug. No, I don't know why. That's just her. She's a PIP, that's all, and I love her like nothing else.

I am five. She smells of Youth Dew—her signature scent. I remember IT before I remember ME. "Bathe in it, darling!" she would proclaim. "Really make a stink of it! Always let them know you're coming!"

She needn't worry. She is nothing if not noticeable.

Today she is wearing a black leotard, black tights, a black cape, and a black turban with a single, soaring egret feather. It's all just TOO, TOO DIVINE of course. BEYOND THE BEYOND. She is the most beautiful woman at the Woolworth's lunch counter. Well, obviously.

It's our weekly "gourmet" luncheon date. We are both enjoying a relaxing Tab, oblivious to the stares of the GODDAMN ABORIGINES that have absolutely RUINED the place for the both of us. We've just eaten grilled Velveeta cheese sandwiches cut into squares and "frosted" with Hellmann's Light mayonnaise—"PENSACOLA PETIT FOURS," she calls them, and absolutely ROARS every time she says it. I do, too— JUST ROAR—although I'm not sure why.

Suddenly, she grabs my face in her heavily jeweled hands, looms closer, then closer still, choking me with her hot, cheesy, mayonnaise and nicotine breath. "Always remember this, Junie," she whispers, "DAM-NAN QUOD NON INTELLIGUNT. That's Latin, dear: THEY CON-DEMN WHAT THEY DO NOT UNDERSTAND."

She is referring, of course, to the growing crowd of GODDAMNED RUFFIANS that are pointing and staring at us. Of course.

VII

So. There you go. There it is.

It was just ME and HER. Muv and June. Together forever. Circle of two.

Other people are "Mongols" and "Huns" and "Visigoths." They are "unruly Hessians" and "bloodthirsty savages." Connecticut is full of them. It's true! Don't let their country club manners fool you.

"Blackhearted fiends!" she cries, and shakes her fists. "Out to loot and pillage us all! Never forget it, darling. They'll plunder your goddamn SOUL if you let them!"

It was an odd thing to tell a child, especially a child as delicate and impressionable as I was. There were bound to be repercussions, and there were: bedtime hives, cold sweats, creeping paranoia, self-mutilation. The usual.

VIII

MORE DETAILS

We live in the town of Darien, Connecticut — pronounced Dar-i-ENNE! Yes! With ZING! Muv loves that about the city. I think it's the only reason we moved there. "Oh, you gotta dress things up, babe! Gotta polish that apple!"

She has a theory that if Florida called itself Flor-i-DOO! it might not be such an armpit, and we'd still be there. Or FLAIR-a-day! Who wouldn't want to live THERE?

"Create your own glamour, Baby Boy. Grab it where you find it."

"Ever let your fancy roam!" she says with a flourish. And oh, we do.

Her Monday night meat loaves, shaped like hearts or bunny rabbits and frosted with mashed potatoes dyed pink or blue, were certainly fancy. "Pretend it's cake instead of meat loaf! Pretend it's a party for you! This world is hard enough, Junebug. It's not all canapés and cuddles, I'll tell you THAT. It's full of ugliness and fear. Suffering and misery! Get your frosting where you can!"

Sometimes we wear boas and brooches and enormous hats, and talk in fake British accents. LA DEE DAH we say, and OH, MY DEAH! We do each other's nails, drink our tea from the forbidden Limoges, and toast to the good life. "Cheers, Big Ears!" she says.

And it WAS a good life.

But then. Well. Nothing stays the same. Things change. She changed.

She started drinking. A LOT. Nasty, complicated drinks with names like Bloody Guatemalans. Cranberry Clots. Peek-a-boo Plops. "Darling, be a lamb and make your muv another Gassy Gin Cramp." (And I DO make a mean Gin Cramp, if I say so myself.)

So she was often drunk. Knee-walking drunk. "Muv has a case of the dropsys," she'd say, and I'd carry her to her room, which was no easy thing. I was only eight years old, and small for my age.

"Life is hard!" she'd say.

And I'd smooth her hair and say, "I know."

"If it's not chickens, it's feathers" she'd say, and I'd agree, CLUCK, CLUCK, CLUCK.

"I'm just a chrysanthemum in a coal mine," she'd moan — and I would wipe away the falling tears.

"I know, Muv!" I'd agree. "Me too," even though, of course, as usual, I HAD NO IDEA what she was talking about. It all just sounded tragic and glamorous, and I wanted in.

More and more, she was wistful and watery, and sensitive as an eyeball. "Oh, Billy, Billy, Billy," she'd sigh, and tug at my arm, "Tell me: Have you ever been happy? I mean, really, REALLY happy? BIRD-HAPPY?" This, in the middle of my tenth birthday party. Well, it brought things down a notch, I'll tell you that. BIRD-HAPPY? What could it even mean?

Occasionally, I would catch her muttering to herself odd little snippets of long-ago conversations, maybe, or secret fantasy scenarios that she kept *hidden from me. "They might think I will, but I won't," she'd say. Or: "If they do THAT, then I'll just go the other direction!"*

And that disturbed me.

Her outfits got progressively nuttier as the years passed. Then, zip, zip, they went from nutty to just plain batshit berserk: Christmas lights in her hair. Bells on her toes. Lots of swirling purple capes and scarves and ponchos. By the end, she was adding beaded fruit to the colored lights in her hair and drugging the cat and wearing it as a fur stole.

I could only watch helplessly as she floated farther and farther out of my reach. It seemed she was already just a speck on the horizon. I could hardly see her. Every day she was getting smaller and smaller. Soon she'd be completely gone, and then what would I do?

IX

My point, and I do have one, is this: It was always me and Muv—Muv and her Junebug—just the two of us. We were separate. Special. Different from the common man, and thank God for that. I had always been very proud to be included in her short list of acceptable companions, and secretly terrified that one day she would tire of me, and banish me from her charmed little circle forever.

Which, of course, is exactly what happened.

I should have seen it coming; I should have seen the signs. I knew her moods, or spells, were getting darker and lasting longer. She was often angry, confused, paranoid. Given to fits of froth and frenzy. WATCH OUT!

But that shouldn't have affected US. We still needed each other. I wasn't jumping ship. I was used to her behavior. Besides, I enjoyed her company too much. I'm not like those kids who hate their mothers and need to rebel. That's not me. I loved my muv. I secretly found her madness exhilarating. A LOT OF WORK, and not always appreciated, but exhilarating. So I was perfectly fine with US. Apparently, she was not.

Because.

One day.

THAT day.

She turned on me.

CHOKE.

But that.

That.

That I don't remember.

That I can't see.

It's covered in darkness.

Just darkness.

The memory is gone. Mother is, too.

Once again, it's just me and the inky black silence of the void.

A little boy lonely as God.

FADE OUT.

Part Two

THE BLOOMING OF FLIP KELLY

I

BACK TO LIFE

My eyes fluttered open.

Tick, lick, lightning quick.

Here's what I saw: Flip asleep on a chair next to my bed.

Here's what I thought: *Well, that's it. I'm dead, then. And I made it to heaven. I'll be damned. Who'd have thought? And look! There's my angel. Flip. Why, that God thinks of everything!*

Then—

DING! DING! DING!—my quarter was up.

My eyelids rolled back down. The thought was gone. I was gone. Even the memory was gone. I was back in the Billyverse, tumbling and twirling into the Great Whatever.

La la la.

Then . . .

(*A minute or maybe ten years later.*)

"He's waking up!"

The shades came back up. My eyes focused, and *THWAP!* mind and body were merged again. This was not a good thing. Seems there was a slight problem upon reentry.

Pain. Ow.

Bone-crushing agony.

I felt like Anakin Skywalker in the lava fields of Mustafar.

Had I just been in an atom smasher? Had I been attacked by a herd of wild steamrollers? If this is heaven, give me hell.

But there was Flip again. In his football uniform. *Awww*. And hey, look—it's Flossie in HERS. And . . . um . . . wow, there's Dad. Yes, Dad! And he's SMILING AT ME.

Note to God: *Not exactly the afterlife scenario I had been hoping for.*

Then it hit me. Like a dozen fists.

This wasn't heaven. Or hell. I WAS ALIVE!

ALIVE!

"He's alive!" Flossie shouted, and gave Flip a hug.

(Flossie smiling? Happy? Happy to see ME?)

I tried to speak, but my tongue felt like a hairy soft taco. There was continuous gag, like I had swallowed a ball of yarn in my sleep.

"*Aaaarrrggk* . . ." I made a strangled little rasp and crackle, and everybody smiled encouragingly and leaned forward to hear my first words.

YES? YES? WHAT IS IT? IS ANYTHING WRONG?

They strained closer, closer still . . .

Then, FINALLY, I managed to speak!

"Just . . . a little . . . lip gloss . . . please."

Flossie rolled her eyes. Father's thin smile looked stretched to the limit. But Flip, God bless Flip, let out a whoop. "That's Billy!" he screamed.

Well, I had a million questions, of course, that I was dying to ask. What happened? What day is it? What YEAR is it? Are there flying cars yet? Have the Morlocks taken over? What is Flip doing here? Why are he and Flossie talking together like old drinking buddies? And what's up with the new Smilin', Chill-out Dad? What's he doing here in the flesh?

All of it. Too fascinating.

But my biggest concern: "Muv?" I whispered.

She must be so worried.

There was a crack in Dad's big, toothy smile when I mentioned her name, but it was so quick, so subtle, that it might just have been a bit of coma-lag.

He patted the cast on my leg. "She couldn't be here, son, but she sends her love."

The doctor came bustling in. "How many fingers am I holding up?" he asked, holding up one.

"Un," I grunted, and passed the first test.

He shined a light in my eyes. "Any blurred vision, headache, or nausea?"

"Aul off the abuvvvv."

He scribbled furiously on my charts for a moment, then gave me a thorough, if slightly rushed, exam.

"Open!

"Close!

"Look up!

"Turn left!

"Lift up!"

He poked and prodded. He peeked under blankets and bandages, then reached RIGHT UP MY HOSPITAL GOWN and gave me the old "cup and cough."

Really! How indelicate! In front of Flossie! And giving Flip an eye-ful, I'm sure!

He continued to lift and squeeze and mutter and make notes.

It was all very thorough. I'm sure he was just doing his job. But. Oh my GOD, man, ENOUGH! CUT TO THE CHASE!

"Su . . . pleazzzze . . . , what's wrrrrong . . . with me?"

The doctor rattled off a list of all the various injuries I'd sustained. He explained, in great detail, each and every break and crack and compound fracture . . . the various fissures and abrasions and contusions and concussions . . . the bruising and swelling and bloody discharges . . . all the various soft tissue damage and organ trauma . . . BLAH BLAH BLAH . . . hematoma THIS and big hemorrhaging THAT. . . .

After a while I stopped listening.

YEAH, YEAH, YEAH—I GET THE POINT: THEY DIDN'T LIKE THE DRESS!

On the bright side, though, I was going to mend, sure enough, with the help of at least a month of bed rest, twenty-six kinds of pills to be taken at random intervals, and a little physical therapy as the weeks went on.

After twenty more minutes of small talk—HEY! YEAH! YOU'RE OKAY!—Dad and Flossie excused themselves. "Flip wanted to be the one to explain what happened, so we're going to leave you two alone." They said good night, and before I knew it, I was alone with Flip.

ALONE?

WITH FLIP?

And oh, how I've dreamed of JUST SUCH a moment.

Well. You know.

It was slightly different in my head. Replace "hospital bed" with "rolling fields of heather," and "coma" with "champagne picnic," and we're almost there.

(*Slightly awkward.*)

"Your dad's a great guy," he said. "He's been so worried."

Yeah, right.

"I'VE been so worried," he said, and that was even harder to believe.

But there it was.

Since the day he carried my limp and lifeless body into the emergency room here at Plantation General Hospital, he's been by my side. It's true! The nurses will back him up. He's been coming here every day, straight from football practice, and sitting with me, willing me, by God, back to health. He's been talking to me nonstop, he says, telling me stories, details about his life and his plans, anything at all, hoping that maybe the sound of his voice would guide me back.

And now his prayers have been answered.

Well! How about THAT?

Of course, I'm WILDLY jealous of myself for spending SO MUCH TIME with him and hearing his stories and GETTING TO KNOW HIM like that. I wish I'D been there. I wish he would tell ME stories. It's not fair!

COMA BILLY HAS ALL THE LUCK!

But he suddenly got very quiet and serious.

"Okay . . . um . . . ," Flip started. "Do you remember what happened in biology?"

"Sort of . . . It's all a little muzzy. I couldn't really see, remember? Or move. Damn eyelashes. And I was wrapped in those vines; oh my God, what was I thinking? I just remember Bernie giving the order. Then . . . nothing . . . until . . . here. Today. You."

He took a deep breath. I think he had been rehearsing this for a while.

"Here's what happened . . . ," he said.

And then told me the whole story.

∽∾

TIME-OUT: NOTES ON TEXT

Of course, I can't even begin to capture the fizz and crackle of Flip's speech. I'll try to print the actual words when I can, but even then, that's just half the show. There's a whole lyrical package with Flip that could never be translated onto the page. For instance: he has this supersexy "Sucking-of-the-Excess-Saliva" sound that punctuates the end of certain trains of thought. Basically, whenever there is a beat to be emphasized in his delivery, he sucks in the corners of his mouth and makes an inhaling sort of slurp. A THHFFSH sound.

I think it's a hip-hop thing, but how would I know? It could be Elvish. Or emphysema. Whatever. It's still impossible to duplicate on the page.

Oh, and his voice, for the record, isn't that deep. It's surprisingly soft, with a slight rasp. There's a little Surfer Dude in the delivery, mixed with a crackling kiss-my-grits Southern twang. And of course, that maddening, homeboy patois (straight outta Pompano, yo).

And that's Flip.

So. Back to the takeaway points of Flip's explanation. . . .

☙

FLIP'S VERSION:

"Yo, honest to God, Billy, it was just a prank. No one was supposed to get hurt. They were just going to scare you. 'Scare the faggot'—that's what they said. It was just going to be a little pushing. A few taps on the arm. Some tough talk. That's all."

So apparently, it had all been very carefully planned. For weeks. Down to the fake emergency phone call to Mr. Reamer. Everyone knew. The whole school.

Flip was against it from the beginning. "Swear to God! You gotta believe me, Billy. I was looking out for you. Fer real." (And he gave a mighty saliva suck to show his sincerity.)

He tried to talk his teammates out of it. Even threatened to tell me. And almost did that day by the lockers. Finally, he dropped it, stayed quiet, and decided to just be there, you know: to step in if things got out of hand. Act as a referee, of sorts.

So it was all planned out. Real quick, right? One, two. BAM! BAM! Done. There shouldn't have been any problems. BUT . . .

But then: "MY GOD! BILLY! Who knew you'd choose THAT day OF ALL DAYS to show up looking like a big gay monster? In that DRESS! I mean, what were you thinking? I'm not saying it's your fault or nothing. But you gotta know, that threw everything off."

Indeed. I knocked everybody for a loop, all right. I decided to push the envelope, cause a sensation, and see just how far I could push my enemies, on the absolute worst possible day. I decided to TRY and piss them off the very same day they were planning to let out their hostility on me.

"But that shouldn't have mattered," he said.

Here, his eyes started filling with tears.

No, he explained, things still shouldn't have gotten so out of control. And the reason they did? Because he wasn't there.

"I wasn't there!" he said, so obviously distressed. "I'm so sorry!"

I then watched as Flip fought back those tears. I watched as his eyes filled up with water, getting higher and higher until it was a solid wall of water, until you couldn't believe an eye could hold that much. And yet the tears kept rising! Defying gravity! Higher still! Then PLOP, one gigantic tear zipped down his face, leaving the sexiest streak you ever did see.

Flip Kelly was crying? Curiouser and curiouser! His reactions were more fascinating than the story.

He was certainly turning out to be very different from what I originally thought.

Anyway.

And WHY wasn't he there to protect me?

"My godamned car wouldn't start!" he rasped.

"Stupid, goddamned car! Stupid, goddamned car!" he repeated angrily, and pounded his thigh—a flawed response, I thought, as he seemed to be missing the entire point of *"Stupid, goddamned Bernie! Stupid, goddamned Bernie!"* or even: *"Stupid, goddamned homophobia! Stupid, goddamned homophobia."*

But whatever.

Don't let me interrupt his story.

"I mean HOLY SHIT! What could I do?"

Well, what COULD he do, poor thing? IT WOULDN'T START. . . . WOULDN'T START . . . WOULDN'T START. . . . All of a sudden it was nine o'clock. He was late for school. Late for class. Nine ten, and without him anything could happen. Anything was possible.

After finally getting a jump start from his neighbor, he hauled ass to make it to class in time to save me.

"I drove one hundred miles per hour—swear to God—all the way here. Running red lights. Running stop signs. And when I got to you . . . well, you know . . . things were just about over . . . and, well, I'm so . . . sorry. . . . See, it's all my fault! Yo, I understand if you never want to speak to me again. But I TRIED . . . I TRIED, BILLY. . . ."

He was an absolute puddle now, full-on blubbering, so even though I was the one who just came out of a coma, I felt like HE was the one who needed comforting. Poor little thing. All he went through.

WAY TO MAKE THE STORY ABOUT YOU, DUDE.

"Flip, stop," I rasped. "You saved my life. I'm grateful you did all that for me, my God. I'm not mad."

And there you have it.

A FEW LOOSE ENDS:

Oh, and maybe you're wondering, like I did, what the rest of the class was doing during the zombie beatdown? Where were they when I was bleeding on the floor, gasping for air and crying for help? Well, apparently, the other students were SO APPALLED that they couldn't even watch. They had to look away. LOOK AWAY! It upset them THAT MUCH! The cheerleaders turned their backs altogether on the carnage and practiced a new cheer TO THE WALL. How's THAT for a statement? A handful of students left the room in protest. They went to McDonald's and had some McGriddles and hash browns. MMMM. I'm sure they were delicious. The Bible Belles all claimed they prayed for me, but they must have been lying because I did not feel His protection AT ALL.

Even more disappointing: No action was taken by the school. Nobody was disciplined. Not one suspension. The prime suspects were all Manatees, you see. And no one saw a thing. In that crowded room. They were all studying very hard. Well, of course they were. The final game of the season was coming up. Of course they got off scot-free. Did you doubt it for a minute?

AND FINALLY:

What does Flip think of his fellow classmates now? That they're essentially good kids, you know, just a little misguided, Oh, yeah, he's totally Anne Frank that way. I learned that about him later. In Flip's world people are good, evil will be punished, and hope springs eternal. BLAH BLAH BLAH. Also, gumdrops grow on trees, elves live in his TiVo, and the Pattycake Princess watches over the children of the world from her castle in the clouds.

I respectfully felt like spitting on his optimism. I had just seen something really rank in human nature, had my face shoved in it, actually, and I wasn't in the mood to be generous or forgiving. I wanted to grab him by his shirt and scream: Listen to me! The school is a snake pit and the students, YOUR FRIENDS, are bloodless, heartless, baby-eating, grandmother-raping, puppy-killing, bottom-feeding vermin who are utterly repulsive and totally devoid of any redemptive qualities! But I kept my mouth shut, for the time being.

Anyway, that's as far as we got. I was tired. So very tired. Confronting such soul-sucking malevolence isn't easy. Flip said good night and promised he'd be back first thing in the morning, "as usual."

II

ALONE IN MY HOSPITAL ROOM

Alone in the dark.

Lying on a mattress stuffed with gravel. Trying not to cut myself on the sheets. (Estimated thread count: three.)

Listening to the wails of what could only be the LEPER WARD next door. Very NAUGHTY lepers, by the sound of it. Obviously having their noses pulled off by the evil night nurses.

I mean, my God, listen to them: howling like the damned! Their anguish is almost unbearable!

What to do? What to do? Concentrate, instead, on the buzzing fluorescent light just outside your door.

Yeah, that's nice and soothing.

A real lullaby.

And what's up with all the fluorescent lighting, anyway? SO

UNFLATTERING! And why? It's the sick and disease-ridden that NEED forgiving light, for God's sake.

And of course, the Gatorade-colored walls don't help either.

Hospitals. Ech.

And nurses! Don't get me started! I mean, what is it with those mannish hairdos of theirs? I can think of no other profession where looking like HANK HILL confers status on a woman. Ladies, why not consider a flattering Anna Wintour bob, instead? I beg of you!

So. What now?

Still can't sleep.

I started taking inventory of my injuries, isolating each body part, beginning with my toes.

I said each boo-boo out loud: "Two broken ribs . . . bruised collarbone . . . ruptured spleen . . ."

On and on. What I could feel, and what I could remember.

"Hematoma . . . hairline fracture . . . extensive bruising . . ."

I touched what wounds I could, finger-exploring their defining characteristics.

I pushed at each bruise. Felt under every bandage and Band-Aid. Sometimes when I came across a particularly big and painful sore, I would wiggle my index finger around in it a bit and make myself cry.

I isolated my legs, pelvis, hips, chest, arms, and face.

I discovered: a full cast on my left leg, a cast on my lower right arm, a neck brace, splints on four fingers, and some sort of body support thing, like a body corset, probably for the broken ribs.

Until finally:

Sleep. Sleep.

Swirling, sweeping,
Streaming, screaming,
Full of fever and fear,
I dreamed of faceless assassins, and fists that never stop pounding.

III

I was a bit wifty yesterday, when I first regained consciousness, and well, who wouldn't be? In my fog, though, I just accepted everything I was told and thought it was all perfectly natural, perfectly normal.

WELL—OF COURSE I was in the hospital, *where else would I be?*

OF COURSE I had been in a coma. *I hear they're all the rage now, darling.*

OF COURSE Flip and I had become best friends while I was asleep. *I'm sure I was a scintillating companion.*

It never occurred to me to question what was going on. I was just thrilled to be ALIVE. When last I checked, it was all over but for the worms.

In the light of a new day, though, and with a much clearer head, I was looking at the bigger picture. The bigger mystery. The real story.

And that would be my new FLESH-AND-BLOOD FATHER—I mean, what was THAT all about?

Who was this Suddenly Smiling Dad—*and smiling with his TEETH, no less!* I'd never seen THAT before.

FREAKED. ME. OUT.

Some sort of robodad, obviously.

A Pod-Poppy.

It was just TOO BIZARRE. I couldn't get over what the hell my father was doing here!

I know we haven't talked about him much, and really, why bother? One thing you can be sure of, though, that was not his usual demeanor. OH NO, NO. NO. Not by a long shot.

USUALLY he's about as pleasant as pickle pie.

USUALLY he's about as compassionate as a cattle prod.

It's a fact: My father is a thundering bully, a gristly old goat, and a bellowing boogeyman.

Harsh words? Well, these are harsh times, my friend.

Up until now, remember, he's shown precious little interest in me. I've yet to even see him more than half a dozen times since I got here, and when I do, it's usually just for a quick:

"TAKE THAT OFF THIS MINUTE!" or, "BY GOD, THERE WILL BE NONE OF THAT IN MY HOUSE!"

Lots of, you know: "NO SON OF MINE, GODDAMN IT! . . ."

And so on.

I can't win with him!

He hates everything about me! It's always something!

He doesn't like my poodle perm, say. Or nail polish color. He has a problem with the fishnets under my jeans. And the JLo perfume I'm wearing. He doesn't like when I do my AbFab imitations at the country club. And hates it when I perform songs from *Rent* for visiting relatives.

I mean, I could end world hunger, and he'd bitch about my mango lip gloss. I could pull him from a raging river, and he'd say I tug like a sissy.

"Hey, Dad, I just won the Nobel Peace Prize!"

"DID YOU PLUCK YOUR GODDAMNED EYEBROWS?"

"Look, Dad! I can make diamonds from old potato peelings!"

"WHAT DID I TELL YOU ABOUT WEARING WOMEN'S JEWELRY, BILLY?"

Papa don't preach, indeed!

And this little attitude problem isn't new. Not by a long shot.

It all goes back to when I was twelve and announced at the family barbeque that I really didn't care for the stuff. "None for me, thanks," I said. "It's too messy," and I made an unpleasant face. "I'll just have myself this little piece of quiche, here, that I brought with me. . . ."

It was the first time I stopped a room cold.

DID HE JUST SAY . . . ?

I THOUGHT I HEARD . . .

DOESN'T LIKE BARBEQUE?

Why, you'd have thought I said, "The hog ate Grandma," the way they reacted.

I mean, the earth's rotation skipped! Ocean levels surged! Gravity spiked! The tectonic plates shifted!

People gasped and choked and coughed up perfectly good bites of food.

"WHY — THE BOY'S NOT RIGHT IN THE HEAD!"

"IMAGINE A BLOOM BOY NOT LIKING BAR-B-QUE!"

"I'VE ALWAYS SAID THERE'S SOMETHING ODD ABOUT THAT BOY!"

While my father clutched his chest and fought for air I blithely yammered on: "In fact, I don't believe in ribs, at all. LIFE'S TOO SHORT FOR BONES, I always say. You won't find ME sucking the gristle off some sparerib, no siree. I have better things to do. Just give me a nice filet mignon, thank you very much. Anyway, Muv says barbeque was invented so the lower classes could cover the taint of their spoiled meat."

Several of the women fell to the floor. The men had to be restrained from whuppin' my butt on the spot. "HE CAIN'T SAY THAT! NOT ABOUT RIBS! I WON'T LET HIM!"

Father never recovered. You know how Southerners are about their barbeque. It was a mortal wound. And after the first death there is no other. He never treated me the same after that. It was a hurdle we could never get over.

Any chance for a father-son relationship was gone. Poof. In the limp of a wrist. I dashed his every dream.

Ever since that day, he's always had SOMETHING to criticize me about. He can always find SOME fault to pick on.

So, to recap: my dad.

Bad dad.

Not really a nurturer, if you know what I mean. Lacks a certain parental warmth. Doesn't much like "the gays," I suspect.

He's a dream squasher, a style assassin, and a spoiler of the arts.

He scares me, you see. And that's not unusual—"For fathers are disturbing," wrote the poet Rimbaud.

IV

So then, who the hell was that guy last night?

Why wasn't he upset? AT ALL?

This should have sent him careening over the edge! Spiraling into a whirling vortex! He should have absolutely blown a gasket! Cartoon steam should have shot out of his ears!

COME ON! Think about it: His son—that blazing Technicolor faggot, the SHAME OF HIS LOINS—was taken to the hospital in a sparkly and freakishly accessorized dress the size of a small gazebo. COME ON! RIGHT THERE! STOP! I mean, never mind the leafy green wig and glowing tentacles on his face. How can he even get past the dress? And NOT ONLY was I wearing a DRESS the size of a HYUNDAI, but I WORE IT TO SCHOOL, for Christ's sakes! WHERE PEOPLE COULD SEE ME!

COME ON, DAD! STEP UP TO THE PLATE!

I DON'T UNDERSTAND. Isn't there enough to work with there? Not one detail to get all shouty-crackers about? You're just going to let this slide? And SMILE about it?

WHO ARE YOU?

"We're just glad you're better," he said yesterday. With a THUMBS-UP!

Somebody has kidnapped my father and replaced him with a look-a-like.

I don't necessarily want the real guy back, but if some group cares to step forward and take responsibility, I'll send him a care package of fresh underwear, good scotch, a dozen of Flossie's pecan sandies, and some clean tennis whites, just in case y'all have a court.

It's the least I can do.

V

THE NEXT MORNING . . .

The nurse told me I had a visitor, but that she couldn't catch her name.

"Did it sound like Blah Blah Blah?" I asked.

"That's *exactly* what I heard."

"Send her in."

My only friend, Blah Blah Blah, bustled in, arms spread, voice full of concern: "Billy!" she cried.

"Buttercup!"

"I brought you some cold mush. My own recipe. You'll love it."

Why, I was just craving mush, too! How thoughtful!

She couldn't stay but a minute. Her friend Mumble Mumble was outside in the car. She just wanted to say she was SO SORRY, it was TOO TERRIBLE; but rest assured, EVERYONE WAS TALKING. I was a hero and a "martyr to the cause." (Of what? Swamp Zombies?) There was even talk of giving me some sort of award or medal. ("Most Loathed!")

She pulled up a chair and began furiously whispering all the news from school. Such an odd duck, right? Always whispering. Always scurrying about. But God bless her for it. She knows everything about everyone.

Of course, I had probably heard all about the assembly they had recently, right? (UM . . . NO.) Well, it was about the "hate crime." Although my name was never mentioned. Anyway, a "sensitivity speaker" was brought in, and he showed a filmstrip about tolerance. (THAT'LL SHOW 'EM!) And the upshot of everything is that the school now has a zero-tolerance policy on hate crimes of any kind. So that's progress, huh?

And what most people didn't know, she whispered, was that Flip BEAT THE CRAP out of Bernie the day after I was attacked! It's true! KNOCKED HIM OUT COLD. It caused quite a rift with the other Manatees, and now he and Bib aren't getting along, either. They practically tackled each other to death during practice the other day, and ended up wrestling in the locker room afterward. The coach is frantic, what with the big game coming up . . .

Then, quickly, quickly, what else? What other gossip did she know? Well . . . seems Lynnette Franz broke up with Bo-Bo Peterson, but nobody knows why. (I DIDN'T EVEN KNOW THEY WERE

GOING OUT!) Oh, and you know Sesame Blixon's monster snoobs? TOTALLY FAKE. A seventeenth birthday present from her dad. EW, RIGHT? And apparently, word on the street is she got the boob job specifically to get Flip's attention. In fact, she's planning on asking him to homecoming next month. Ten-to-one odds he doesn't accept. Of course, he never accepts. He never even seems interested in any of the girls at school. HE'S SO MYSTERIOUS.

Once she had exhausted her gossip supply, she was off and running.

"Kiss, kiss," she said as she scooted out the door. "Feel better!"

"Yeah, thanks, I feel much . . . better. Yeah."

VI

DISCHARGE—THE GOOD KIND

After five more days I was discharged from the hospital and sent home to finish my recovery on sheets NOT made of sandpaper. WHOOOO! I must have the most exfoliated bedsores in town.

Before I left, though, I had Flip steal one of those wildly erotic backless hospital gowns, some needle-free hypodermics (to make a punk-rock tiara), a commemorative bedpan, and enough tongue depressors to finally build that detachable stegosaurus spine I've been dreaming of.

There was not a lot I was going to miss about this place. CAN ANYONE SAY: SPONGE BATH? My God! The final indignity!

Once home, it took the combined efforts of Flip, Dad, and Flossie to get me up the stairs and into bed. We finally figured out that if I sat in a chair and they lifted it, rickshaw-style, they could carry it up, one step at a time. It would still be a slow and jiggly process, taking almost

FORTY MINUTES, but finally I was home and back in the safety of my own room.

Thank God.

VII

And true to his word, Flip has come by EVERY SINGLE DAY. We've gotten to know each other quite well, in fact.

And based on my keen observational skills, my vast knowledge of human behavior, and incorporating the new data I've been able to gather, I'm revising my opinion of Flip. I've learned something shocking.

Lean in.

(*Whisper.*) *He's not cool AT ALL.*

WHAT? WHAT? HOW CAN THAT BE?

Oh, he's many, many things, don't get me wrong. All of them wonderful. He's wildly exciting. Wildly attractive. He's so handsome, he'll burn your retinas. He's got that white-hot white blond hair, with those killer bangs . . . a nose like a ski slope . . . those blazing, dragon green eyes . . . and a smile so white and so bright, it guides Santa's sleigh in dense fog! It's true! He exudes charm and charisma and sex appeal like no one else in the world. Go on, I dare you not to fall in love with him! I dare you!

And NICE! Whooo-eee! You'd think he was running for office. Why, he's on friendly terms with EVERY SINGLE STUDENT at the Eisenhower Academy, even Stinky Jo Blunchly, who wets himself if anyone get too near. Anyone but Flip, that is. For Flip he stays dry! That boy gets RESPECT.

So he's all of these things, ON TOP of being Flip Kelly: football hero, local saint, and role model.

But cool?

Nah. He's a dork. Too wide-eyed. Too earnest. Too easily impressed.

ALSO—and I mean this kindly—HE'S A BIT OF AN IDIOT. A lovable idiot. A saint among idiots. He makes idiots look hot. But an idiot all the same.

Look into his eyes. I know. It's hard. You get so dazzled by their size, color, and clarity. You could get lost in them. Sometimes you swear you could see forever.

That's because there's nothing behind them! It's true! It's an empty cave in there! Not a thought in his head. Not one. Those eyes shine so brightly because there are no brains in the way to block his inner glow. They are, then, just very pretty curtains.

So in summary: Flip Kelly, not cool. Not smart. . . . Instead, sensitive moron. Dashing dork. Yummy bumpkin. . . . And I love him even more because of it.

VIII

SOMETHING ELSE: The more time we spend together, the more I get to know him, the more I begin to think that MAYBE BEING FLIP KELLY isn't all it's cracked up to be, either. WHAT? I know! Pretty bold statement. It's true, though! I'm beginning to think it's all just surface sparkle and twinkle-twaddle with him. And that underneath that whole swoon-doggy–surf-hunk exterior, he's really pretty dark and cloudy. Troubled, even.

What makes me think that?

For one thing, he sure spends a lot of time here. With me. Don't get me wrong. I'm not complaining. Hubba-Hubba, right? But it makes no sense. I mean, this ain't no "Big Rock Candy Mountain," I can tell you THAT. And I'm no Fipple Flute Fairy, if you know what I mean. . . . (Just go with me here.)

And HE'S FLIP KELLY!

Why isn't he out being a superstar? Why isn't he out partying, and getting laid, and doing all those cool things that cool kids do? You know. Like . . . um . . . illegal drag racing . . . and break-dancing battles . . . oh, I don't know. You've seen the movies. Whatever cool kids do when I'm not around.

My point: If it's so great being Flip Kelly, why does it seem like he's hiding here?

Here's a clue, perhaps: He doesn't talk about his parents or home life. At all. When I ask, point-blank, he gets all monosyllabic and changes the subject. Word on the street (by that I mean, Blah Blah Blah) is that his father rides his ass, really pushes him hard, like, to the point of abuse. He demands absolute perfection. And doesn't seem to recognize it when it's right in front of him!

So THAT sucks.

Then factor in the whole hero–saint–role model complex, and the expectations everybody places on him, and the inability to deviate from his image . . .

Yes, yes—all things considered, I'm thinking it's probably pretty difficult being Flip Kelly, the boy king.

Heavy is the halo, you know.

HOMEWORK

Every day after football practice he brings me my homework, as well as his own, and we tackle it together. I help him as often as I can because he struggles, I mean REALLY STRUGGLES, bless his heart, with most subjects. And remember, his teachers are BEYOND generous when grading his work.

Now, it's not that he's totally hopeless. Not exactly.

From what I can tell, he just panics, easily—like with each new question. Give him a simple true and false, and he'll go statue-still and stare at nothing with those big, boiled-egg eyes. He'll think and think, and think some more. He'll chew on his bottom lip. He'll furrow his little brow. He'll make a bunch of sucking-saliva sounds. He'll be so quiet and so tense that you'll think he's bending spoons with his mind. Then a full ten minutes later, he'll scream out: "FALSE!" Then: "NO, TRUE!" Then: "NO, WAIT, FALSE!" Then he'll punch himself in the face and call himself an idiot for the rest of the night.

It's on account of the weird DOOMSDAY SCENARIO planted in his head:

He thinks if he gets just ONE bad grade on just ONE pop quiz, then CRASH!—there goes his final grade, and with it his GPA, and then he'll lose his scholarship, and the whole house of cards will come tumbling down. Suddenly, he's disappointed everyone who's ever believed in him. The school. The team. The coach. The fans. His teachers. His parents. And, I don't know, Santa Claus, Oprah. . . . Doesn't matter.

The end result: He's a loser and a fake, and he's responsible for sending his parents to the poorhouse.

I think it's kind of sweet, and I just want to chew that lip for him, LORD, but it must be paralyzing inside his head.

X

MONDAY EVENING

I was working on an oral report for American lit about Zelda Fitzgerald—the talented but tragically unstable wife of F. Scott Fitzgerald—and having a perfectly marvelous time. WHOOO! Who knew she was such a loon! A gorgeous, fabulously doomed loon! I think I've found a new role model!

"Hey! Listen to this!" I yelled over to Flip, reading from my book. "It says here, she spiked her Coca-Cola with spirits of AMMONIA 'to give it a slight kick'! That's HARD CORE, right? LOVE THAT. Let's try it sometime!"

He looked up, all Bambi-eyed and quiver-lipped. Clearly, he wasn't having as much fun with his "Teapot Dome Scandal" paper.

"Oh my God!—Listen to this!" I said.

"Billy! I can't!"

"Just this one thing: Guess how she died?"

"Stabbed by her study-buddy because she wouldn't shut up?"

"NO. The mental institution she was in caught FIRE, and she was locked in her cell! CAN YOU IMAGINE? Crazy AND on fire? That's like being allergic to your shark bites! It just makes your death ten times worse!"

"Yo, yo, yo, from now on, you are only allowed to discuss things related to Warren Harding, is that clear?"

"Warren Harding thinks Zelda Fitzgerald and I sort of look alike. What do you think? Same fiery red hair! Same impertinent nose! Same devil-may-care hauteur!"

"Were both of you clobbered with a teapot dome? Because I'm THIS CLOSE—"

"Are you threatening an invalid? JEEZ. Buzzkill. Okay, give me what you've done, Flipper. Let me take a look at it."

"Thanks, Billy-boy!"

XI

Sometimes when we're together, I forget time and place.

I pretend that we are man and wife, living peacefully in the hills of Northern Ireland. He is a shepherd. I am his plain-but-sensible wife, who stays at home all day making meat pies. He has a ruddy complexion from so much time spent on the moors. I have wobbly jowls, common to the women of our region.

He is gruff and drooly, and smells of sheep.

"I love you," I tell him, and we live happily ever after.

Sure I loved him. That was the easy part.

But I fall in love at the drop of a hat. At least a hundred times a day: I love the fry cook at McDonald's. I love Kelly Clarkson. I love balsamic vinegar on my vanilla ice cream. . . .

Love is easy; it's when you actually start to like someone that it gets difficult. Putting up with their odd little idiosyncrasies. The way they suck their teeth after dinner, say, or the way they change perfectly good lightbulbs. It's when you like somebody despite the fact that they have every season of *Reba* on DVD—that you know it's something special. It's about liking someone in spite of the gaping flaws in their personality. . . .

And that's how it all started with Flip. It's when I actually started to LIKE him—as a person—despite the fact that he's a bit of a mouth-breather, possibly an idiot, and is waaaaaay too enthralled with *Charmed*—that I realized how much I cared.

It's true! He was soft and sweet, and my eyes went blurry when I looked at him. A friendship began. And it was like an old half-forgotten song. It started quietly, and I couldn't quite place it; but with each refrain, each time we saw each other, it became clearer, and the tempo picked up. Suddenly, we were both singing along, and it was sweet and natural. There was a rhythm that was full-bodied and exciting. And a robust chorus that added layers and textures. When we recognized it, we felt good. We were friends.

Isn't that nice?

XII

Father is, of course, just beside himself with this new friendship of mine. BY GOD, it seems I did something right for once! Never in a million years could he have hoped for such a thing!

This is what he said to me today: "I'm proud of you, son. Flip Kelly is a very good friend to have."

This is what he was thinking: *I'm shocked as shit somebody like Flip Kelly would even give you the time of day.*

Here's what he's hoping: That somehow just the sheer proximity to a manly man like Flip will knock the sissy out of me, and maybe now I'll join the football team and give him grandchildren.

Strange enough, but then it was FLIP who brought DAD back into MY life. Like, in a major way. No more absent dad. No, sir. Now he's almost always around.

Always somewhere, always underfoot.

He's constantly "just checking in" and "seeing how you are"—passing off stale clichés as fatherly advice. "Now, don't overdo it, son," he'll say. "Think positively." I guess he's trying, bless his heart. He's just seventeen years out of practice.

I find it all painfully awkward. Our conversations always seem so stilted. So forced. Full of uncomfortable silences. There's still so much that remains unsaid. For example: We don't discuss the beating AT ALL. We also don't discuss the dress, the wig, or the tentacles. And we certainly don't talk about the big gay elephant in the room that started it all.

And with no common interests, and not much of a shared past, either, all we talk about is—Flip.

And this is the weird part:

(*Whispers.*) It's really all about him. Yes! He seems happy for HIMSELF! It's like HE has this great new friend, Flip! It's like HE has a crush on this guy, Flip!

IT'S WAY CREEPY.

And when I noticed THAT, well—DING! DING! DING!—everything just fell into place. Suddenly, that confusion over the Suddenly-smiling, Suddenly-hangin'-out dad was solved. This new-and-improved Billy-buddy dad (now 90 percent less shouty!) is due to the Flip Effect.

Apparently, it happens to a lot of otherwise normal, heterosexual, middle-aged men when they find themselves around FLIP KELLY: ALL-AMERICAN. Reflected in Flip's glory, they see the boy they once were, the life they let slip away, the son they wish they had, and hope for the future of America.

So, yes, my dad has Flip fever.

He's been Flipified! Flipperized! Flipinated! (It's so Flipical!)

Now whenever Flip is around, he turns into this gushy, girly, fan-man, instead of the growly old goat of yore.

As soon as Flip arrives, he's all gaga, rah-rah, Go! Flip! Go!

It's all: Sis boom bah! "Ring the bells!" and "Isn't Flip fantastic?"

Naturally, I'm mortified.

I can't believe my father is such a total spaz.

The first time I saw him transform into this stammering, yammering FRESHMAN GIRL, I thought: *Who IS this freak? Why does he insist on embarrassing me in front of company! It's just TOO WEIRD.*

But then, after a while, it just became standard operating procedure.

And now you can't escape it. You can't escape HIM. He's everywhere, remember?

So there's lots of THIS:

"Hey, fellas! Thought I'd just check in, see how you're doin'?"

And: "Stayin' for dinner, Flip? Flossie made her famous Alabama fried chicken!"

And most embarrassingly: "Hey, Flip, if you got some time later, maybe we could toss the ball around out back?"

I usually roll my eyes loudly when Dad does this, but Flip is always charm personified. He gets it a lot, he says. He gives a little groan that only I can hear, and promises he'll be back as soon as he can. Then he'll go out and rock Dad's world by letting him catch a (supposedly) difficult pass or two and telling him how good he was a dozen or so times.

"No, really, Mr. Bloom, that was amazing!"

"Still got it, huh?" Dad wheezes and puffs.

"Oh, yeah. You must have KILLED back in the day!"

Then Dad blushes and stammers and kicks at the dirt.

And between you and me, it's wearing a bit thin.

Yes, Flip is fantastic. Yes, it's nice having him around. I'm president of the fan club. But, JEEEZ. He's just a kid! A high school kid! I mean, you'd think it was the LORD GOD, TOM BRADY himself, who had dropped out of the sky to admire dad's old trophies and give him a backrub.

(Well, OF COURSE I know who Tom Brady is, ding-dong! Give me SOME credit. He's only the dreamiest Visa spokesman EVER!)

XIII

Flossie, on the other hand, was suspicious from the start.

"What do you really have in common with a pretty-boy football hero from South Florida? What can you even talk about?"

That really burned me up.

"Well, if I want intelligent conversation, I'll talk to myself."

"I don't know," she said ominously. "Doesn't seem right, is all."

(Which sounded like a curse.)

Flossie, of course, knows everything about everything. Oh, yes, she's quite a sage, that maid of mine, lecturing to me from her ironing board. Always SWIMMING with insight. Not this time, though.

"Oh, but Flossie, we're just friends, and I'm not miserable," I said with as much conviction as I could muster.

"Really," I explained, "it must just be a heavy gravity day in my room—that's why I'm stuck to the floor."

And: "I don't need there to be more to the relationship," as I confidently polished off another Entenmann's double fudge chocolate cake. My third one that day.

"Really, I don't need sex. Or love. Or physical attention." (This I confided to the rubber tree plant as I dry humped the banister.)

"I'm very happy with things as they are, thank you," I said as I lit some black candles and spit three times at the moon.

Okay, so maybe I was lying to myself. And maybe I wasn't that happy. But what could I do?

XIV

I am sometimes secretly convinced that he was raised in a cage, possibly by Frankenstein monsters. Or that he's a time traveler from the Dark Ages. How else to explain why he's so new to so many experiences that the rest of us take for granted?

EXAMPLE:

Often while doing homework, I'll intercom Flossie and have her send up some of whatever is in the fridge. Usually it's Southern stuff. Dad stuff. High WASP stuff. Broiled grapefruit. Melon with tomato ice. Eggs with crab sauce. Salmon Wiggle. Nibbly things to get us through till dinner.

WELL! Flip looks at whatever she brings us as if an enchanted fairy pulled it out of her ass. Why, you'd think the boy had never seen a pickled walnut before!

To his credit, he tries everything, though, and takes his tasting very seriously. Very solemnly, he brings each new morsel to his mouth and chews thoughtfully, carefully, really trying to discern each individual flavor. Then his eyes go all golly-gosh, like Orphan Annie, and he either shouts with alarm or groans with bliss.

ANOTHER EXAMPLE (AND THEY *DO* PILE UP):

We watch old movies, classics mostly, that he's never heard of. *What Ever Happened to Baby Jane?*, *Sunset Boulevard*, *Breakfast at Tiffany's*, —You know, camp standards. Well! He is transfixed. Hypnotized. Mouth slightly open, saliva pooling in the corners. Doesn't even blink.

One afternoon we watch *Gone With the Wind*, and it affects him to his very soul. "How could Rhett just leave her?" he asks over and over again. It's a genuine shock. I think he cried in the bathroom. Days later he's still upset: "Does she get him back? Is there a sequel?" Sometimes in the middle of school, he furiously texts me at home: "Ashley Wilkes—what an ass hat," or "Melanie died! ☹"

AND THIS:

He's endlessly fascinated with my room and the various odds and ends he finds. When I couldn't move around as much, he would bring me various wigs and feathered bed jackets, and help me into them. Now that I'm starting to get up and about, he leads me around the room, asking me to explain and try on various things. "What's that?" he'll say, and point.

"Surgical adhesive."

"What for?"

"If you want to glue something metal onto your skin, then regular spirit gum won't work."

This genuinely perplexes him. "Why would you want to glue metal to your skin?"

"Well, why WOULDN'T you?" I ask. "Now, let's say you want to wear these antlers here. They have a metal base. Now I can attach them to my forehead, like SO. Or maybe I want to do a 'robo-tranny' look tonight. Well, that calls for three or four dozen little mirrors on my face, like a disco ball. . . ."

"Yo, do it! Do it!"

My hands are shaky, and I get tired easily, but I do it, and it's fabulous, and now he's a world-class expert on adhesives and robo-trannies.

Sometimes I give him some Vulcan ears or glue a fake wart on his nose to keep him entertained. And, oh! if that isn't just the living end! Have you ever? HE LOVES IT. No, really. He'll stare at that wart in the mirror for absolute hours, unable to believe how realistic it looks, checking it out from different angles, posing with different expressions, wondering how his life would be different if it were a real wart. "Should I wear it to school?" he asks about everything.

It's hard to believe he is so easily awed. I mean, was he not invited to many masquerade balls as a child?

One day he came LEAPING and BOUNDING into the room, fresh from football practice, proud as a pup and bearing a mysterious package. He had gone to the costume store on Sunrise and gotten me a little something to wear around the room.
     "I hope you like it. . . ."
     It was a tiara! "Oh, Flip, it's FABULOUS!"
     "I thought you could wear it today, right now."
     OF COURSE! YEA! And I was Queen for the Day.

XV

Alone in the cupboard, I let the sticky black darkness drip over me and dream that I am inside a giant cut-glass perfume bottle, like the one my mother had on her dressing table. With me is my husband, Flip Kelly, and together we roll around the world, secure inside the crystal ball. We safely tumble off mountains, roll down hills and into the ocean. Nothing can touch us; no one can hurt us; the glass is unbreakable. We see the world pass by through a dazzling prism of colors. And as we roll around, we are

thrown together right side up, upside down, always into each other's arms,
over and over again until the ball stops and we rest, lying like spoons on
the smooth, cool floor of our home. And then the ball will move again—
somebody will push us, or a wave will wash us away, and we are off again,
tumbling into the future. Me and Flip Kelly.

XVI

In the meantime, have you noticed? I am healing, healing . . .

Up and moving around!

Bruises gone!

Swelling down!

Leg cast off!

Tomorrow? The arm cast!

Every day I am more myself.

Every day I am more aware, merciful heavens, that this room is an absolute boar's nest! I can't believe that Flip has seen me living in such squalor! WHAT must he think?

XVII

FRIDAY—

Flip was coming over, possibly to spend the night, so it was vitally important that I scrape the dried bugs off the windowsill. AT LEAST THAT. I didn't want him to think I was always this unclean or anything. Being an invalid gave me an excuse to be a slob. But now I needed to show him how together I was. That meant I needed to change my underwear, deodorize myself, and take down the Chad Michael Murray posters I had posted around my bed.

There was a strange smell coming from the northwest corner of the bedroom. I made a mad, impetuous dive into the pile of clothes there and prayed it wasn't a family of possums, or something even more sinister. (Monster slugs? Fresh body parts?) Thank goodness, it was just a couple of fossilized hamburgers and a plate of old moo goo gai pan. From last summer.

I only had two hours to make up. Not much time. I was going for that difficult "real girl" look . . . you know, subtle and pretty . . . a whisper of bisque here, a touch of russet there. And maybe just a soupçon of ecru eye shadow. When the doorbell rang, I answered it in a seductive cream-colored camisole and a pair of Seven Jeans that gave me the ASS OF DOOM. My hair just happened to be in a gorgeous cascade of "natural blond" curls. My complexion was flawless, as usual. God had blessed me tonight.

"Oh, Flip, I look just terrible!" I lied. "You caught me off guard!"

"No, man, you look good. If you was a girl, I'd get busy wit choo," and we both laughed uproariously at his joke.

(Flip: impossibly hot in baggy jeans, faded tee, and bangs way too long in that "I'm too cool to see" way. He did a little pimp roll up the stairs and into my room. "Wassup?")

"What are we going to do tonight?" he asks.

"*Buffy*, season six?"

"Nah. I've seen it too many times."

"Oh! I know! We can steal some vodka from the bar!"

"Okay."

"Are you hungry? Would you like something to eat while I finish getting ready?"

He nodded vigorously, and I went into the kitchen to see what we had. Not much.

"Um . . . tomorrow must be grocery day. Let's see. There's some melba toast. Or I could make a Bundt cake!"

"Nah. Let's just do shots. C'mon."

How many times has this happened to you:

For some strange reason that can only be explained after twenty-six consecutive shots of pepper vodka, you've decided to finally set up that home karaoke machine you got three Christmases ago and perform your signature song: "I Believe I Can Fly" by R. Kelly. IT'S THE SONG THAT'S BEEN BUILDING UP INSIDE OF YOU FOR A LIFETIME, and you absolutely MUST SHARE it with an audience . . . RIGHT NOW. There's no time to lose—no time to rehearse—just peel your new best friend, Flip, off the floor and thank God for the "Emergency drag bag" you keep next to the door. (It contains a full costume change, complete with makeup and accessories, for no-brainer quick changes like this—it's a drag queen's lifesaver!) Hurry! You'll change in the bathroom. . . .

Things get a little blurry.

You remember changing into a gorgeous floor-length polyester cocktail gown with an empire waistline and gorgeous Pucci-esque swirls of ocher, cinnamon, and puce. You don your Suzi Wong wig—but it sits at a jaunty angle that's not quite right. . . . In your haste you glue one eyelash to your nose and the other onto your forehead, for that delightful "Qu'est-ce que c'est?" look that's so popular now.

Of course, unbeknownst to you, your best friend, Flip—who from now on will be referred to as The Hurlmeister—has just barfed into your drag bag before handing it to you, and as you take to the makeshift stage (a foot locker) you are covered in Whopper chunks and regurgitated melba toast.

I believe I can fly
I believe I can touch the sky

See me running through that open door

The audience (Flip) is wildly receptive. They are—okay, he is—throwing things at you: wigs, pencils, keys, and beer bottles (Isn't that sweet?), and screaming, "Take it off!"

Hmmm . . .

It wasn't meant to be a sexy number, but what the hell, you're feeling saucy, so you show 'em a shoulder, give 'em some gam, then let your booty bobble and bounce—and you, sir, are NO LADY!

In your confusion you've fallen a beat or two behind, and in your struggle to stay on pitch, you begin braying like a herniated yak. (Use your imagination.) But nobody is paying attention to you, anyway, because the audience has begun throwing up on some old wizard robes and dashikis, which were probably ready for the trash, anyway, and before you know it, the two of you have both passed out on the staircase—sick and ashamed of yourselves.

How often has this happened to you?

I would hate to think I was the only one.

Eventually, he poked me, picked me up off the stairs, and wiped a few vomit chunks from my dress.

He slung his arm around me and slurred in his straightest voice, "You know what? You're okay, dude."

"Glad to hear it."

"No. I really like hanging with you."

"Right back at ya, babe."

"You aren't like a fairy or anything. You know what I'm sayin'? You aren't like a fairy or anything."

I wanted to mention that my "fairy phase" ended when my mother stole my wings and elf ears for herself, but I didn't want to ruin the moment. He was trying very hard to explain our friendship in straight terms.

"I mean, you dress like you're from freakin' Mars, man." He looked critically at the eyelash glued to my nose. "I don't care or nothin'. You are who you are, and I think that's cool, man. . . ."

We walked outside, and as we walked, we talked. Without realizing it, we walked the length and width of the compound, along the sea wall, through the garden, around the guesthouse, finally ending up back at the house, the main house, with our arms still slung chummily around each other, feeling closer than we ever had before.

Once upstairs I excused myself to the bathroom, where I quickly brushed my teeth and washed my face. When I came back into the room, ten minutes later, I saw that he had fallen asleep on an old pile of wigs. *SIGH.* I set about making him comfortable, propping up his head and wiping his nap-drool.

I took one last look at him, my lovely Prince of Pouts—So perfect! So sweet!—turned out the light, and retired, regretfully, to the bed.

XVIII

5 A.M. BLUES

He's asleep now. On my mattress. In his underwear. With an erection. It's very early in the morning. The sun is slowly spotlighting the room. He must have gotten up and moved in the middle of the night. Now I'm perched on the side of the mattress, breathless, holding a Dr Pepper, staring at his chest, his nipples, the thick tufts of hair under his arms. . . . I'm all moist and oozy just looking at him. I couldn't possibly go back to sleep. Could you?

I stare at him, hard, until I am unable to focus clearly on a detail. If I blur my eyes, try to take in the whole image, he seems to bend and shift. He's not solid somehow, more like the memory of something solid, something forgotten.

He is a wave, maybe, that you can touch but never hold—moving, changing, disappearing and reappearing. I am suddenly aware that this moment will be with me forever. I will carry this vision to my death.

If I bend down, if I get close enough to him, will I be able to smell him? In my mind he smells like a stable boy, reeking of horse sweat, cut grass, and olive juice. In my mind he smells like a caveman fresh from the hunt: bloody, murky, dark, and primordial.

If I lick his nipple, will I taste the testosterone that drips from him?

I crawl closer to him. He won't mind. I stare at the birthmark on his shoulder, the one shaped like Michigan's Upper Peninsula. When he moans and turns onto his stomach, I get a pen and connect the freckles on his back.

This is love.

If only he would wake up. If only we could roll around in each other's arms for a couple of years. Playing games and giggling. Writing words with my finger on his back, and letting him try to guess.

I could have him now, you know. If I really wanted to. Really, who turns down sex once it's already underway? Afterward he'd probably never talk to me again. At best. At worst, he'd beat me up, he liked it so much.

But no.

Instead, I shove a couple of Flossie's cigarettes up his nose and take a picture for posterity. Using a wire coat hanger, I try to open the flap of his boxers and get a peek. Then I leave and go out into the living room to see if Regis and Kelly are on yet.

XIX

LATE MORNING—

I watched him lace his boots in that cute way that he has: across and across rather than letting the laces crisscross over each other. It requires skill that way, he told me, and concentration. His forehead crinkled in childlike frustration as he tried to show me, and then his eyes lit up with satisfaction when he was finished.

I marveled once again at how he's changing. He doesn't hang out with the other Manatees as much—he says they don't understand him anymore. He seems quieter now, more introspective. He doesn't talk in that tough-guy wigger way as much anymore. (Although it did return in full effect last night, when he was drunk, huh?)

He acts increasingly protective toward me. Dare I say tender? When we're together at night, he jokingly refers to me as his bitch. Isn't that sweet? In private he tells me I'm the best friend he's ever had. Sometimes he holds my hand when we are out walking in the gardens, and that just makes my LIVER QUIVER, I'll tell you THAT.

XX

SATURDAY NIGHT—

It is almost midnight when I make my entrance.
Spotlight, please.

My gown is glimmering, shimmering. A gorgeous piece of craftsmanship. One hundred thousand Japanese silkworms pooped it up, and twenty-seven blind nuns beaded it while locked in a castle tower somewhere in Tuscany. It's unlike anything you've ever seen before. Under different lights, at different angles, it moves, it undulates—it SINGS THE BODY ELECTRIC! Is it real? A mirage? Perhaps a holy vision? If so, then it's, quite literally, TOO DIVINE.

My wig is enormous, at least two feet high. It has a nautical theme tonight: "Under the Sea." It's blue and white, like foam on waves. It's swirled up here and curled down there and then piled into a glamorous, cascading topknot. It is pinned with pearls and tiny shells and even starfish. . . . But the pièce de résistance—are you sitting down? Look! There! From a circular swirl at the center of the topknot, BUBBLES EMERGING! Yes! From a hollow hole deep within the mound of curls, my hair is blowing out a continuous stream of bubbles! I call this my GLUG GLUG wig. I see your mouth visibly drop. "Am I underwater?" you ask.

No! I rigged a bubble machine to the base of the wig! I'M A GENIUS!

"You look awesome, Billy," Flip shouts when he sees me. He leaps to his feet and gives my outfit a standing ovation.

"Thank you. Thank you."

Eventually he stopped clapping.

Then he looked at me.

And I looked at him.

We looked at each other for a few moments.

Then.

I . . . um . . . got nothing.

That's when—TOTALLY OUT OF THE BLUE—Flip raises his hand like he's asking a question at school, and blurts out: "So . . . um . . . then . . . tell me: Are you gay? Or what? Bisexual? DON'T WORRY.

You can tell me. I can take it. I have an uncle who's a stewardess."

I was thrown. Clearly, this was something he'd been thinking about. And possibly worried about? What if I scared him off? What if this was a test? What if he wanted me to say yes so he could come out, too? Um . . . maybe not. But I needed time.

So I stood there—in my beaded dress; my bubbling blue wig; and six-inch heels—looked him straight in the eyes, and said, "Me? Oh. Um. Sort of, kind of, maybe a little bit bisexual. Kind of. Maybe. Sort of. You know."

He wasn't buying it. "So you're saying you're NOT gay, then?"

I laughed and punched him in the arm, real manlike. "Nooooo, silly goose!"

He arched a brow. "Hmmm." And he shuffled through my CD pile. "A LOT of straight guys collect Kylie Minogue B sides and bootlegs, huh?"

Not such a dim bulb after all! "Um . . . I don't know what you could mean by that."

"So, if you're so straight," he continued, "who's your ideal girl? If you could have hot monkey sex with any GIRL in the world, who would it be?"

"Um . . . um . . ." (*Don't say Liza! Don't say Liza!*) "Um . . . um . . ." (*Don't say Martha Stewart! Don't say Martha Stewart!*)

I hemmed and hawed for a solid three minutes until I came up with: "Beyoncé!"

He made the sound of a buzzer. "Yeah. Um. No. You want to BE Beyoncé, Billy, not bone her. Nice try. And besides, according to you, she's already technically a drag queen, anyway, so she double doesn't count!"

Wow. He's a quick study.

Then, innocently, as a simple matter of course:

"So, what kind of BOY do you like?" and "Who's your ideal boy?"

DANGER! DANGER! Uncharted territory! Potential land mines all around! All previous experience useless! Emotional compass going haywire! Turn around now!

How to answer?
  The truth?
  Be honest?
  Tell him you like impossibly blond superboys? Heartbreakingly pretty quarterbacks? Power-pouting teenage saints? Emo-eyed Bambiboys?
  What about: Guys named Flip?
  What about: YOU! YOU IDIOT!
  KA-BOOM!

But no. I went with: "Donnie Darko."
  Flip chewed on that for a moment. "Yeah. Hmm. Donnie's dope. Hey, but what about Captain Jack Sparrow? That nizzle is off the hook, right? He's gotta be up there, huh? Pirates are the shit! And Johnny Depp is the MAN!"

Oh my God! Oh my God! Oh my God!—I had to pinch myself. Was this really happening? Were Flip and I really gossiping about cute boys? And was Flip just totally crushing on Johnny Depp? We were! He was! Oh my God—we're not boyfriends, WE'RE GIRLFRIENDS! This is SO tween slumber party. All that's missing is the popcorn, headgear, and a new pom-pom routine.

The next question, then. "How far have you gotten with a guy?"
  This could be potentially creepy. Luckily, I'm a teenage spinster, so there's no icky reveal. "Nowhere. Nothing. No one. Ever. Really. I am so totally homo-challenged, I might as well be straight. I mean, I am clueless. What's a bottom? What's a bear? What's a chicken? I may never find out. I'll probably die a virgin. I'm just going to her-

metically seal my ass now and save future archaeologists the problem."

"No one? Ever?" He was silent about that for a very long while.

Then we continued on.

Like so, you know.

Ha-ha-ha.

La-la-la.

Things took a sinister turn, though, when Flip introduced a new game—Who Would You Rather Do?

The rules were simple enough. He would list two options—A or B? This one or that one? Tom or Dick?—and I chose the one I'd rather "do." ("Dick.")

Well, that was easy enough!

Sounded like good fun.

But wait! Not so fast! It wasn't as simple as that! There was a hitch! A glitch! A bump in the road. A blackfly in the chardonnay!

For some reason Flip's choices almost always consisted of "Bib" and someone else. And that someone else was almost always someone like Gary Shandling, Comic Book Guy, Stephen Hawking, Carrot top, Chris Farley's corpse . . . you get the picture. It was all very strange, and I wasn't quite sure where he was going with it.

"Who Would You Rather Do? Bib or Jar Jar Binks?" he asked.

"Bib or Richard Simmons?"

"Bib or Mini-Me?"

So it went. Until . . .

"Bib Oberman or . . . Michael Moore," he said. He paused, then added, "And Michael Moore has advanced flesh-eating disease. . . . And he's only wearing spandex hot shorts and a sports bra. . . . And while you're deciding, he's hard-core krumping, and as he pops and spins, large, crusty, infected chunks of rotting flesh are flying every-where, pelting you in the eyes and mouth."

Oh my God. This was so retarded. I said nothing.

"Well? Who? Come on?"

"Bib!" I finally groaned. "I'll do Bib!"

He LEAPED into the air, eyes blazing, finger pointed to God: "AGAIN! AHA! I KNEW IT! Five Bibs in a row! You have a thing for Bib, don't you?"

This shit was bananas. Where was it coming from? I never knew he was so jealous of Bib!

"Okay, Flip," I said. "You're so smart. You got me. It's true. I love Bib Oberman. TLA. True Love Always. We didn't want to tell you, so we concocted the whole months of torment and coma thing to throw you off the track." I started making out with my hand, "Kiss, kiss. Slurp, slurp. Oh Bib! Bib! You're so hot!" I stopped and turned to him, and here's where I forgot about the potential land mines.

"Now, I have a question for YOU! Okay—who would you rather do? ME? Or STAR JONES? And Star Jones has a nasty-smelling yeast infection. And humongous hammertoes, which she insists you suck. Oh! Oh! And she likes to use her old liposuction fat as . . ."

Well, that shut him up.

"That's different," he said, sulking. "I'm straight. You have to give me two females."

"Oh? Oh? Is that THE RULE? Is that how they've been playing it for GENERATIONS now? Is that written in the bylaws of the charter of the HICK RETARD IDIOT GAME LOVERS CLUB? Well, tough crap, straight boy. So? Well? Who's it going to be? Me or Star Jones's hammertoes?"

"I'm outta here," he barked, and slammed down the stairs.

"Yeah! Well, FUCK YOU! GET OUT!" I screamed. "GET OUT! GET OUT! GET OUT!" I was angry and hurt. He couldn't have just been polite? He couldn't have been a gentleman? Who knew I was somewhere beneath yeast infections, hammertoes, and recycled body fat on the Table of Sexual Desirability. I felt rejected and monstrously, hideously ugly. I'm grotesque!

XXI

Maybe the air was getting a little thin, or maybe the peanut-butter-and-Robitussin sandwich was finally kicking in. At any rate, I was hot, nauseous, and cramped. I was spending the day in my footlocker, with my snout against the airhole, whimpering like the dog I was.

This was my penance for being mean to Flip.

I closed my eyes and prayed to Mary Hart, the symbol of all that is good and pure in my life. "Please, Mary, deliver me from madness, passive-aggressive hostility, and hetero-hating."

Amen.

According to the *Big Book of Symptoms* I found in my dad's library, that heavy feeling in my chest, pressing down on me, was a terminal case of angina pectoris. And all this time I thought it was a broken heart.

(*Sniffle.*)

I took to my bed, yet again, and piled on layer after layer of foundation to cover the pain of rejection. I propped myself up to receive visitors, like Garbo on her deathbed in *Camille.* . . .

Oh. Oh dear.

Anyone?

Anyone?

Oh, people. GARBO. Greta Garbo! Swedish movie star of the 1930s! Heart-stopping beauty! "I VANT TO BE ALONE!" Frequently lampooned in Bugs Bunny!

It wouldn't kill you to watch a little TCM once in a while, you know.

Anyway, in *Camille* she is a nineteenth-century courtesan who dies of tuberculosis, and it's just the saddest thing you'll ever see. Sadder than *Titanic*.

SO THERE I WAS.

I had propped myself up to receive visitors, like Garbo on her death-bed in *Camille*, and bravely offered my hand to be held by the various imaginary friends who stopped by to see how I was doing. "Just a little lip rouge, darling," I said, "and I'll be just fine."

But as the week plodded on and wore me down, I realized that no, I was not going to be "just fine." Frankly, I was a mess. I wasn't eating. My weight was plummeting. I weighed about eighty-three pounds (in platforms and hairdo). I was a rag and a bone and a hank of hair. I was sinking into filth and sinking into ennui. I stopped caring about Pop-Tarts, Jake Gyllenhaal, and *Days of Our Lives*. I didn't sleep. I didn't moisturize. I didn't even bathe for a while there. Even Flossie began avoiding me. And it's HER JOB to put up with me.

XXII

"Margaret!" I said in the thick Irish brogue I revert to in times of distress. "Go fetch Father Pete and tell him MY TIME HAS COME!"

Then I remembered there is no Margaret, and I've lost my mind.

"You've always been so good to me," I said to my imaginary boy-friend.

"I'M DYING!" I shouted to the world, and sobbed pitifully.

With my last ounce of strength, I crawled to the phone and called Flip.

"Hello?"

"Flip!" I croaked. "Oh! Flip! Help! Please!"

"Billy! What is it? What's the matter!"

"Just . . . get . . . over here . . . before . . . it's . . . TOO . . . LATE!"

"OH MY GOD! I'M ON MY WAY! HANG ON!"

He arrived in less than twenty minutes. "WHAT IS IT? WHAT'S THE MATTER? DID YOU HURT YOURSELF? SHOULD I CALL THE DOCTOR?"

"This is it, Flip," I said in a hoarse whisper. "I'm dying. DYING, EGYPT, DYING!" (*And no, I'm not babbling. That's what Cleopatra said as she clutched the asp to her breast.*)

Flip sighed and sat down, realizing he'd been duped. "Okay—I'll play along. What is it this time?" he asked.

"Um . . . I think I'm allergic to myself. Or the universe. Either way, things don't look good. I'm afraid I'm not long for this mortal coil, old chum. I just couldn't go without seeing you ONE . . . LAST . . . TIME. . . ."

Then I coughed and whispered, "Good-bye."

And that's when I died.

Or tried to, anyway. I thought I did a pretty convincing job. I rolled my eyes back into my head and spit up on myself. I wheezed and gasped and flailed about. My audience, though, remained unconvinced.

"Hey, Drama Boy, get up. Enough dying. I'm not mad at you. And if you wanted to see me, all you had to do was call."

HUH? I came back from the dead, sat up, and asked: "You mean, we're still friends?"

"Yes, Billy," he said, and brushed the hair back from my face. "You are one crazy little homo, you know that?"

XXIII

BACK TO SCHOOL

Time heals all wounds.

There. I said it.

I could have done a whole tap-dance extravaganza about the passage of time, the changing of the seasons, how the world keeps spinning and nothing stays the same. Hi-ho. I could have pointed out a dozen senior-class milestones that came and went while I recovered—midterms, SATs, senior pictures, my driving test, college applications—to show the passage of time. I could have charted my physical progress, shown when each cast came off, each bone mended, each bruise healed. You could have looked at the before and after pictures—witnessed my transformation from the throbbing gob of rotting meat that arrived at the emergency room to the luminous Julianne Moore–like beauty in front of you—that would have effectively done the trick.

But, no.

I did not do that. "Time heals all wounds" just about covers it. Not every sentence has to sparkle with originality. Some just have to get you from point A to point B.

In this case: Point B being the first day back to school. Almost a month later. It's mid-October.

And yes, I'm going back.

Back to my old boggy Gulag!

Hee-Haw High! Swampworth Academy!

I was promised things would be different, this time, though.

The principal laid down the law: If anything happened to me upon my return—any accident or threat of any kind—then I held the power to have that student suspended immediately.

The coach held a private meeting with the Manatees and told them not to screw this shit up. Personally, he didn't care if they stuffed and mounted me on the locker-room wall—but just to wait until after the season was over. Otherwise, he would have no choice, and they'd be off the team.

The deciding factor in my return was Flip, though, who promised to be my bodyguard and personally escort me to and from every class, holding my hand if it would make me feel better. HELL, YEAH!

He would also make it very clear to everyone that I was off-limits. Flip was riding a personal crest of the winning season, and at this point he could tell everybody to jab flaming sticks into their eyes, and they would do it.

XXIV

So.

First day back.

Walking through the courtyard, onto the campus, Flip at my side.

TOP OF THE WORLD, MA!

FAGS RULE, OKAY!

DON'T TREAD ON ME!

I AM THE TEFLON QUEEN.

There was a banner welcoming me back, and that was sweet, I must admit.

The principal was there to greet me (i.e., please don't sue). "Great to have you back . . . blah blah blah . . ." "Whatever I can do . . . blah blah blah . . ." (Translation: No more trouble out of you, please.)

And I thought: *Yes, THIS is how we do it, do it . . . . VIP all the way!*
The Full Diddy!

In the hallway students stopped and smiled and said hello. Many asked how I was and expressed their outrage at what happened.

I was dressed in flowing white, like a young Gandalf the Gay. Saints should always look their purest, don't you think? And because I was rather glowing with holy light this morning, I started blessing my well-wishers. "Peace be with you." And: "Let the healing begin."

Oh, I'm just such a good person. (*CHOKE.*) It's true. Not many people could be as big as I'm being. I'm like Oprah. I give and I give until I'm just an empty husk. . . .

XXV

It was 9:03 — class was about to begin. I took my seat.

Flip had a surprise for me.

"Hey, Billy!" Flip shouted. "Come sit back here between me and Bib!"

Bib screwed up his face, and said in a flattened monotone: "Yeah . . . Billy. . . . Come sit . . . with us."

Oh my God! Bib Oberman! Did you hear that? Can you imagine? Bib, who is usually as tender as a tazer, darling as a dingo, and about as inviting as a riptide, wanted ME to sit with HIM! HOW THRILL-ING! Granted, it was Flip's idea, and yes, Bib looked to be experiencing extreme intestinal duress, but why quibble?

YES! YES! YES! I'LL DO IT!

"BERNIE! Get Billy a chair," Flip said sharply. And lo and behold, Bernie did it! He got me a chair!

And so I walked the ten feet, but million miles, to my new seat. Well, all right! Look at me! I've joined the exalted ranks of the Back

Seat Boys. Not too shabby! ON THE KNEES OF THE GODS, and all that. I must say, the view was mighty empowering.

Flip gave me a knowing little wink.

"Yo, Bernie," Flip called out again. "Billy doesn't have a pencil. Give him yours, will you?"

"But . . . but . . . Yes, Flip. Here, Billy."

I took it and gave him a saucy wink.

"Could you sharpen it, too?" Flip smiled sweetly.

"Yes . . . Flip . . . ," he growled, without moving his lips.

When Mr. Reamer arrived and, in front of the class, again apologized for his absence that day, I smiled beatifically and said, "YOU ARE FOR-GIVEN," then made the sign of the cross. He looked vaguely annoyed.

When class was over, true to his word, Flip escorted me to the seat of my American lit class. And when the bell rang fifty-five minutes later, he was there to pick me up and escort me to the next class.

XXVI

Lunch—I sat with the Manatees at table one, the most prized piece of cafeteria real estate. Sitting there was Flip's idea; he said it announced to the world that I had made it. It sent a message that I was untouchable.

The murderous goons of the Hitler Youth Brigade all behaved like perfect gentlemen. They included me in their conversations and politely refrained from kicking the crap out of me. I couldn't have had a lovelier time.

In fact, I thought I pulled off the transition from punching bag to luncheon date quite graciously and was a sparkling addition to their table. Yes, yes. It's true!

However, as I was telling Bib and the Takaberrys all about the Marc Jacobs spring collection, and how they could translate some of the trends into their own spring-summer wardrobes, I noticed that they were kicking Flip under the table.

"Floral is back, you say?" Bib smiled, and there was an audible CRACK! from below. Flip winced.

"Gingham for night?" The ugly Takaberry asked in disbelief. There was another KA THUNK! And again Flip's face registered discomfort.

Heterosexuals are so rough with each other! I'll never understand them!

Anyway: I counted lunch as a great success, and a major social coup on my part. Definitely better than getting fish sticks up my nose.

I even went so far as to hug and air-kiss Bib good-bye. He looked a bit stunned, like he was holding down a powerful emotion.

I think he was touched. Probably not many people hug him. Hard to cuddle a walking sledgehammer, you know.

XXVII

AFTER LUNCH

It was all rather exhilarating. People smiled and said hello. I received compliments on my hair, my smile, and my new boots (octopus leather!). One girl even asked for makeup advice. ("Big felt eyebrows for fall," I told her. "And a reversible wig. Oh, yeah, it's ALL ABOUT the reversible wig for fall.")

Why, I felt like a real person, not some windy warthog to be avoided!

Flip was giddy as all get-out. "What do you think? Isn't it cool?"

"Oh my God," I agreed, "everybody's being so nice! It's tripping me out!"

"I know! I told you things would be different when you came back! You can do whatever you want! You can dress however you want! Nobody can touch you!"

"Yeah, well, I think I'll lay low with the freak flag for a while."

"Naaah, man. Now is the time! Send a message! Show them how fabulous you are!"

Well . . .

Hmmmm . . .

A perfectly marvelous idea HAD been bubbling up in my head for a while.

A way to put a little POW! into tomorrow's oral report on Zelda Fitzgerald.

"I'LL DO IT!"

Later: "You're SURE you'll be by my side ALL DAY?"

"I'm there like back hair."

I guess that's good. But just to be sure, I asked again: "EVERY-WHERE?"

He held my hand. "To the urinal and beyond, babe."

Well! THAT'S PROMISING!

Now where's my Coke and ammonia cocktail? I have a lot of work ahead of me.

XXVIII

NEXT MORNING

I pulled up a chair, and began ceremoniously gluing Grape-Nuts onto my face and covering them with great gobs of greasepaint. Yes, again with the cereal on the face. Grape-Nuts can be molded into textured bumps and anthills. It gives your skin a wonderful Freddy Krueger–like finish that's just too, too fabulous. See? Oh—admit!

I latexed some open wounds onto my cheeks and stippled them with black, giving them a "just singed" look.

A little ooze.

Maybe a bruise.

La-la-la.

I finger-waved my fiery red mane . . .

Added some perfectly bee-stung lips, painted with Scarlet Temptation lip rouge . . .

Tossed on a little beaded flapper gown that I had set fire to last night, then quickly stamped out before the flames ate through the fabric. Then, a single peacock feather in my headache band and a cigarette holder, and VOILÀ! you've got "Zelda Fitzgerald—After the Fire."

Yes! Yes! Too fabulous! I thought I might reenact the fire in the mental institution that killed her!

Give them beauty AND talent!

POW! POW!

XIX

THE OBLIGATORY NONFAN'S REACTION

Flossie clutched her heart when she saw me. "Oh, Sweet Jesus!"

I did a zippy little Charleston for her and batted my eyelashes demurely.

"Child, what is wrong with you? Have you been licking light sockets? Have you already forgotten? You need to be locked up! You are a danger to yourself and everyone around you! I'm calling your father. We are not going through this again . . ."

"Relax. It's for school. It's homework. Besides, I have Untouchable status now. And Flip is by my side the entire day."

She shook her head. "That boy doesn't have the brains God gave a squirrel."

XXX

Once again the hallways filled as people pushed to catch a glimpse of the freak. Students jumped and jostled and jockeyed for position. They hung from lockers and clung to poles, straining to see for themselves the loony homo in his latest outfit.

As I walked through the halls the murmurs rose to a mighty roar.

Let's listen:

"Don't you look pretty?"

"I love your makeup."

"You go, girl."

"Fab dress."

"Lookin' sexy, yo."

"You always look SO great!"

"Did you have a makeover?"

"How do you do that?"

"Can you teach me?"

"Doesn't Billy look nice today?"

"You should be a stylist."

"Is that your real hair?"

"Hot."

"New outfit?"

"Billy! My man!"

"Come to my party this weekend?"

"Sexy Momma!"

"Wow!"

"You crack me up!"

"BIL-LY! BIL-LY! BIL-LY!"

"I swear, if I wasn't straight, man . . . MMMM-MMM."

And on.

What a difference a couple months makes, huh?

With the quarterback by my side, and their enthusiam still ringing in my ears, I should have been over the moon. I should have been crowing about "freak power" and "the trumph of the tranny" and planning my victory lap.

And yet . . .

And yet . . .

"I told you they were great guys!" whispered Flip. "See, they love you! It just took a little time, that's all!"

I bit my lip and wondered.

XXXI

Lights off.

Strobe light on.

A tape recording of radio static, howling wind, and a piano key (D minor) plunked over and over. And over.

Chaos. Dissonance. Aggressive black noise.

I started on the floor, hunched over with a flashlight shining up, under my face, illuminating the Grape-Nuts to horrific effect.

"Oooh! . . . Ooooh! . . . The pain! . . . The pain! . . . Do you feel the flames . . . Do you feel the hellfire licking at your feet?"

I moaned and writhed a bit.

Then: "I am the ghost of Zelda Fitzgerald! When I danced upon this mortal coil, my husband, F. Scott, and I knew boundless joy and unfathomable pain. Our larger-than-life escapades and violent, gin-fueled tantrums defined the Roaring Twenties. I still remember how we danced and drank and fought and loved like there was no tomorrow. Now . . . as my skin bubbles and blackens, scorches and curls off the meat . . . I realize there is NOTHING BUT tomorrows . . . and tomorrows . . . and tomorrows . . . stretching to infinity. . . . Oh, the agony. . . ." And I began rocking side to side. "And with every blistering flame-lick that I endure, I am reminded of my own personal damnation! This is my story: From MADCAP to just plain MAD—I am Zelda Fitzgerald!"

Oh, I was good. Yes. I was ON. I didn't just tell her story; I didn't just act it out. No, BY GOD, I LIVED IT. The glory years—the dancing in water fountains, the drunken fights with F. Scott, then the descent into alcoholism and madness—the works! For the big fiery death scene in the insane asylum, I took it to another level.

I really went there.

In my head. In my heart. I WAS THERE.

It was BEYOND method acting, I'll tell you THAT.

Why, I might have been actually channeling the REAL SPIRIT of Zelda Fitzgerald, it felt THAT authentic.

I spun and shrieked and cried and banged against the window, begging for death. I THREW myself against the wall (*THUD!*) then the door (*KLUMP!*), truly feeling the unbearable panic and frenzied agony of this poor madwoman. I dropped and rolled and tried to put my burning flesh out. I choked and gagged until I gasped my last breath. I was dead. BUT THEN, as my soul plunged into the fiery depths of HELL, I rose up again—SPINNING and SCREAMING, laughing and crying, as I embraced damnation!

When I finished, there was a moment of silence when I worried that . . . maybe . . . I had done it again.

But no.

There was a burst of enthusiastic applause—the real deal, not feigned or forced. These preppy princesses—who openly dislike me; find me repellent, in fact; and think I should be burning in hell—genuinely liked it! Tiff Tarbell smiled! Baba Deschler mouthed: "Wow!" Lynnette Franz was not scowling! Even Holy Roller Dottie Babcock looked impressed!

The teacher was equally blown away. In all her twenty-seven years of teaching, she said, THAT was the most surprising and thrilling book report she HAD EVER HEARD!

I picked my burned and battered little body off the floor.

"You are all TOO KIND!" I said, and gave a deep bow of thanks.

I excused myself to the restroom to scrape the Grape-Nuts and goop from my face. I must have scrubbed for fifteen minutes. I changed into my gym clothes and went to meet Flip and tell him of my theatrical triumph.

I must say, it felt pretty damn good. I could get used to this.

XXXII

But. From the highs and the lows, to the . . . um . . . ups and downs of daily life . . .

THURSDAY

I need to tell you about a particularly humiliating episode. I'll try to be delicate, but if you don't care for lurid stories about inappropriate yet entirely natural body functions involving hormonal boys and Speedos, read no further.

You have been warned.

Mondays, Wednesdays, and Fridays, I have gym class.
Tuesdays and Thursdays, health class.

Gym class, as you might imagine, is not one of my best subjects. I have a profound lack of hand-eye coordination that makes me unusually girly and spastic. Yes, MORE SO. I haven't mentioned it because I've been humiliated in gym for as long as I can remember, so it's no big deal.

However.

I always have a few moments of GAY TERROR in the locker room. Well, of course.

I know that one lingering glance at the wrong behind, one too many quick checks of my neighbors' vitals, or GOD FORBID, any sort of accidental physical contact would spell instant death for me.

My strategy?

Avoid all temptation.

For me it's IN, OUT, eyes down, think about tumors and tongue cancer.

(*Tumors and tongue cancer, tumors and tongue cancer . . .*)

And then get the hell out of Dodge.

But remember:

It's always there. A bit of gay terror. Bubbling under the surface. Threatening to pop up and expose you. I mean, you can't un-gay yourself whenever it's inconvenient for you. Despite what Republicans seem to think.

So this month we're swimming. And on this particular day it's diving practice. My doctor says that the exercise will be good for me, so I'm forced to participate. *GRRRR.*

We were all in line, taking turns on the diving board.

In an endless loop.

Dive. Swim. Back in line.

Dive. Swim. Back in line.

In front of me was my new best friend, Bib Oberman.

You know Bib. But do you have a good mental image handy?

Let's recap, just for the sake of the slower kids.

He's a big boy. Big enough to choke a cow. Captain of the football team. Looks like, well, Superman.

Broad chest.

Muscles on his muscles.

Granite jaw.

Wavy blue-black hair.

In a nutshell: a perfect specimen of blossoming manhood. A classically handsome young man. No one can deny that Bib is easy on the eyes, no sir.

So there he was, standing in front of me in his WET, WET, WET school-issued black Speedo—so Kleenex-thin that you could see every dimple, crack, and bulge—and it was impossible not to notice that, well, everything was perfectly visible. EVERYTHING. WAS. PER-FECTLY VISIBLE.

Now we were standing in line.

Going up the ladder.

And Bib's big old bubble butt was poking me in the face.

Over and over again.

Step after step.

And there was no place else to look. It was THAT big and bubbly.

Frankly, it was hypnotizing. Can you blame me for closing my eyes for just one second? Not even. Half a second. I just closed my eyes and WENT THERE. You know what I mean. SNAP! Just a micro-mini-fantasy. SNAP! Then eyes back open.

And then it was my turn to dive.

And, um . . .

How can I say this without being too graphic? Let's just say that my President Johnson was saluting the troops. If you know what I'm saying . . .

Yes, yes, I introduced the entire gym class to my good friend Buster McThunderstick.

The old Zipper Ripper . . .

Kaptain Kielbasa . . .

My Little Pony . . .

The Big Dripper. . . .

And I'm not going to lie to you: it was enormous. I know, I know. Too much information. But what the hell, you've come this far.

So everybody saw what I was thinking when I closed my eyes.

And everybody broke into peals of laughter.

"Holy shit!" "Check it out!" and "Hey, Bib, Billy's got a present for you!"

Bib looked physically ill when he saw what I thought of him. "Ahhhh, MAN!" he said.

Well, I wanted to JUST DIE, of course. I MEAN, MY GOD, if ever there was a good time to be hit by a meteor shower, this was it. And the more I tried to focus on, ahem, MINIMIZING the situation, the HARDER it became. Um . . . Yes.

The teacher had to even acknowledge the situation and put an end to it before it got out of control. The whole staff was on high alert, remember, where I was concerned. Nothing could happen to me.

"Okay, Bloom, you're excused for the day," he said quickly. "Hit the showers. The rest of you chuckleheads, quiet down! Now back in line! I don't have to tell you that these things happen to everybody."

And as I was standing at the end of the diving board and the line had already resumed, I couldn't go back the way I came and climb down. CAN YOU IMAGINE? Banging each guy on the head as I went? So I had no choice but to dive in, swim over to the ladder, and get out AT THE END OF THE LINE, then walk the entire length of the building back to the shower-room door.

It was the ULTIMATE walk of shame. I was made to parade my float, as it were, in front of, and close up to, each and every one of them, ONE AT A TIME.

Instead of a "perp walk," it was my "perv walk."

There was a deafening silence as I made my way to the locker-room door. As I closed the door to the showers I heard them all exhale and mutter amongst themselves: "Groooosss" and "FAGGOT" and "Dude, what is wrong with him?" and laugh about my chances with Bib.

I finally made it to the showers, where I was alone, humiliated, and still turned on.

Probably one of the most horrible, confusing days of my life.

I didn't go back to the gym class. I just couldn't face it.

And for the next couple of weeks, the teacher didn't look too closely at the notes from my "mother" excusing me from swimming due to "swollen glands."

THE REPERCUSSIONS

NOW, DON'T FORGET: I still had my veto power to expel people—

And because Bib Oberman was involved and would share in any ritual humiliation by association, the incident wasn't shouted down the halls or screamed across the classrooms. I wasn't really teased about it. Not openly, at least. Besides, every guy there had probably experienced something similar at some time or another, and I'm sure most of them were just relieved that it hadn't happened to THEM.

So it was quietly dropped.

Except.

There was one repercussion, one life-changing bit of kickback—so wicked, so unexpected that no one could have ever foreseen.

XXXIII

LATER THAT AFTERNOON

THWAP!

Flip materialized, in that way that he has, as I shut my locker door. I jumped and let out a little girl scream: "Oh!"

He smiled THAT smile and looked at me with an arched brow. "So. Bib, huh? I was right all along," and then he playfully (but NOT so playfully) punched me in the arm. (OWW!) "HEY, if you want, I can maybe put in a good word for you."

"Don't you dare! I mean, it's not what you think. Please, just leave me alone."

"Relax, I'm kidding." And he gave me the old puppy-eyes.

"Well, don't. It's really embarrassing."

"No, it's all cool. I won't talk about it ever again." He paused for a moment, then started talking about it again. "So, Bib, huh? I don't get it, personally."

"No, not Bib, really. Let it go. It was just an unlucky coincidence. A total accident."

"Sure, sure. Accident. Whatever. But you DO know that Bib hates you, Billy? I mean, that's sort of sick on your part. Do you like being treated like that? 'Cause if you do, hey, that's your deal. . . ."

"I DO NOT LIKE BIB OBERMAN, MR. KELLY! NOW WILL YOU PLEASE!"

(*Is he jealous? Is this flirting? Are we flirting? There seems to be an underlying joke . . . something funny we're dancing around. Yes, I do believe this is flirting. Oh my God!—this is so* Degrassi High!)

"Good. I just don't want you to get hurt," he said. His leg brushed against mine—accident? He leaned over and whispered in my ear: "I take care of you, bro. Lookin' out for my buddy."

He smiled and winked, and then he was gone.

OH, THAT BOY!

He always left me hot and shivering. Dead calm and quivering. On the floor and on the ceiling. I could still feel his hot breath in my ear. "I take care of you," he whispered, and my ear has never known such spasms of pleasure. I swear, it moaned. It grew a mouth and moaned. True story.

❧

It is suddenly ten years in the future. We are a man-and-wife trapeze act in a small traveling circus that tours through Romania and the Bal-

kans. We call ourselves the Flying Kellikoffs. He has changed his name to Vladimir, and I am now Natalia. By day he leads the caravan across the countryside, while I sew new spangles onto the spandex hot shorts that we each wear onstage.

By night, we swing through the air, soaring from bar to bar and into the safety of each other's arms.

Every time he catches me, the audience applauds loudly.

Every time he catches me, our love is confirmed again. He loved me enough to catch me tonight, I tell myself.

"I take care of you," he whispers. "You are mine."

XXXIV

LATER THAT NIGHT

BANG! BANG! BANG!

"Billy! Open up! We need to talk." It was Flip.

"What's up?"

A lot, apparently. He hit the stairs full gallop, full speed, talking a blue streak, forgetting to even take a breath, so that he just kept going and going and going until he ran out of air and wound down like a tin woodsman. Then, BIG GULP, and he was off and running again. He didn't even notice my pretty new dress or the enormous conehead I was wearing.

He seemed genuinely upset. And this time, there was no good-natured undercurrent. No possibility of flirting.

"I'm sorry, Billy, I can't just sit back and do nothing. I know you like Bib. Don't bother to deny it. It's obvious. People have been talking about it since the beginning of the year."

THIS WAS MADDENING! HE WAS LIKE A BROKEN RECORD!

"Flip, Flip. Whoa. What is this? Calm down. Look in my eyes. I PROMISE YOU, I DO NOT LIKE BIB. Why does this upset you so much? Why can you not accept that?"

"Come on. It's so obvious. You sneak stares at him all through biology. I see you. We all do."

Now THIS was the very definition of irony. Because when I look at Bib, I'm looking to see if HE caught me staring at FLIP! I spend the whole hour trying NOT to make puppy eyes at Flip, but when I do, I get paranoid that Bib's noticed, so I have to quickly check HIM out!

There was more: "You were hanging ALL OVER HIM at lunch this week. It was disgusting. I was embarrassed for you. You HUGGED him the other day. What was THAT about?"

"I want Bib to like me because he's YOUR FRIEND! I didn't want your friendship with ME to be a strain on your friendship with HIM!"

And I shook my head at how RETARDED this was.

It's all just weird, plain and simple. There was absolutely no RATIO-NAL way to explain Flip's behavior. He was acting like he was jealous of Bib! Like he felt threatened by him!

By God, it felt like we were having a lovers' spat!

So, hey, you know what? I decided I was just going to treat it as such.

What the hell, right? When nothing makes sense, acting sensibly isn't going to get you anywhere. So: DEEP BREATH.

"It's not Bib," I said firmly. "And you need to calm down."

"Not until we work this out," he said.

"Work WHAT out, Flip? What don't you get? It's you! I'm always looking at YOU in biology! Not Bib."

His eyes opened wide as he absorbed what he must have known all along. "But . . . but . . . in gym class . . ."

"An accident! Like I told you the first time! I can't help that it was Bib's ass in my face. It could have been anybody's ass. Bernie's. Mr. Reamer's. I'm a freakin' teenage boy! What do I care? Flip, it's you. It's you. It's you. You are the only person I think about day and night. You gotta know that. It can't be a surprise. It's you. It's ALWAYS you."

He got all golly-eyed, "Wait. Wh-what?" he stammered. "Why are you saying this? You know I'm straight."

"Then why are you so jealous of Bib?"

"JEALOUS?" he asked. "AM I . . . JEALOUS?"

He was walking back and forth now, shaking his head. "I don't know," he said. "This is wrong," he said. "I'm straight," he said, but with a little less conviction. He didn't understand what was happening to him.

He paced around my room, and the words kept coming faster and louder. Over and over again he said he was lost; he was confused; he didn't know what to do. This wasn't supposed to happen.

This feeling was wrong.

That's when I did it.

YES!

I grabbed him.

I grabbed him and pulled him close to me.

I kissed him, quick, just once, then pulled back.

He looked at me. I looked at him.

Both shocked.

But then . . .

Our heads moved slowly back together again. Closer, closer . . .

His lips brushed against mine. Softly. Quickly.

My world stopped. I stopped. Our mouths met, two people joined.

As he slowly gave in to his feelings, his tongue did a slow pirouette around mine. He drew me closer, kissing me harder. I turned into Liquid Billy and slid down his throat—happy, happy, finally happy.

I danced in his mouth, dangled from his epiglottis, and did a delirious free fall into his stomach.

I bathed in his gastric juices, nibbled on his semi-digested food, and played tickle games with his intestines. There I was; I was inside him; I was a part of Flip now—small at first—timid, shy, unsure of a rhythm, but with each passing moment, I felt my confidence grow. I became fluid, buoyant, growing larger, like a balloon, filling up inside him, until I was just beneath his skin—and he was my shell. My skin. He was mine.

Mine.

He stopped. The balloon popped.

"Yo, Billy. I don't know . . ."

No, no, no. I pulled him close again and let my tongue trace the line of his lips—they were soft, juicy.

I kissed him harder, pushing him down, climbing on top of him. I didn't care who we were anymore. I kissed him harder because I was happy, yes, finally truly happy. Who cares if the whole school hates me? Who cares if the WHOLE FUCKING STATE hates me? Flip Kelly was kissing me! I did it! I'm happy! And I deserve this moment.

I couldn't help myself. I kissed his eyes, his nose, his cheeks. I opened my eyes and looked at the most gorgeous boy I'd ever seen.

Did I go too far, cross some invisible line? Had I forgotten myself and become overconfident? Like Oedipus Rex before me (or was it Vanilla Ice?), I was so caught up in my own satisfaction, I ignored the warning signs and various red flags.

"Hubris leads to nemesis," my history teacher said the other day—whatever that means. It's probably Latin for "Don't molest straight boys."

Because . . .

Just as I got his shirt off and was working on the jeans . . .

And while we were falling against walls and leaning on tables and rolling over couches . . .

Really surrendering to the moment, you know . . .

Yes, just when he finally seemed fully committed, and all his doubts and misgivings were swept away in a great and glorious tide of homo-passion, that—

TOOT! TOOT!

YES!

That's when two hundred slack-jawed Yankees pointed and gasped and lunged for their cameras.

Within half a second, we were literally blinded by the explosion of flashes as the *Jungle Queen* sailed past.

Yes! Caught in the act!

Look! There was Flip, shirtless, his jeans around his ankles. And there I was, splayed out on a table, dress hiked up, bodice pushed down, in the unladylike process of licking his armpit.

FOR THE LOVE OF GOD, BOYS—HAVE YOU NO SHAME? COVER YOURSELVES!

Hoping against hope, I said, "Who cares?" and I lunged breathlessly back for more.

But no, no. The spell was broken.

He jumped up and ran for the door.

"Go away," he cried. "Get away from me. I can't do this. I can't believe you . . . after I told you . . . And in front of all those people. . . ."

"What do you mean?"

"No, Billy! I gotta go. I can't. . . ." And he grabbed his shoes and searched for his shirt, and never finished the sentence, he was out the door so fast and taking the steps five at a time.

"Where are you going?" I screamed. "What are you doing?"

Oh my God! I'm having an aneurysm! Yes! And a stroke! . . . BRAIN . . . POPPING! . . . MELTING! . . . TURNING TO FOAM! . . . Everything's going black. This is it. I'm dying.

"Flip! Come back here!" I screamed. "Goddamnit, you can't do this to me!"

But he kept on running.

And like every great woman of tragedy, I frantically followed him out the door, pointlessly screamed his name from the patio, and furiously ripped my dress off. Then I fell to my knees, looked up at the stars, and screamed, "WHYYYYY?" as he peeled away in a cloud of dust.

XXXV

SATURDAY

"Hi, this is Flip. Yo, I'm not here right now, but be cool and I'll get back with you as soon as I can."

BEEP!

"Hi, this is Billy. Listen, I wanted to apologize for the other night. I think we SHOULD just pretend it didn't happen. I didn't mean to upset or weird you out. I didn't mean to. That's really the last thing I wanted to do, you know, is upset you. Your friendship means a lot to me, Flip. It's sort of all I have right now. I hope I wasn't out of line. I just couldn't take it if I did something stupid. Let's just not make any final decisions yet. You're the only friend I have. I don't want to sound possessive or anything. I just want you to know how important you are and—"

BEEP!

". . . That I miss you already."

Entr'acte

I

WAIT!

WAIT!

STOP!

HOLD IT RIGHT THERE!

Nobody read another page!

You there! Hands off the book! Put your reading glasses on the ground where I can see them!

We have a problem.

I can't go on!

My conscience won't let me.

I've been living a lie. IT'S TRUE! Everything I've told you has been a lie. EVERYTHING! Well, not everything. Just the foundation. JUST THE FOUNDATION? Don't you see, then? Don't you get it? What I'm trying to tell you is this whole book has been based on a lie.

What lie?

What am I blithering on about?

Remember back on page . . . ten . . . when I told you I had no idea why mother threw me out? That she just lost her mind for no reason and couldn't deal with me, and I COULDN'T FIGURE IT OUT FOR THE LIFE OF ME?

And then again, when I was in the coma and remembering bits and pieces about my life with Muv . . . but I couldn't quite remember that last little part?

Lies.

All lies.

Nothing but plop and twaddle.

Horseshit and hooey.

It was blatantly false. Patently untrue. Nothing but complete and utter nonsense.

Yes, yes. I looked you straight in your collective eyes and just out-and-out lied. Lied like the dog I am. I'm such a sociopath sometimes. Bad Billy!

I know EXACTLY what happened.

I can give you a second-by-second account, in fact, of that afternoon, complete with flow charts and graphs and annotated footnotes and full bibliography. I could tap it out in goddamn Morse code if you'd like. Backward.

My God, how could I ever forget something like that? It's seared into my soul. My brand of shame. And yet in light of recent developments, it seems a minor thing to keep from you.

You need to know the truth.

You DESERVE to know the truth.

When we last left the story, Muv had just lost her mind and started dressing like a deranged bag lady, remember?

Okay—see, right off the bat I have a slight confession.

Gosh, this is so mortifying.

Yes, she was an eccentric dresser. And she certainly piled on the crap. But she never wore the cat as a stole. That was Elinor Glyn, a lady writer from the twenties, who invented the phrase "It Girl." I must have gotten them confused.

It could happen.

And the Christmas lights in her hair? That would be me. I do it all the time, and it's FABULOUS, not crazy at all.

WHAT?

IT WAS A DREAM! I WAS DREAMING! IN MY COMA! YOU WEREN'T WATCHING A DOCUMENTARY!

There are no guarantees here, people.

You pay your money, and you take your chances!

But that's it!

That's all the white lies!

I swear!

Everything from here on out is unequivocally, undeniably, 100 percent true. Polygraph-proof. May I spend an eternity in Evan-Picone casuals if I'm lying.

You can trust me.

HERE WE GO:

You have to remember that growing up, I was mother's own little "mini-Muv," parroting her every outrage. Aping her every gesture. Trundling along behind her, echoing her thoughts, repeating her grander-than-thou pronouncements on life and how to live it.

"Dar-LING!" she'd say.

"Yes, dar-LING?" I'd reply.

"EGOMET MIHI IGNOSCO," she'd pronounce.

And I'd translate: "I, myself, pardon myself!"

"That's Horace, darling! You, alone, have the power to forgive your-self! You have only to answer to yourself!"

I didn't understand then, but I do now.

You'll see.

But of course, I wasn't just mindlessly imitating her—monkey see, monkey do. I was learning, processing, absorbing it all—oh yes, I was quite the little sponge. Yes, yes, I was always busy editing, reformatting, and refiguring everything she said and did.

Whenever I was alone, I would try on my own variations of her outfits. Tweak it a little. Take it down a notch. Or up the glam factor.

Adding my own unique touches. Butt pads, sequined skullcaps, ears painted gold, clown noses. Bits of whimsy.

I was finding my own style, my own individual way of expressing myself through clothes. The outfit might be Muv's, but the look was pure Billy. I was big, bold, cutting-edge, like her. But cleaner lines. Simpler. Not as fussy.

Behold, the birth of creation!

The beginning of me.

Billy in Bloom.

But hush, now.

Keep it quiet. Keep it mum. Keep it FROM mum, oh yes, by all means.

Let's not send out announcements just yet. Let's not alert the media of my newfound penchant for drag.

I couldn't quite pinpoint why I was uneasy with her finding out. I just doubted she would be overjoyed.

It wasn't exactly a betrayal.

It wasn't really a rebellion.

It couldn't have been much of a shock.

I just thought it was wise to lie low for the time being.

I know it seems odd that I would worry about the reaction of a woman like Muv—an artist! Who's educated! Worldly! A staunch nonconformist! Who looks down on the provincial rubes that cross our paths! And yet, a child knows. . . .

I knew she'd been at the bottom of a bad cycle for a while—months!—so moody and erratic that I'd never seen her this bad. She seemed lost, paranoid, muddled, defensive. Prone to anger and hysteria, easily threatened, thinking everyone was out to get her.

I was walking on eggshells, ANYWAY; I just knew she was not in a warm and fuzzy place for any major lifestyle shake-ups.

And I was right.

When she finally turned on me, it was such a major blowup over such a minor misunderstanding!

It all went down over a dress—a silly, bias-cut Ungaro number of the floatiest beaded chiffon—that belonged to my mother.

I was just trying it on while she was at the store. And for the love of corn, it wasn't even REALLY a dress. More of a shapeless shift. Why, one might even go so far as a LONG BLOUSE. Okay, that's too far.

You know how a few years ago, all those B-list starlets—like, oh, Lisa Rinna—always seemed to be photographed wearing those flirty-but-casual chiffon dress and jeans combos? And how in the beginning it brought just a funky whiff of anarchy to the red carpet? "I'll conform to your dress code on top, but from the waist down, I'm a REBEL" is what it screamed.

Well, I thought to myself, *why shouldn't men be allowed to enjoy the same quirky mashup of casual wear and elegance?*

So I tried on my mother's Ungaro and wore it under a suit, a white satin tuxedo jacket of the sharpest order. True it was Muv's, and nipped and fitted to a fare-thee-well, but it could totally pass as a man's jacket. Totally. And the effect was UNBELIEVABLY FABULOUS! A WHOLE NEW LOOK! Why, I had single-handedly revolutionized the men's suit.

As I was admiring my cunning work, who should pop back in but Mother. She had left her purse.

"I left . . . my . . ."

And she never finished the sentence.

Now, let me reiterate: I WAS NOT IN DRAG. I was tweaking the men's fashion silhouette, which is an ALTOGETHER different thing.

Okay—so I ditched the jacket. I confess.

And the pants were really white tights.

And, well, all right, I had a wig on, as well. And a little pink lipstick. Okay, maybe it was Scarlet Temptation. Who knows? It was just to pull the outfit together. BUT I WAS DEFINITELY NOT IN DRAG.

But there I was, I suppose, in my mother's stunning, showstopping, gold, beaded Ungaro number, and I was working it better than she ever could. So perhaps she was a little jealous. . . .

There was a moment of total silence in which all the air was sucked out of the room.

Nothing to do but:

"Oh, hullo, dar-LING!" I said, and struck a pose. *"Quel surprise,* right?"

(*Hold pose, and smile desperately.*)

Just brazen it out.

And:

Silence.

She said nothing.

Her mouth open, O, but no sound came out.

Not good. Not good.

My smile started to crack. My ta-dah pose began twitching and jerking.

Beads of sweat drip, drip, drip down my face.

She looked at me. I looked at her.

Then she darkened.

Her whole posture changed.

When she finally opened her mouth, she just ERUPTED in blood and thunder. Foam and fury. Her voice was a great and terrible trumpet blast, a mighty bellow, full of misplaced rage. It was the voice of a monster, a Leviathan, a mighty pissed off *Tyrannosaurus rex.*

She took my cross-dressing as an act of betrayal, and completely blew her stack.

She stopped making sense.

She raved and ranted, and generally acted as if I were the enemy, that I had been out to destroy her from the beginning. According to Muv, I was the cause of everything wrong in her life. I was the very embodiment of chaos, the face of random violence. I was a walking earthquake, a living disease, an epidemic that needed to be quarantined.

According to her, I steamrolled over lives, flattening everyone in my path. My greed was boundless, unending. I took and took with such great, grasping urgency, such gulping, gobbling hysteria, it was ugly and animal-like—embarrassing to witness. I was a razor-toothed succubus. A bloodthirsty jackal.

In the History of Mothers and Sons, I stood alone in the Pantheon of Ungrateful Children. She would rather have raised a 9/11 terrorist, a death camp general, or a butcher of babies—they would have been less trouble.

Which I thought was all a bit harsh. . . .

"And THIS!" she screamed, her voice raw. "This latest stunt!" and she ripped the dress off my body and threw it to the floor.

This was THE LAST GODDAMN STRAW! Did I understand?

She kept on, her voice rising in pitch, her anger swelling, her reason slipping away:

"Who do you think you are?" she bellowed.

And: "Did you think you could get away with it?

"Did you think you were above common decency? Respect?

"Do you like breaking my heart?

"Are you trying to humiliate me?

"Well?

"Why don't you answer me?

"HOW DARE YOU JUST STAND THERE AND LOOK SMUG?

"Does this whole thing strike you as funny?"

Silence.

Dramatic tension as she built up to:

"OUT!" (And I heard the blood rushing in my ears.)

"I WANT YOU OUT!" (And my mouth went dry.)

"I don't even want to look at you! Just go! I don't want to see you again." (My bowels constricted.)

She walked to the kitchen.

"You have ten minutes."

I suddenly felt faint and collapsed, but only briefly. Instinct took over. A lightning quick assessment of the situation concluded that it was probably a wise idea to do as she said. Now wasn't the time to argue or explain or apologize.

Just go.

I quickly, blindly, began shoving items into a garbage bag. Anything. Everything. No time to organize. THIS and THIS and THIS and DONE. I took one last look around, then got the hell out of Dodge.

So there you have it.

Not a pleasant tale, but there you are.

That's how I came to Fort Lauderdale.

She called dad and said it was HIS turn to deal with me. That maybe he would be a better influence on me.

And honestly, after all that I had been through, I actually looked forward to the quiet life with Dad. (Although I never would have admitted it at the time.)

We now return to our regularly scheduled story.

Where were we? Oh, yeah—barrel's bottom, SCRAPE, SCRAPE.

Flip had just abandoned me. And I was feeling lost and alone and teetering on the very brink of sanity myself.

Now, without further ado, we rejoin our gender-squashing heroine's plight, already in progress. . . .

Part Three

HERE COMES SUPERFREAK!

I

LIFE AFTER FLIP, DAY ONE

I move about, free from myself, free from my thoughts. My movements are automatic—opening drawers, looking through cabinets. I am looking for something—I don't know what it is, but I will recognize it when I see it. Until then I pause, maybe, and listen to my breath, then continue . . . under the rug, behind the bookshelf . . . I am shuffling and breathing, and listening and looking. Always looking. I am not myself these days. I am not myself, nor am I anybody else.

Can't you see? Don't you get it? Without Flip, I'm just a shell, a hat stand all dressed up. Why, if I weren't wearing these platforms and this sombrero, I wouldn't exist at all. I'd dissolve. PLIP PLOP. Down the drain.

Look here, I can cut myself and nothing happens. It's just corn syrup and food coloring pouring from make-believe veins. It's not even mine.

I retire to the safety of my cupboard and continue slowly fading away.

II

DAY TWO

There are days when even the cupboard is too roomy, too wide open. There are too many variables in there, too many chances for things to go wrong. You need something more secure. A better fit. On those days, when you just want a giant Ziploc sandwich bag to slide into, I find there's only one practical thing to do:

Lock yourself in the guest room and fold yourself into the sofa bed.

Yes, only then can you discover the absolute bliss of total restriction. Only in your new hideaway heaven can you finally feel safe from the pain of the outside world.

And if you never leave, you'll be just fine.

III

DAY THREE

And it's time to admit defeat. Yessir. Time to throw in the towel.

From deep within the bowels of your sofa bed, you come to a momentous decision: You're not going back to that wicked place.

Never, never, never.

There's no point. There's no use. You can't fight a school. You can't battle a belief, a way of life, a deep-seated hatred. You can't win. If a two-ton boulder is barreling toward you, you can either try to stop it and face an almost certain flattening, or step aside and live to tell the tale. And I'm sick of feeling like a goddamned Fruit Roll-Up.

So that's it. There you go. The bad guys have won.

IV

DAY FOUR

Tides are turning. A new day is dawning.

And you just might pull through, after all.

Sure! You've been through hard times before. Your mother threw you away, like an old Choo! You're no stranger to heartbreak.

And worse things happen at sea!

So what do you do? How do you cope?

First of all: take it easy. Be gentle with yourself. Don't rush back into the world just yet. You still have a long ways to go.

Rule number one: nothing beats a big bowl of mashed potatoes when you're feeling this depressed. Anything soft, in fact, will do. Chewing is for go-getters. Chewing is for people who have it together. You are not one of those people.

I know, I know, you probably don't have much of an appetite, anyway.

But eat you must. You need to keep up your strength.

I find it helps to picture yourself eating your lover's body parts. Spaghetti? Take a mouthful of his arteries, dear. Tapioca? Those lumps are his eyeballs . . . let them float around in your mouth, then CHOMP! Grind them to a pulpy membrane! With a little imagination marinara sauce becomes his blood. That water bottle is full of the tears he's shed now that you are gone.

It's okay to cry while doing this.

You may feel like masturbating twenty or thirty times a day during this period. And that's . . . okay! Go right ahead. You deserve it. But never, ever, let the image of you-know-who slip into your head while you're doing it. Think about your eighth-grade gym teacher. Think about the lawn boy. Watch *One Tree Hill*. Fantasize about anyone, ANYONE except your beloved ex–Flip Flop.

(It's okay to cry while doing this, too.)

NOW THE CLEANSING RITUAL:

He may have broken your heart, but it's time to reclaim your life. You are going to take control of your emotions. First, gather together all the little mementos of your time together! Yes! Each and every keepsake! The souvenir bedpan! The empty bottle of pepper vodka! The pencil he chewed on! And the little wart you glued to his face! Now TOSS THEM INTO THE DUMPSTER!

Trust me! It's for the best!

Next, the clothes! Yes! Make a pile of all the precious little outfits you wore when you were together! Then, tear them all up! Tear them to shreds! EGAD! ARE YOU SURE? Yes! Yes! And spare no costume, no getup, no snappy little suit! That includes the ocher and puce dress! The bubble wig! Zelda Fitzgerald! Preppy 3000! Yes, even the Vivienne Westwood pirate outfit! Rip it all to shreds! Be brutal! Destroy that dress! Obliterate those jeans! NOW, BRING OUT THE GARDENING SHEARS!

When you are through, it's okay to collapse in a sweaty pile of tears and self-loathing.

Sleep it off. The worst is over.

V

DAY FIVE

Today you begin your journey back into the light.

To ready yourself, you will need to be relaxed and free of all tension.

I suggest you rent a couple of *Care Bears* movies. Sure!

Most people hate the Care Bears on principle. But then, most people hate *me* on principle—so I say to hell with people and their principles!

Pay them no mind!

Might I suggest *Clan of the Care Bears*? Oh, you'll just love it.

Trust me: those perky little buggers can turn your whole day around.

Then? A new task. A confidence builder: Make a list of your strengths. Your selling points. All your most noble and majestic qualities. Here are mine:

- I make a great Bundt cake.
- I can parallel park like a demon.
- I'm great at refolding maps.
- I can wiggle my ears.
- I arch a good brow.
- I do killer '80s eye makeup.
- I know the complete scores of *Rent* and *Hairspray*.
- I lend an aura of quiet dignity to any gathering.
- I'm a people person.

Not exactly the stuff of the coming messiah, but it's a start.

VI

Now for the most important part of your healing process:

Light a candle. Summon forth your most tranquil and positive energy.

Then when you are feeling at one with the goddess within, approach the slash heap and acknowledge what it represents to you. Acknowledge the loss you feel.

Shed a tear at the mess you've made! Go ahead! Look at that big old pile of rip-rot and snip-slop, and tell it how sorry you are. Apologize to each and every outfit that you destroyed.

Now, say a prayer of resurrection.

You are going to give these rags a brand-new life. Yes!

Pick through the saddest little snippets, one by one, and hold each one up to the light.

Really look at them.

You are going to bind these separate pieces together. You are going to build a unified SUPER-SUIT from these sullied, ripped-up memories.

Ask yourself: Could *that* be an armhole? Yes!

Could you get your head through *there*?

And if you wore that bit underneath something like . . .

Say . . .

THAT.

And belted it with THIS strappy glitter thing . . .

And, oh! that's fab! That's fierce, huh?

Now, if I could safety pin these two pieces together and tie it into a sort of sarong around my waist, and then RIP IT A LITTLE MORE here . . .

Yes! Yes! Keep going! More! More!

Loop it!

Twist it!

Let it flap in the wind!

Pin this to that; knot that there, firmly; rip this up to there.

Then . . .

Voilà!

Look at what you have created! A new look!

Yes, the scraps of clothes that were once ripped and shredded beyond recognition have found a new life when cobbled together. It's a "patchwork punk" look. And in it you will be a glorious gutter princess. In fact, it's a wilder, more daring look than anything you have ever worn before. Sliced up to here and slashed down to there, the overall effect is of a violent but fabulous young monster.

So you complete the look by painting yourself an angry, mutant green. It's what any plucky heroine would do.

You are, after all, an angry She-Hulk! *RAR!*

And now you look in the mirror, and you like what you see. Yes!

You are a raging, ragged shock of a girl, and that feels good. Yes!

They tried to destroy you, but they didn't succeed. Oh no! They tried to tear you down, but you refused to give in. For that, you will wear these ripped and ragged clothes! For that, you will SASHAY SHAWNTEE these shredded outfits! And they will be your BADGE OF COURAGE.

They will say to the world: "I SURVIVED AND I'M STRONGER FOR IT!"

And wearing the rags that misery made while wrapped in the shroud of your anguish, you have turned your self-loathing into something FABULOUS, and it feels good. It feels right.

You are owning your martyrdom, and defying it.

You stand tall on the rock of righteous fury and pump your fists in the air.

"I will show the world what has been done to me," you scream. "From this day forth, I wear these rags as a reminder to all the haters in the world. For every faggot who has suffered, let me bind your wounds with my rags. For all the trannies out there who haven't yet found their strength, let them tether themselves to me!"

You vow: "I wear it FOR THEM! And whenever I wear this freakish garb, I will strike fear into the hearts and minds of redneck rich kids everywhere!

"Yes, they shall learn to fear my holey, ragged shadow!

"FOR I AM SUPERFREAK!"

And the gods applaud.

You have moved into the light, and your healing has begun.

So this is it.

The BIG BOOM!

REBIRTH!

A LIGHT SHINES DOWN!

THERE IT IS!

LOOK UPON THE GLORY!

GAZE UPON MY SUPERNATURAL BEAUTY!

REJOICE! THROW FLOWERS!

LET THE RAPTURE BEGIN!

GIZZLE-GAZZLE! DIZZLE-DAZZLE!

BOW DOWN!

FOR I AM SUPERFREAK!

BOOM! *KER-PLOW!*

(*And the world sings of salvation.*)

VII

I am SUPERFREAK!
  Watch me go! Check me out!
  A whole new world! A whole new me!
  And—what's this?
  A plan!
  A reason to be!
  And a powerful new alter ego!
  It's TOO DIVINE!
  Let the dark clouds pass!
  I'm livin' on the edge! Dancing on the lip of a volcano!
  No longer afraid. No longer living a half-life!
  Nothing can hold me down.

VIII

I am Superfreak.
  Defender of girly-boys, scourge of flat-faced homophobes everywhere.
  Wrapped in the purple cloak of midnight.
  I come and go undetected.
  My every move whisper quick!
  A wig on the wind!
  I move about free from glaring eyes. Hidden in shadow. Covered in darkness.
  A creature of the night. Prowling. Growling. Ready to pounce. WATCH OUT!

IX

Then a flare. A flash. A crashing new idea.

A ray of light.

A dawning realization.

If, as SUPERFREAK, I'm all powerful . . .

And I'm finally in control . . .

If it's up to me . . .

Then. Well . . .

And I knew what I had to do.

I knew why I was put here in this godforsaken red state.

The reason for my newfound strength.

What my special purpose was.

I was the light of dawn.

I was the blazer of trails.

I was given this newfound strength to right wrongs and build a better future.

Suddenly, I understood: With absolute freedom comes absolute responsibility.

And so I had to go back.

Because, to be truly free, you can't be running from anything, or tied to what-ifs. Or have regrets.

Ironic, isn't it, that at the moment when I could do anything, when the world held limitless possibilities, I saw only responsibility?

It took a million choices to show me I had just one.

Sure, I could keep running, and never look back. But then I would never know how it all turned out, if I had what it takes to survive in that world, or possibly even triumph.

X

AND SO IT'S . . .

Once more into the swamp, dear friends. Once more!

Or you might as well fold yourself back into the sofa and wait for death!

This vacation, this brief respite, has been lovely, no doubt—doing nothing, lying back, indulging the goddess for three whole days. It's been rejuvenating, hasn't it? It's brought you back to yourself.

But don't you hear? The blasts of war? The call to honor?

It's time to go back to battle once more, and this time, to prevail!

Be strong now, Billy! You have a new mission! Rise up from the ashes of your old self! You are a new species of drag queen, like nothing the world has ever seen before! Look at your sinewy magnificence! Feel this newfound courage surging through your body!

When the alarm is sounded, you must set aside all that is gentle and good in your nature. You must answer your destiny in the guise of the great and fierce drag queen warrior you know you can be!

Yes! You are a tough little queen! Stronger than you knew! You are able to absorb the blows that life keeps giving you! Yes! You are a righteous and mighty She-Hulk!

Now get mad!

Look mean! Real mean!

Give your enemies the hairy eyeball! Stare them down! Look directly into their souls!

Frown! Ferociously! Now grit your teeth! Pull back those glittering ruby lips! Let's see those fangs! Those flesh-eating incisors! Those bone-crunching molars!

Breathe in and out! Let those nostrils flare! Stretch 'em wide!

Pull yourself up to your full queenly height! Rise higher! You are a goddess! A Superfreak! An artist! An iconoclast!

Others have come before you—proud warriors, beautiful she-males. Say their names! RUPAUL! BOY GEORGE! They are legend! PETE BURNS! LEIGH BOWERY! Sister soldiers! DIVINE! SYLVESTER! Call upon their strength and styling skills! HOLLY WOODLAWN! CANDY DARLING!

Rise up now—for all the countless freaks before you who lost, who suffered, and who died at the hands of redneck bigots. And for all those who continue to fight, be a beacon of light in their darkness!

Come on, then. Now is not the time to shirk, to shrink, to fade into the mists of morning.

Let me see the passion in your eyes!

Now, onward, ever onward—to Eisenhower, ho!

GOD SAVE THE SUPERFREAK!

ALL HAIL SUPERFREAK!

XI

BUT FIRST: As a new superhero, I knew that I needed a sidekick.

And if I wanted to go back to the academy, I knew that I'd need some help and protection.

So, my choice was obvious.

Yes.

Why, Blah Blah Blah, of course! My first friend!

Why, she'd be perfect! I've always considered her a rhinestone in the rough!

And I sort of owed it to her, don't you think?

Poor Blah Blah Blah.

No really.

Bless her little blank heart.

Can we all agree that I've been somewhat less than committed to the relationship? That as far as friends go, I rate only slightly better than a Furby? I mean, I've known her for how many months now, and I still have yet to learn her name? Could I be any more odious?

Hey, have I ever even told you what she looks like?

No?

(*I'm such a stain.*)

That's where we'll start, then.

She looks like Harriet the Spy. Yes, yes. One of those hamster-faced girls with bright, inquisitive eyes, who are pretty in spite of themselves. And I mean that in the sweetest way possible. You know, the kind of girl you always think is a bit pudgy, but one day discover it was just the cowl-neck sweaters? And the sexless, full prairie skirts?

And here's something that helps lift her out of character sketch limbo:

Originally, she's from Boston, and when she's not whispering, her voice is a great and glorious East Coast honk—all flattened *a*'s and nasal *e*'s. You didn't know that, did you? Yes, in real life she sounds like an angry teamster or a lovesick sea lion.

THAT explains all the whispering and the scurrying about, and the way she always looks like she's dodging imaginary pigeons, see? It's a way to camouflage herself from the various cat cliques who prowl the halls looking for outsiders to eat for lunch.

See, she's an outsider, just like me.

Perfect sidekick material.

But how could I get in touch with her if I still didn't know her name? I couldn't very well call 4-1-1. I couldn't ask the school office. ("She's a girl, maybe sixteen or seventeen, with brown hair, medium length. No, I don't know her name. But it sounds like . . .")

Then, of course! D'OH!

I didn't know why I hadn't thought of it before!

Where was it?

Searching, searching . . .

Ah, there it was! On the fertility altar!

MY OLD EISENHOWER YEARBOOK!

AND LO! THE ANSWERS I'D BEEN SEEKING WERE AT HAND!

Finally! The great mystery was about to be solved!

I felt like I was about to enter the tomb of King Tut for the first time.

Somewhere on these pages was a picture with a name underneath it. That picture would be of the mysterious BLAH BLAH BLAH, of course. And the name below? Anybody's guess.

And here we go!

I began flipping through the pages of the sophomore class.

Not there.

Or there.

Page after page. Nothing.

There were pictures of Bib and Lynnette and Flip (awww) and Baba and Bo-Bo and Tiff and Kristin and on and on . . .

AND STILL NOTHING!

MORE NOTH—

Wait, wait.

There! Stop!

Was it . . . ?

Yes! Finally. There it was. Plain as the nose on my face. Her name was . . .

DEEP BREATH . . .

I closed my eyes, steadied my hands, EXHALED . . .

And looked down at the page.

OH. MY. GOD.

NO.

IT CAN'T BE!

IT MUST BE A TYPO.

SOME SORT OF MISTAKE.

Look. There. Written in firm block letters:

MARY JANE MCAFFERTY

Huh?

MARY JANE MCAFFERTY? What in the hell was THAT? Some kind of JOKE? Her name was Mary Jane McAfferty? How the hell did I hear Blah Blah Blah over and over again? Why, it wasn't even close! You couldn't slur a name like Mary Jane McAfferty. You couldn't be lazy or mush-mouthed about it. It was all fricatives! Nothing but crackle and spit!

Here, all this time I thought that her name would turn out to be something like Blondie Blahnik or Blossom Blodgett, and that I would have been in the right general area, or at least on the same map. BUT THIS? THIS?

It's too crazy!

(*Looks again at yearbook and shakes head.*)

MARY JANE MCAFFERTY.

I'll be ding-donged.

If that wasn't the most goddamned thing.

You just NEVER CAN TELL.

About ANYTHING.

XII

Tracking down her number was easy, once I had a name. (Apparently that's how it works.)

I called, and within twenty minutes the former Blah Blah Blah was banging on my hall door. "Oh, BILLY! BILLY!" she honked, and threw herself into my arms.

"MARY JANE, my *liebling*, how ARE you?"

"Wonderful, wonderful. Wicked pad, my dear!"

"Thanks. I'll give you the grand tour later. I love your shoes, by the way."

"Miu Miu."

"Well they are TOO TOO . . . !"

We chatted amiably about this and that for a couple minutes more before she finally screamed: "SO TELL ME, ALREADY, WHAT THIS BIG NEWS IS! You said on the phone that you wanted to bring me up to speed. You can't tease me like this, and not follow through! I'm LACTATING, I'm so excited!"

"Okay, okay. Got a few minutes, though? Can I tell you the whole story? It all goes back to that coma, remember . . ."

So I sat her down and I told her everything—from the coma to the kiss to my Billy Scissorhands breakdown. And because I actually KNEW HER NAME, I used it every chance I could. So this is pretty much how the conversation went:

"So then, MARY JANE, Flip said . . ."

"NO WAY!"

"It's true, MARY JANE! So, I said to him . . ."

"STOP! YOU DID NOT!"

"Oh yes, I did, MARY JANE. And he was all . . ."

"OH MY GOD! I'M DYING!"

"Don't die, MARY JANE. But see, he totally seemed like . . ."

"GET OUT! GET! OUT!"

And so on.

When I got to our big kiss, well, I thought my new friend MARY JANE MCAFFERTY was having a stroke, I honestly did. That's when her face got all twisted and twitchy, and she got this freaky Joker-from-Batman smile that was too big to really be a smile—I thought it must be some involuntary muscle reaction that occurs when your brain explodes.

I literally thought my gossip was so juicy, it killed her.

But then she bolted upright and screamed: "YOU MADE OUT WITH FLIP KELLY?"

"In front of God and two hundred slack-jawed witnesses aboard the good ship *Jungle Queen!*"

She choked on an imaginary bite of food. "YOU MEAN . . . THERE ARE PICTURES?"

Oh. Hm. I hadn't even thought of that. But yes. "Yes, I suppose there are."

She was already scribbling madly in her to-do book.

I LIKE THE WAY THIS DAME THINKS!

We then spent a while chatting about this and that, and getting reacquainted and caught up on all the latest gossip, until I felt confident enough to tell her why I asked her to come.

I laid it all out for her.

I filled her in about my new alter ego, Superfreak, and my new calling in life, and how I thought I needed to somehow use my drag to challenge the system (She nodded vigorously at this.); and that I needed to go back to the Eisenhower Academy one more time, but for ME this time, and give it a clear, concentrated effort, you know; and that I felt like I needed to conquer those rich swamp rats once and for all (She pumped a power-to-the-people fist in the air.); that I was going to earn their respect and their acceptance, or die trying; and, along the way, drag them into the twenty-first century, right? and teach them that being gay does not mean that God hates me or if I sneeze, they're going to get AIDS; or that just because they all have penises DOES NOT MEAN I want to lure each and every one of them into the broom closet. (Here she jumped up and hugged me. "YOU GO, SISTA SOULJAH!" she screamed.)

Emboldened, I went so far as to show her my Superfreak costume, and explained the meaning and power behind the rags.

She was suitably awestruck. "Those are SOME HOLY RAGS, then, huh?" she whispered.

Then I mumbled that "maybe, if you wanted, you could be my side-kick."

She accepted on the spot.

"OH MY GOD!" she squealed. "I've only been waiting MY WHOLE LIFE for someone to ask me that! OF COURSE! OF COURSE! What's my name? What's my shtick? What do I wear? I'm not so good with the tying old rags together, though. I'm going to need something preassembled."

I pulled out the bedraggled circus outfit with a timid "ta-dah!" "But picture it clean, of course, and totally glammed out with new spangles, new sequins, and all new feathers. It will be rejeweled and reglittered and reborn, better than before! We'll do it together! I'll show you how! And we'll get you a really fab wig and a mask, and you can be WIG GIRL!"

"Do you really think I could pull it off?"

"SURE! That's the thing about superheroes and secret identities: They're SUPPOSED to be opposites so nobody will ever suspect . . . You are the meek-and-mild whisper chick by day, and the bold, audacious FEATHERED FIST OF JUSTICE by night! It's a classic paradigm! You can't lose!"

"Let's do it!" she said. "Let's change the world!"

WHEEEEEEEE!

XIII

MY SUPERHERO ACADEMY

Mary Jane McAfferty, from the get-go, proved to be a very proactive sidekick.

With her everything was all "Chop-chop!"

"Hup! Hup!"

"Down to business!"

"Dawn of a new day," and all!

WHOOEEE. YES, SIR. With her on board I was on the fast track to begin getting things done. Things were really moving right along.

We spent almost all of our spare time together—early mornings, weekends, secret late-night rendezvous—whenever we could squeeze in a meeting, there was always just so much to do!

But now, instead of describing each of our courses and activities in mind-numbing detail, I thought that we might just have a quick, *Rocky*-style montage of the high points, set to inspiring music:

LA-DA-DA! DA-DA-DA! (That's the music.)

There we are doing Tai Chi on the beach at sunrise . . . and running and jumping hurdles in high heels. . . . That's Mary Jane, practicing dramatic entrances and advanced cape swirling. . . .

On the split screen, there's Mary Jane reading Machiavelli and *The Art of War* by Sun Tzu while I'm watching *Cruel Intentions* and studying old episodes of *Pinky and the Brain.*

DA-DA-DUM-DEE-DUM! LA-DA-DEE!

Here, Mary Jane has turned an unused room in the southern wing into our war room. As you can see, there are chalkboards and poster boards and overhead projections of diagrams and secret game plans, as well as perky strategy slogans to keep us inspired and on track.

"BE BOLD!" she has written in large orange and pink letters.

"COURT ATTENTION AT ALL COSTS!" she instructs on another board.

"TRANSFORM YOUR WAR INTO A CRUSADE!" she advises.

"KEEP YOUR MESSAGE SIMPLE," she warns.

"ELEVATE YOURSELF ABOVE THE BATTLEFIELD," she extols.

And so on.

LA-DA-DA-DEEEEE!! DUM-DA-DA-DA-DEEEE!

Oh, here I am, building a better superhero outfit . . . because let's face it: The "tatter-monster look" was okay for quick public appearances and photo ops. But it wasn't built for the general day-to-day things we do, like swinging from rooftops, scaling walls, and chasing villains through sewer systems. And no matter how it's tied together, it has a tendency to unravel at the most inconvenient times—just as you're bursting into villains' lairs, for instance, or standing in line at Arby's.

And I know I said all that crap about wearing those rags as a symbol of my oppression, BLAH BLAH BLAH, but . . . um . . . ew—they're RAGS! You didn't think I was really serious?

So here I am: altering the Batgirl costume. I've glued a red wig ON TOP of the masked headpiece, as sort of a hair hat—SO CHIC!—and changed the insignia to a silhouette of a GIANT BOUFFANT wig. . . . Oh! Oh! And I've shortened the cape! Now it only falls about halfway down my back, which is THE hot new length in crime-fighting capes this season. It's true! Shorter than a poncho, longer than a capelet. Yes, that's how EVERYONE'S wearing them.

Oh, and there's Mary Jane, still diligently working on her Wig Girl outfit . . . bless her heart; there are a LOT of spangles that need resewing on that thing before it's ready for its debut.

BUM-BUM-DUM-DUM-TA-DUM!

And there you have it! Superhero boot camp! The two of us diligently preparing for my triumphant return!

But as wonderful and energizing as Mary Jane is, we don't always share the same vision. In fact, sometimes we are on completely different pages of completely different books.

For instance: One of our top priorities is making sure that I'm not attacked again, if and when I return to classes. We were each supposed to brainstorm ideas and bring our lists to the table for discussion.

These were HER IDEAS:

- Self-defense class? Brazilian jujitsu? Kickboxing?
- Secret Bully-cams hidden in each classroom?
- Carry pepper spray?
- Alert the school board of potential threats?
- Hire a bodyguard from one of the students on the wrestling team?

And these were MY IDEAS:

- Tiara that doubles as boomerang.
- Bullet-deflecting bracelets (Chanel).
- Hypno compact! No. Wait. Maybe a hypno belt buckle! Yes! And then knockout powder in my compact! YES!

Then one day, quite out of the blue, Mary Jane said something incredibly odd. We were discussing various strategies for outmaneuvering the enemy when she said: "'Lay low, sing small'—that's the motto of the shadow people, you know, and it works for them."

THE WHO?

THE WHAT?

"Oh, Billy." She leans in conspiratorially. "I've wanted to tell you about them forever. I mean, FOREVER! But I was bound by oath to keep their secret until they told me it was okay to let you in. . . ."

SHADOW PEOPLE?

Yes, apparently there is a secret population of shadow students who survive on the fringes of the academy. According to Mary Jane, they live under the radar and out of the spotlight. They are ghost kids, taking the long way to classes; scurrying noiselessly along forgotten paths, behind the overgrown hedges, down dark, unused corridors.

"A secret underground society of closet rebels and misfits?" I asked incredulously. "You mean like *Beneath the Planet of the Apes*? Do they look like us? Or are they all *C.H.U.D.*-like? Do they have great, glowing goggle eyes to see in tunnels? Have I ever seen one? Would I know one if I did?"

"Oh, you are SO FUNNY!" She laughed. "Relax. They're just regular students, like you and me. You see them everywhere. You just don't LOOK at them, because they know how to blend in. The trick, you see, is to be not attractive enough to attract attention, but attractive enough so as not to stand out in a sea of physical perfection. You have to be a strict seven and a half. . . ."

It was a lot to wrap my head around.

Imagine! All this time! Drama students! Geeks! Nerds! An actual lesbian! And one or two possibly bisexual boys! It was outrageous! Remarkable! A complete and utter shock! According to Mary Jane, there were even a couple of them in my biology class!!

"Get OUT! Who?"

"Payton Manners and Louis-Don Pettigrew."

I had absolutely no idea who they were.

"SEE? That's how good they are! I'll try and set up a meet 'n' greet for you with a couple of them. They're very anxious to throw their support behind you and offer whatever technical expertise you might need to help you sock it to the "preppyarchy." Oh, and just so you know: Their help would be STRICTLY BEHIND THE SCENES. Whatever you do, DON'T ACKNOWLEDGE ONE if you see them on campus. They've worked very hard to pass unnoticed. One swooning air-kiss from you, and all their anonymity goes down the crapper. *Capeesh?*"

"Wow. I don't know whether to be honored or insulted. But it's not an issue either way, because I'm ALL ABOUT the cloak-and-dagger scene. I LIVE for that stuff!"

"Well, I'll arrange for something interesting, then."

XIV

So far, our main focus has been the development of a vague blackmailing scheme, wherein we would target the various students who constituted threats: gathering the goods on, say, Baba's incontinence, Bib's boy-band past, and Dottie's cutting for Christ.

I didn't like it.

"Don't think of it as blackmail," she'd say. "Think of it as an insurance policy."

And: "Even Batman resorted to vigilantism."

I thought it seemed like bad karma. I know what shame feels like; I didn't want to inflict it on others. It seemed counterproductive and un-Superfreakish. I didn't want to inspire hate. And besides, Batman is SO NOT a role model for us! Way too grumpy and gloomy.

But NOW!

Well, this just changes EVERYTHING, doesn't it?

I mean, the existence of an underground network of support suddenly opened up a whole new world of opportunities. . . .

Knowing I had the support of others got me to thinking. . . .

HMMMM . . .

Just maybe . . .

I looked at the calendar . . . then went online to check out a few things. . . .

I took my still vague, still unformed idea to Mary Jane. "Wow," she said, and whistled, when I laid it out for her. "That would really be something. But is it feasible?"

I showed her my preliminary research, and she took it from there.

Within twenty-four hours she had devised a fully workable plan of action.

So it was Mary Jane who took my embryo of an idea and gave it form and substance and made it into a real possibility.

It was Mary Jane, for instance, who realized how big it could really be, and how far we could take it.

And most important of all, it was Mary Jane who contacted Clancy Duckett.

Clancy Duckett?

The Channel 7 Action News anchor?

I never would have had the nerve!

I never would have thought my little announcement was newsworthy!

But Mary Jane had once done an interview with "the Voice of the Southland" for the *Eisenhower Dispatch* and had kept her phone number and e-mail address for just such a reason.

And Clancy's response, God bless her, was one of immediate support.

XV

A LITTLE BACKGROUND

"Fancy" Clancy Duckett is anything but.

It's one of those jokes, like calling a fat guy "Slim," or a tall guy "Tiny" (oh, ha-ha).

So let's get it straight: There ain't nothin' fancy about her.

She's an "earthy" gal.

A real Peppermint Patty.

(And a dyke, to boot.)

NOT A PRETTY WOMAN, you understand. We're clear on that?

After a lifetime of playing golf in the brutal Florida sun, Clancy Duckett looks like a coconut. Yes, yes, look: the skin on her face is hard, hairy, and brown. CRACKLE CRACKLE. Put a spiky wig on a coconut, prop it up at the news desk, and see if viewers can tell the difference. And, bless her heart, she's WAAAAY past the point where a little hydrating serum or RevitaLift could help, so don't suggest it. And even IF she wore makeup, which she doesn't, ever, not even on the air, but even if she LOST HER DAMN MIND one day and allowed a makeup woman to "paint her up" I suspect it would be like nailing Jell-O to a tree. It would not stick. No. No. No. It's too late. Of course, she wouldn't even notice. She doesn't know M•A•C from crack, or NARS from Mars. HELLO! SNAP!

So no, no, no . . .

"None of that glop for me," she booms. "If the viewers don't like my face the way God made it, well then, lump 'em! When the image becomes more important than the message, that's the day I'll retire to my poodle farm in Peru!"

And nobody wants THAT.

And fashionwise? Let's just say she's not going to set any red carpets on fire. No, no. She dresses with all the panache of Jim Belushi.

But Clancy Duckett didn't need any of that. She had a charisma that transcended the phony trappings of other newscasters. She told the truth, see. She was a straight shooter, and for that she stood out in a sea of bubbleheaded bleach bunnies.

As the leader of the Action 7 news team, she was the venerable voice of South Florida, a respected community leader whose nightly commentaries shaped public opinion, changed attitudes, influenced politicians, and swayed elections. That she was also an out-loud lesbian, out proud for twenty-seven years and a great supporter of the local GLBT community, and was accepted by just about everyone. She had been a part of South Floridian's lives for so long, and had so completely earned the public's trust and respect, that even the most conservative viewer was willing to tolerate her alternative lifestyle.

To say she was a good ally would be an understatement.

So when Mary Jane told me she had taken a personal interest in my story, and was planning on filming my announcement LIVE, well, I just about DIED.

XVI

We met for coffee an hour before school.

"You're Bloom, then?" she asked when I walked into the Denny's.

"Yes, ma'am."

"Clancy Duckett, Channel Seven," and she shook my hand, giving me two firm pumps and a business card. "You've taken on quite a challenge. I'm impressed."

"Thank you. And thank you for covering it."

"Okay, Bloom, before we get into the preinterview, there's a little paperwork here. Standard rights and agreement—name, image, story. No union, right? Good. Sign there, there, and there, date there and there, and initial this. And then this. And then this, this, this, and this. Yep. Yep. Okay, and I need to ask a few questions before we begin. Purely technical. Bloom is spelled *B-L-U-M-E* or *B-L-O-O-M*?"

"Double *O*," I answered.

"And how do you want to be identified?"

I must have looked blank, or taken too long, because she added, "Under your name? You know: Gay? Bisexual? Transgender?"

"Oh . . . um . . . Well. Hmm . . ." I thought for a minute more, frowned, then brightened. "Hey! I've always been partial to 'preen queen.' Yes, yes, that's good! That pretty much sums me up!"

She shook her head. "We should stick to established terms. Maybe something like 'Gender-bender'? 'Transvestite'?"

"What about 'TRANSVISIONARY'?"

"Okay. Too vague. Could be a moving company. What about 'gender illusionist'?"

"'Gender obscurist?'" I countered. "Or 'GENDER OBLIVIATOR!'" I shouted, maybe a little too wild-eyed.

"Wooo. Wrong direction, Billy. Network. Keep it friendly. What about the standard 'drag queen'?"

I closed my eyes and shook my head. "'Twinkle queen?' 'Tinsel queen?' No. No. Nothing old-school. More forward. Oh, hey! What about 'GLITTEROID!' That's hot! Oh my God! That could actually take off!"

She was obviously getting frustrated. "Okay. Hey. I get it. Don't like labels, huh? I hear ya. What about 'visual artist?' 'Performance artist?' Yeah? Okay?"

I was almost ready to give in when . . .

The fry cook looked out from the kitchen and did a double take when he saw my breathtaking androgyny. "FREAK!" he hissed under his breath—and we both looked at each other. Yeah?

"Oh, I'm totally down with 'freak.' I'm pretty used to it around here; in fact, I was already trying to reclaim it as my own."

"Okay." She smiled. "The title will say, Billy Bloom: Self-proclaimed Superfreak."

We went through the questions she planned to ask, and walked me through the shots. She then looked at her watch, took a last gulp of coffee, and said: "We'll start shooting in about half an hour. Does that give you enough time to get ready?"

"Oh, yeah," I said, and ran off to find Mary Jane and begin the process of my drag.

XVII

DAY ONE, SCENE: COURTYARD, EISENHOWER ACADEMY

The students started crowding around the minute they saw the Action News van.

Clancy was busy barking orders to her cameraman. "Roger, bump in with a long shot. I'll be in front of the school sign for the intro. We'll do a head and shoulders, first. Cut to three quarters medium shot for the interview, then pan to crowd. . . ."

By now, every student was on the courtyard lawn, struggling and straining to see what was going on. *Push, push.* What was Clancy Duckett doing here? *Nudge, nudge.*

"What'd she just say?"

"What's going on?"

They murmured and rumbled and mumbled and surged forward and pushed backward and jostled for position. They jumped up and down.

The camera lights went on.

A hush fell over the crowd. All eyes were on Clancy as she made her way to the Eisenhower Academy sign and lifted her microphone to speak.

"WHAT IN HEAVEN'S NAME IS GOING ON OUT HERE?" Principal Onnigan boomed as he sprinted across the courtyard, and 787 students actually shushed him.

At exactly five minutes to eight, I emerged from the library bathroom in my best monster-meet-the-press drag, and made my way across the courtyard, working my way through the crowd of looky-loos. "Pardon me! Excusez-moi! Coming through! Watch your back!" as I inched my way toward the front gate, where Clancy and her crew were waiting.

There was a rolling groan of horror when everyone got a load of my outfit and saw Clancy wave me through. Obviously, I was behind whatever was about to go down, and they were suddenly a little bit nervous.

Here's what they said:

"Jesus Crap!"
   "Not again!"
   "What now?"
   "What's he up to this time?"
   "Oh, here we go again."
   "Yawn."
   "Ho-hum."
   "Such an attention whore."
   "He just asks for it, doesn't he?"
   "Why doesn't he ever learn?"
   "No longer shocking."
   "BOR-ING!"
   "Overkill."
   "We GET it—you're different!"
   "Yeah, yeah, yeah."
   "Whatever."
   "Lacking his usual polish."
   "Makes me miss the Swamp Zombie."

"He's up to something, though."

"Why would the Channel Seven news come just to cover an outfit?"

"This can't be good."

"Maybe he's announcing his engagement to Flip."

"Oh my gaaaaawwd—stop! Someone might hear you!"

"I bet he's suing the school."

"Or about to go Columbine on our asses—LIVE!"

"He's never going to go away, is he?"

"I guess we're stuck with him."

"Give him credit: He doesn't give up."

"Tougher than he looks."

"You WISH you had his cojones, dude."

PICTURE ME LOVELY: I was wearing a new dressy dress, a pretty lace number that I found at a thrift store the other day, with a real "special-day" feel to it.

I sported a heaping helmet of frosted hair . . . proper pageant hair, don't you know, the likes of which they don't do much anymore, except in the darkest depths of the deepest South.

I carried a festive bouquet of assorted flowers in my arms.

And to top it all off—a big, old twinkly tiara on my head, and a regal-looking sash across my chest, which was, strangely, still blank.

Oh! Oh! And of course, how could I forget? The most important detail—the crowning touch, the splash of colorful whimsy that ties it all together, gives it depth and meaning—I was spattered, no, drenched, really, with chicken blood. BOO! It's true! Dripping with honest-to-god chicken blood! In all its scarlet fury! (Okay, okay, really just a mixture of corn syrup and red vegetable dye, but with the same sticky consistency and overall look as the real deal.)

So I made my way through the crowd: "Pardon me! Coming through! Watch your backs!"

Dripping. Drizzling.

Sloshing forward.

Staining the very ground with my crimson gore.

Anybody figure it out yet? Anybody? You in the back?

Carrie! Yes! The movie *Carrie!*

The classic horror flick about a killer prom queen with telekinetic powers. She's the class freak, see, who brings down the prom in a fiery blaze, killing everyone who made fun of her.

GOOD STUFF.

Real feel-good kind of movie.

Does anyone see where I'm going with this?

Clancy mouthed, "roll it" as soon as I reached her side.

XIX

After her introduction I began my speech.

My voice quivered and wavered and barely rose above a rasp. But it rallied as I did, and grew in pitch, in clarity. It started soft, then grew with confidence, and finally rang out like a clarion call to arms. "For too long I have suffered in silence," I said. "I thought being an outcast meant I had no voice. I accepted the role of victim that was assigned to me and was shamed into martyrdom. No more! All that changes today. Today I take control of my destiny; I reclaim my birthright. Once again, I will be fabulous. Ladies and gentlemen, I have an announcement to make . . ."

Here, I paused to put on my EISENHOWER ACADEMY HOMECOMING QUEEN sash.

There was a sharp gasp from the crowd.

"Yes, I'm here to announce my candidacy for homecoming queen!

It's time to put a real queen in charge! I want the students here to under-stand that GENDER IS A CHOICE, NOT A LIFE SENTENCE. I'm going to change the world, one dress at a time!"

Well, that was it.

The world exploded in a mushroom cloud of horror and outrage. The collective "NO!" of every student there sent a sonic boom circling around the globe seven times, flattening everything in its path. And when the dust finally settled, it was as if common decency and two hundred years of Southern tradition had been dealt a deathblow.

The crowd turned ugly.

Torches were lit. Pitchforks were raised. Cries of "KILL THE MONSTER" were heard.

Here, Clancy stepped in, reminding everyone that the cameras were still rolling.

"Tell us about your platform, Billy. What do you want the students to take away from your campaign?"

"My platform is simple: I'm pro-glamour and anti-khaki. I support total artistic freedom, and I'm against conservative backlashes. I intend to stamp out redneckism wherever I find it, and fight discrimination and Christian intolerance, using only my beauty, wit, and wig-styling skills. I'm going to try, single-handedly, to bring about an end to the hatred I've found here at Eisenhower. And it's not just for me, Clancy, no. I feel AN ABSOLUTE OBLIGATION to change the way the stu-dents here think about GBLTs. In fact, by running for homecoming queen, I feel I'm carrying the flag for a whole culture."

Here, I looked straight into the camera, raised a fist to the sky, and shouted: "TEASE HAIR, NOT HOMOS!"

Clancy moved into the crowd to get their reactions.

They ran the gamut from: "It's wrong. He's sick and needs to be stopped," to: "Why not? He'll never win, but let him run."

Why, there were even a few: "You gotta give the kid credit. He doesn't give up."

And that was slightly encouraging.

The cameras then turned to Principal Onnigan. He cleared his throat uncomfortably and said, "Well, while there's no OFFICIAL rule that limits the position of homecoming queen to just females . . . ummm . . . errr. . . . We will certainly have to look a little more closely at the issue in the days to come and see if it's feasible or advisable . . . but . . . um . . . as of now, Billy does fit the eligibility profile: He has collected the requisite twenty-five signatures, he has the support of a school-sanctioned club, and his GPA is certainly higher than the needed two point eight. . . . And let me also state, for the record, that the Eisenhower Academy is clearly not sexually biased, and as always, we support Billy's . . . um . . . creative approach to school curriculum and campus traditions. . . ."

"And there you have it!" Clancy said. "Dawn of the 'drag queen' at one area high school. Despite overwhelming opposition, one out-proud young drag queen seeks to eliminate gender-based discrimination through that most archaic and sexist of institutions — the old-fashioned beauty pageant. Will he succeed? Will gender identity become a nonissue at this elite private school? Stay with Channel Seven as this story develops. I'm Clancy Duckett, reporting from the Eisenhower Academy in Plantation. Now back to Rick Rock in the studio with the weather."

"And we're out!" said Roger, the camera guy.

"Good stuff, Bloom!" she boomed, and gave me a punch on the shoulder. "You're a natural. It'll be on the news tonight. The six o'clock, definitely, and possibly the eleven o'clock, as well. And we'll be following the story, of course, so this isn't the last you'll see of us."

XX

And LO AND BEHOLD, I was on BOTH the six AND eleven o'clock newscasts!

AND all the commercials, as well! ("Day of the drag queen at one area high school, controversy at six!")

And it must have been a slow night because I was the SECOND PIECE of the night! The granny suicide bomber got the lead. BITCH! But I managed to beat out the president's pulled groin and day six of the Jessica Simpson chapped-lip crisis!

So, yeah. That's pretty wild.

And I'm just going to come out and say it: I WAS FABULOUS! YES! AND LUMINOUS! AND RADIANT! AND RIVETING! I looked just like Fashion Fever Barbie! Or mid-career Lindsay Lohan!

Even better: I came off as intelligent and likable—a compelling underdog character with a crackling good hook, fighting against intolerance, and a memorable catchphrase: "Gender is a choice, not a life sentence!"

I'm on fire!

Can't touch this! HA!

XXI

I should have seen the signs—the malevolent crackle in the air; the rank, overripe smell of goat genitals; the rain of blood—the Hellmouth was opening. It was the End of Days.

Even as I passed the four horsemen without faces in the school courtyard and looked right at the flaming pentagram on the cafeteria door, nothing registered. What could be wrong?

La. La. La.

Then, up ahead: a bustle in the hedgerow. A commotion in the court-yard.

Something brewing.

Something afoot.

An ill-wind blowing.

Students were buzzing and racing all about. A crowd had formed.

And there, standing in the center of the storm, and looking like maybe she WAS the storm, Lynnette Franz glowered and tossed her hair and generally looked mean and scowly.

No surprise there.

Next to her, though, was a rather big surprise. Tossing HER hair while a makeup girl touched up her lips, and a field producer hiked up her skirt, was none other than Medea del Rio.

Yes, THAT Medea del Rio, Channel 4's best weapon against the Clancy Duckett juggernaut!

The pint-sized Cuban dynamo was as pretty and vivacious as Clancy was earthy and raw. She's got "WOW," and isn't afraid to use it.

She's a real power-sparkler, see.

Treats every assignment like a walk down the red carpet, see.

Why, she'll cover a bus full of dead babies in a clinging fuchsia wrap dress and six-inch leopard pumps. She'll wiggle and giggle and struggle to keep her dress from unwrapping and her breasts from spilling out, and pretty soon you will have completely forgotten that she's knee-deep in a pile of bloody baby carcasses.

Yes, here was "jiggle journalism" at its finest. Finally, news that looked like porn—yea!—with cameras that weren't afraid of the old ZOOM-ZOOM, if you know what I mean.

And for people tired of Clancy's dried-out mutton-face, and those intelligent think pieces of hers (groan!)—Medea del Rio was sweet relief, indeed. A breath of fresh air-freshener.

And now it looked as if she was going to glom onto Lynnette as a way to one-up Clancy's interview with me last night.

"This is Medea del Rio, in Plantation, where it's day two of 'Eisenhower Under Siege.' What's at stake? One girl's dream, and EVERY girl's rights and privileges. Standing with me is Lynnette Franz. Tell us what happened here, Lynnette."

"Well, I was supposed to be the only candidate, right? Nobody else was supposed to run. All the girls in our class knew better than to run against me. They all promised. That was the plan. Since seventh grade! But then yesterday, this sexually confused WEIRDO, Billy Bloom, announced HE was running. I don't know, maybe he doesn't realize he's not a girl, or maybe he just wants to make a fool of himself. Whatever. I mean, of course he doesn't stand a chance—everybody hates him, but WHY DID HE HAVE TO MAKE THINGS SO UNPLEASANT FOR ME? This was supposed to be the happiest month of my life. And now he's ruining it!"

"So you don't think Billy Bloom has a chance?" Medea asked, sensing gold.

"Can you imagine? A homosexual? Representing our school?" Lynnette spat. "Well, my gawwwd, I'd laugh if he wasn't being so disrespectful. It's like he's peeing on the flag or something! I mean, he's a drag queen! He just wants attention. Any kind of attention. Like all gays, you know? So they can advance their 'gay agenda.' That is the God's honest truth. By running for homecoming queen, Billy is trying to destroy the Christian way of life here at the academy . . ."

"Tell the viewers why you deserve to be queen, and how you plan to fight against the threat to your values?"

"Well, Medea," she said, suddenly smiling. "I understand the needs of the student body; I'm prepared for the responsibility; I know what's required of a homecoming queen. I know the image that ought to be presented. PLUS, I have God on my side," she said.

Here, she paused for effect, then continued:

"God hates sinners, you know, and gays ARE sinners. It's like what we studied in American history. . . . What is it? . . . 'Manifold Destiny,' the right to conquer. God wants ME to be homecoming queen, see, because I have goodness in my heart, tradition on my side, and the divine right to be queen."

And she gave her most regal look to the camera.

And THAT lit a fire, I can tell you, when it aired on the six o'clock news.

Suddenly, the drag queen wasn't the ONLY kook in this story. Lynnette gave good quip, I'll say that for her. She knew how to get the audience's attention. And now the press had another angle, and the story grew a little larger.

XXII

DAY THREE

And the ball was back in Clancy's court.

And there was NO WAY that Medea del Rio was going to have the last word on HER story.

She called just as I was running to catch the bus. "Hey, Bloom," she boomed. "GREAT NEWS! The viewers want more. Are you ready for a follow-up?"

Oh hell, yes.

I was loving this.

I took to the spotlight like a duck to *l'orange*, like ugly to Ashlee Simpson, like crazy to Courtney Love.

Quick on my feet? You bet!

I loved the attention. Give me a microphone, and I'm off and running, chattering away about things I know nothing about.

And the camera loved me.

Just lapped me up.

Turns out I don't have a bad angle.

Every new tilt up or tip down revealed new facets of my beauty. I was mesmerizing. So when Clancy's cameras began rolling this time, I soared. I took flight. I came alive.

I spoke winningly of tranny power and the need for tolerance. "Homophobia is SO LAST CENTURY!" I proclaimed. "Heal the world, and vote for the sissy!"

I elaborated on my "cross-dress for success" campaign strategy. "Dare to dream!" I urged everyone. "NOW dare to dream in a dress!"

"Up with wigs! Down with prigs!" I chanted.

All in all, I think I was even MORE fabulous than I had been before.

Then: Clancy announced that since the story first aired, she had been contacted by the Broward chapter of Trans Pride America, and in support of my cause, they had created a line of Scarlet *F*s (for "freak") to pin on one's lapel. They sent a box to the school for students to pick up and made them available on their Web site, as well, so that everyone could support me!

XXIII

DAY FOUR

And the campus is a choppy sea of local media. Everywhere you look, the hustle and flow of a well-oiled machine as field teams set up equipment, compete for space, and scout for fresh angles. . . .

Directions are shouted, hair is fluffed, lipstick checked, the countdown begins. . . . Then: LIGHTS! CAMERAS! ACTION!

On!

"This is Rocky del Gado, WBTU, Kissimmee–Saint Cloud . . ."
  "I'm Blizzard McNeil, coming to you live from Plantation . . ."
  "Mary Etta Thistlewait, KLQ Eyewitness News at Noon . . ."

Some reporters concentrate on the small-but-vocal gathering of parents picketing the entrance of the school. They hold up signs (IT'S A QUESTION OF PRINCIPLE AND WE QUESTION THE PRINCIPAL) and chant, "No justice, no tuition," and "Tradition matters!"

Other camera crews zoom in on Dottie Babcock and her clanging Belles of Doom, who are all frantically waving their hands in the air and singing "We Shall Overcome" and "Nearer My God to Thee." To hear them moan and cry and carry on, you'd think the earth had bounced out of its orbit and was careening toward the sun, even as we stood there.

"Coastal Eddie here, coming to you live from the Eisenhower Academy in . . ."

"It's Jo-Jo Johnson, from the Morning Moo Zoo, here on location . . ."

"Ruby Rae Jessup, WYKJ, your channel for breaking news . . ."

The usual suspects—The Demon Debs, the Stuffy Muffys, the Cruci-vixens, the Aryan All-stars — race from camera to camera doing damage-control by downplaying the controversy. "So silly, really," "Not worth your time, even," "It's such a nonstory," and "Nobody takes him seriously." Working together, they form a single, united front of Sissy Assassins, who attack my credibility to every camera and call into question my right to run.

It doesn't make a lick of difference.

The press keeps coming. They are relentless.

"I'm Marvel-Ann Minzer, reporting live from Plantation . . ."

"This is Ola Brinson for Teen Talk *. . ."*

"'Scoop' Cooper with the Morning Dispatch, *your choice for local news and weather . . ."*

XXIV

And so the race was on.

LYNNETTE'S CAMPAIGN: "THE SOUTHERN VALUES TICKET"

Lynnette proved herself to be a feisty opponent and a tireless self-promoter. She positioned herself as a woman of the people, for the people, and with the people's interests at heart. She spoke their language, understood their needs, and shared a vision for a successful future.

To Lynnette it was a Battle Royale, with the fate of the school, no, the fate of THE UNIVERSE hung in the balance.

It was *"life as we know it"* vs. *"the anal Armageddon."* . . .

It was tradition vs. perdition. . . .

It was decency vs. depravity. . . .

She ran a fierce grassroots campaign—shaking hands, kissing babies, and pressing the flesh of as many Manatees as possible. She personally called each and every Eisenhower senior and reminisced about the good old days, quickly rattling off a few shared memories and private jokes. Once that was out of the way, she got down to the business of calling in favors, forgiving old debts, and making new promises. She giggled with the boys and dished with the girls. She played on the homophobia of some, the religious hysteria of others, and the clannish snobbery of almost everyone else.

No one could accuse Lynnette of not wanting to win, or of not giving it her all. Even if she didn't think I had a homo's chance in heaven of winning, she was still going to make me pay for challenging her, by God, and make sure I suffered a humiliating defeat.

CAMPAIGN BUTTON: BEAT BILLY BLOOM! (Which I thought was rather tasteless and constituted a vague threat.)

SIGNS AND FLYERS:

ONE REAL GIRL—ONE REAL CHOICE

ONLY QUEERS VOTE FOR FAGS!

DEFEAT THE GAY MENACE!

UPHOLD TRADITION! UPHOLD DIGNITY!

And again with the not-funny TOGETHER, WE CAN ALL BEAT BILLY BLOOM

XXV

MY CAMPAIGN: "THE PANTY GIRDLE TICKET"

My campaign was less personal, more ideological—if only because I lacked Lynnette's long social history and A-list clout. My battles were mostly fought in the media, and through school newspaper editorials and my highly visible public appearances.

Every morning I would sweep onto campus, looking fabulous, of course. Then I'd twirl around the courtyard, showing off the dress du jour—usually something in a dreamy silk chiffon, from the Lily Munster–Endora from *Bewitched* school of drag—regal yet camp, you know—then I'd say something perfectly pithy to the reporters, hand out a few Scarlet *F*s, pose with supporters, then float off to class. That was about it.

I was counting on showing the students that I was worthy of their respect and friendship through an upbeat, intelligent campaign. As nasty as Lynnette's smear campaign against me was, I was determined to stay above the fray, and not lower myself to her level of mudslinging.

MY CAMPAIGN BUTTON: TEASE HAIR, NOT HOMOS!

SIGNS AND FLYERS:

A QUEEN 4 QUEEN

GENDER IS A CHOICE, NOT A LIMITATION

SAY NYET TO LYNNETTE!

TRANNY POWER!

SUPPORT YOUR LOCAL FREAK SHOW!

LET BILLY BLOOM!

BILLY BLOOM: EXPERIENCED TIARA-WEARER!

XXVI

Meanwhile, every day after school, more and more shadow kids gathered outside the gates of my house, offering to help with my float.

Ten, then twenty, then thirty or more "invisible kids" made themselves known to me, and went to work on my behalf. They each brought with them their special talent, their own artistic vision, and their own unique input. Oh, and their own tools, God bless 'em for THAT. Lord knows, we are not a crafty household, no sir. Not at ALL.

They were magnificent. There was nothing too difficult or outrageous for them, nothing they couldn't accomplish once they set their minds to it. I told them the concept—they said, "Let's do it!"

I provided the neon tubing, the chicken wire, the float-away fringe, the flowers, the scrap metal, the bags of spangles, the wooden lattice, the lawn mower, and the shopping carts.

Then, like little homecoming elves, they got to work.

Pounding.

Sawing.

Soldering.

Sculpting.

Gluing.

Wiring.

OH, AND VERY QUICKLY:

The rules for the float are simple:

Floats can be made of anything. Flatbeds can be constructed using hay trailers, lawn mowers, four-wheel chassis, golf carts, flatbed trucks, SUVs, or . . .

The maximum length is sixty-five feet.

The width: eight feet or less.

It can stand no higher than thirteen feet, six inches off the ground.

A maximum of twenty people on board.

No gas-powered engines.

And the theme must be approved by Principal Onnigan.

Of course, on the creative end, the bigger the better, and the more eye-catching your float is, the better your chances of winning.

It can be as bold and provocative or loud and loopy as you have the time and resources to make it.

Your float can breathe fire or blow bubbles or shoot Gummi worms into the crowd.

It can be pulled by a hundred bikini-clad blondes, if you can entice a hundred blondes to do so.

I mean, THE SKY'S THE LIMIT, KID.

As long as the float itself conforms to the guidelines posted on the school's Web site, and as long as the theme of your campaign is spelled out clearly, and it's built and decorated solely by students from Eisenhower—with no outside help of any kind—DO WHATEVER THE HELL YOU WANT!

XXVII

"Up there . . . !"

"Over there . . . !"

"Could it be . . . ?"

"Is it really . . . ?"

Yes!

IT'S SUPERFREAK AND WIG GIRL!

Tripping on the wind . . .

Slipping in and out of shadows . . .

Over rooftops and treetops, and behind enemy lines . . .

Skirring out of sight . . .

The super-sleuthy superhero and his bewigged sidekick are hard at work!

Today's top-secret mission: to spy on Lynnette's float committee. A simple recon assignment. Gather information, size up the competition, and gauge their chance of winning.

Every day the candidates and their helpers meet during lunch, see, to discuss float-building duties and take care of other items of business.

Today Wig Girl and I are hidden in a broom closet of the room Lynnette used, nervously waiting for the royal court to convene.

Well, we needn't have worried too much, as it doesn't seem like they manage to get too much work done, what with so many other BURNING ISSUES at hand.

Like the daily date updates!

Because it's GIRLS INVITE BOYS to the homecoming dance, you know! So it's HIGH DRAMA!

And I mean, who has time to glue carnations onto chicken wire when both Bib AND Flip remain dateless?

SQUEEEEEEEEEAL!

(The following conversation is brought to you verbatim, courtesy of Wig Girl's trusty handheld tape recorder:)

"Did you HEAR? Sissy Russett got the smackdown from Flip!" "I KNOOOOW! I was there!" "What IS it with Flip, you know?" "I knoooooow. He never goes out with anyone." "If he wasn't so hot, I'd swear he was gay or something!" "OHMYGOD! Riiiiiight? Imagine!" "Sesame Blixon thinks she's THISCLOSE." "I hope so, y'all, because those accidental 'nip slips' of hers are working my last nerve." "Every single class, y'all. 'OOOPS!'" "Like, if he didn't respond the first three thousand times . . ." "I'm thinking it's her boob acne." SQUEEEEEEEEEAL! "Lynnette, you are SOOOO BAAAAAD!" "Oh my God, I heard Dottie Babcock plans to wear that SAME Jessica McClintock dress she wears to every dance." "That horror with the high collar?" "And puffy sleeves?" "EEEEEEEEW!" "I heard it's a hand-me-down FROM THE EIGHTIES!" "And her sister wore it to every dance, tooooooo!" "And probably her mom before that!" "OHMYGOD! CAN YOU IMAGINE?" "Doesn't Christ want her to look pretty for once?" "Ohmygod, Lynnette, you are so baaaaaad!" "PLEASE, like Christ would even ASK Dottie Babcock, I'm sure!" "You are going to HELL!"

And on.

And on.

And on.

Until you just want to shove a fondue fork in your ear!

XXVIII

AND A QUICK SIDEBAR

Just because I haven't mentioned him lately doesn't mean that Flip has been forgotten. Oh, my dear, no. Far from it.

He's HERE. (*Thump chest.*) Always in my heart. Always in my prayers. (*Sniff.*)

He's just been back-burnered temporarily while I deal with the over-whelming STURM UND DRANG of my BILDUNGSROMAN. Yes, I meant to say that. It's German, darling, and it refers to all the grunt and snuffle I go through coming of age in this crap factory called Florida, and trying to make sense of it all.

So, I haven't seen him except in class, and even then it's secret, stolen glances, for he still won't acknowledge me. (*BIG HEAVING SIGH.*) And it's been almost two weeks now. He keeps quite a buffer of "his crew" around at all times—Manatees and various Aryan Nations boys, you know. Strictly "No Billys Allowed." And the damn Swamp Thugs won't let me get anywhere near him to plead my case.

And with the BIG GAME looming—just around the corner, in fact—Coach Karl has been working him into the ground. RIGHT INTO THE DIRT, POOR DEAR. Before, after, and often during school hours. Getting him in tip-top physical shape. And it's already paying off. He's looking GOOD! WHOOOO-EEEE.

He's Flip 4.0,
Meta-Flip,
Mega-Flip,
Flippus Maximus,
High-performance Flip.

A ripped Flip, to be sure, his hot horse-sweat pouring through his T-shirt and gym shorts. Pushing his endurance to the limit. Muscles rippling like white-water testosterone. Starting at five A.M. and often staying until nine or ten at night, he runs laps, does pull-ups and sit-ups and real-boy push-ups and, oh, I don't know, practices his touchdown jig—I CAN'T WATCH FROM BEHIND THE FLAGPOLE ALL THE TIME!

Anyway, that's the extent of my Flip update.

XXIX

The local newscasters practically lived on campus now. Other stations began slowly trickling in, to weigh in on the story.

It became a ruthless round-robin, a sort of "Row, Row, Row Your Boat" for reporters having a slow news week.

The increased press brought out the protesters and wack jobs, who, in turn, garnered more attention in the press, which only . . .

Well, you get the picture.

And once my family's "founding father" connections came to light, the story made another leap up the news chain and became even more newsworthy.

My cross-dressing candidacy was becoming a big-time, statewide story, moving from the back page "news of the weird" up to the Metro section and on up to the third, then second page. Next stop: front page!

I began getting e-mail and fan mail from people all over, wishing me good luck and telling me they were rooting for me (which is always a day-brightener). I heard from other drag queens and transgender types, who told me about similar ordeals they went through in high school, and the horrific torture THEY endured. (And that's always reassuring.)

I even got quite a number of love letters and marriage proposals from weird old men—HA!—as well as a number of increasingly graphic love letters from someone who claimed to be a student at the Eisenhower Academy! Can you imagine? These letters always started off sweet and gushing, telling me how he's been crushing on me from afar, and wishes he could spend time with me, and possibly more? Then there is a weird shift in the tone, and suddenly, he starts berating me for being too open, too gay. I'm ruining it for him. I make him sick. Then the letters get downright nasty and threatening. . . .

They give me the shivers.

So I just brushed those letters aside when they came, and concentrated on the fun stuff.

⁂

NEWS BULLETIN

With just two weeks left until the election, two new students have announced their candidacy for homecoming queen!

Yes!

Just like that!

Henny Nickerson and Alma Doty have qualified as official write-in candidates, with the requisite number of signatures and club sponsorship.

Henny, of course, is the captain of the equestrian team, Junior League committee co-chairman, and was third-place runner-up in the Pepsi Poem for Peace competition. She plans to attend Radcliffe in the fall, and intern at *Modern Bride* magazine over the summer.

Alma . . . um . . . played trombone in the freshman band and enjoys C-SPAN, bird-watching, and diagramming sentences in her spare time. (That's according to the *Eisenhower Dispatch*.)

Both are considered dark horses. Henny sounds like a threat on paper, but nobody really likes her. She's too horsey-looking—reminds people of Celine Dion. Plus, she smells like manure. And nobody wants an ugly queen who smells like shit. Please. This is Eisenhower.

Alma is, you guessed it, a shadow girl who is stepping out of the darkness for the first time. Sweet little thing. Wouldn't say boo! to a goose. This is a big step for her. "Yea, Alma! You go, girl!" She's way outside her comfort zone here, but feels it's important to bring down the oligarchy and end the tyranny of WASP primacy.

These two new entries are mostly symbolic threats. They show that Lynnette's unanimous wall of support is eroding, and that surefire victory she's been braying about might not be so surefire, after all.

Yes, yes, slowly the tide is turning.

Alliances are shifting. Sure bets suddenly aren't. There are sudden defections, secret backroom pledges, last minute switcheroos.

Every day, people are won over by me or turned off by her. More and more, the Billy supporters are equal to, or outnumber, the Lynnette-lovers.

XXX

Bo-Bo Peterson is the first MAJOR PLAYER to break rank. He is the first of the big boys to stand up and say what the others are secretly thinking. Namely: "Lynnette's a bitch, man."

To his teammates he says, "I don't care who she's running against, I ain't voting for her. If she was running against a goddamn butt worm, I'd vote for the goddamn butt worm."

(That I am interchangeable with a "butt worm," is slightly appalling, but I'll take support where I find it.)

He and Lynette had a bitter breakup, you might recall. It seems he caught her with HIS OWN BROTHER! In his OWN BED! Yet, instead of saying she's sorry or begging for his forgiveness, Lynnette went on the offensive and posted a series of wildly popular and deeply humiliating accounts of their love life on her MySpace page. So, you see, if anyone knows the depths of Lynnette's bitchery, it's Bo-Bo.

And if anyone wants to see her fail, it's Bo-Bo.

So WELCOME ABOARD, BO-BO PETERSON. My unlikeliest ally.

He's quite a catch.

A Manatee. Social A-lister. And all-around standard-bearer.

So when he showed up, with one week left in the race, wearing a Scarlet *F* . . .

Well, the whole Eisenhower hierarchy went KABLOOEY, it really did.

Then when he asked me to sit with him at lunch, well, it sent shock waves through the entire school and terror into the hearts of the staunchest Lynnette supporters.

People have started whispering: "He has a shot! He actually has a shot!"

People have begun to think: "It's not such a lost cause after all!"

And I, myself, have begun to have real hope.

Suddenly, I dared to believe.

It could happen!

I could really pull it off!

"Lynnette really IS a bitch," some people were saying.

"Never really liked her."

"It would serve her right."

XXXI

"Yes, Bo-Bo is a big catch," Mary Jane conceded, "and you should be VERY excited by it. But he is only one person. 'One swallow does not a summer make,' and all. You're on a roll, yes. But you need to capitalize, quickly, on the momentum his defection has started. You need one more big name to solidify it, make it look like a trend. Normally, I'd say Flip was the answer. But that's not going to happen. So. Now is when we need to bring out the big guns. Play dirty. And here's how you need to do it. . . ."

XXXII

So . . .
> After biology class.
> In my pretty, powder blue pantsuit . . .
> A hibiscus behind my ear.
> Not a care in the world.
> Skip to the loo!
> *La la la.*

"BIB! BIB! WAIT UP!" I yelled. He turned and looked at me as if I'd lost my mind, and continued walking.

"Whoooooo!" I screamed again, and LEAPED in front of him, blocking his path. He looked down at me like I was a swishy insect that needed squashing. But before he had the chance, I threw my arms in the air and shouted: "Bib, DAR-ling! Lover! Poodle!"

He looked around in wild alarm, embarrassed and confused—was this some kind of joke? Were the guys playing a trick on him?

"Now, Bib," I continued. "Or should I call you HUGGY DA LUV THUG?"

He froze.

"Get over here," he said, and pushed me behind a bank of lockers.

"What is this, Billy?" he whispered menacingly. "Is this your idea of a joke?" He leaned in close, so close I could smell his sexy, big-boy breath. It smelled like protein shakes and oatmeal. "You better have a good explanation for this."

Well, I was terrified, of course. I was taunting Kong in his chains. But I kept telling myself not to worry, that I was Superfreak, remember? I was invincible. I was a mighty drag warrior, and that he was the oppressor. He deserved this. So I brazenly barreled on, in full auto-queen mode, blithely rattling on in the face of certain doom.

"Well, LOVER, I'm so glad I found you. I had been just WRACKING MY BRAIN trying to come up with a song to play on my float, a theme song that really speaks to me, you know?

"You're still pissing me off, Bloom. Get to the point."

"Well, my theme is RETRO BOY BAND! YES! HOT, RIGHT! So picture my float: it's me on a flatbed, lip-synching in front of a bank of forty television screens, singing along to the sweet, sweet harmony of . . . oh, gosh . . . what were they called? Who were those adorable street urchins that reached #173 on the *Billboard* charts in the summer of 1999?"

"Lower your voice, Bloom. I'm warning you!"

"Oh, now I remember! DA LUV THUGS! YES! With their lead singer, HUGGY THUG! Good stuff, there, huh? Now, I just can't decide between 'Mackin' on da Playground' or 'Sour Patch Girl'? Hmmmm . . . 'Sour Patch,' of course, features one of your best performances, the spoken word love poem at the end, where you start to cry—I COULD JUST LISTEN TO THAT ALL DAY! But then in the video for 'Mackin',' you're all wearing those identical red leather jumpsuits. . . . That's a pretty hot visual. And of course, it will be on the jumbo screen above the football field, as well. And maybe I could be wearing a red leather jumpsuit, too! Hey, do you still have yours?"

"I'll kill you," he said simply.

"What?"

"Look, Butt-lick, I don't know how you found out about the Luv Thugs; but if you don't shut up, I'll pound your faggot face so hard, you'll MISS that coma, got it? You either drop it or you're dead—it's that simple."

"And SURPRISE!" I said triumphantly. "You're on HIDDEN MICROPHONE!"

I opened my blazer to show him the microphone while Mary Jane simultaneously knocked from behind a window, pointed to her headphones and mini–tape recorder, and gave a big thumbs-up.

"That makes THREE recordings of HUGGY DA LUV THUG that I own now! Maybe I can make a mashup and play your death-threat confession over a chorus of 'Sour Patch Girl'!"

I could see the steam rising off his ears, and the whites of his eyes had suddenly turned bright red, so I knew he was about to lose his oatmeal-addled mind, any second.

"What's this about?" he said quietly, instead of ripping out my spleen.

"Simple. I just want us to be friends, Bib."

"Funny way of going about it. Just tell me what you want."

"I need your support." And I handed him a Scarlet *F*.

"NO! NO! NO WAY!"

"Hey, did I mention that if I'm elected, YOU'LL be my king? Queen picks her king, you know! I'm so excited. And that first dance will be just the beginning of our new working relationship. We'll be together at every school function, in all the local papers, as the official representatives of the academy, even on the yearbook cover. And then, of course, we'll be reunited at untold homecoming games in the future. We'll be part of Eisenhower history. Forever linked together."

He punched the locker, denting it and bloodying his knuckles.

"Easy there, Ox. I have a Plan B. If you help me out, I'll drop the whole thing and go with a butterfly-and-rainbow theme. Five minutes of your time, tops. That's it. That's all I want."

"*Grrrrrr.*" Then: "When?"

"The pep assembly, tomorrow, when Lynnette and I give our speeches. You'll be on the platform, behind us. After I finish mine, you hold it up. After I leave the stage, you can put it down. Then you can set it on fire, or piss on it, or frame it and keep it by your bed. I don't care."

"I freakin' hate you."

"I know. It's such a shame. In any other circumstances, we could have been so close."

And that's how Bib came to be on the front page of the *Eisenhower Dispatch* holding a giant Scarlet *F* at the pep assembly.

XXXIII

Preparing for the big assembly . . .
  Busy, busy . . .
  Gotta look FABULOUS!
  Gotta TOP EVERYTHING!
  So . . .
  Right now, I'm putting that flesh-colored bodysuit to use by spangling it with REAL DRAGON SCALES. What? Yes! Dazzling green

and black and blue, with flashes of silver. And a tail! A great big dragon tail! When I'm through, I will be a mighty, prehistoric lady dinosaur— RAR!—and everywhere I go, I will leave a trail of destruction in my wake. SLAP to the left! CRASH to the right! Drinks will be spilled. Tables overturned. Pedestrians knocked down. STOMP! STOMP! STOMP! Car alarms! Fire hydrants! Telephone poles! Why, the earth, itself, will tremble with each step I take. Just look at the big green claws on my hind legs. So powerful! So deadly! And did you check out my big green lizard boobs? How hot are THEY? I am truly a beautiful man-eater . . .

"NO! NO! NO!" Mary Jane shouted when she saw what I was planning. "WRONG! WRONG! WRONG! Think about it: You're running for an election! You're trying to get people to like you. You don't want to alienate or provoke anyone with your outfits anymore. You need more voter-friendly looks. Something that will appeal to the people. That will evoke warm feelings and inspire trust."

Okay . . .

What about . . . the Virgin Mary?

Or a puppy-dog suit?

What about Oprah? Who doesn't love Oprah? Sure! I could stuff a few pillows here and there . . .

"Maybe we're going in the wrong direction here," she said. "Maybe being shocking is no longer shocking. Maybe what's shocking is NOT BEING SHOCKING."

Ohhhhhh . . . I seeeeeeeeee.

Damn, she's good!

XXXIV

Monday, Monday, and game week has arrived! YES! At last, The Big One is here! In just five days: FIGHTING FRIDAY! When the Fighting Manatees finally square off against their sworn enemy, the Okeechobee Beefsteaks!

But first:

Homecoming week officially kicks off with the Monday morning pep rally. WHOOOOOO!

In this delirious three-hour celebration of school spirit, the students pay their respect to the varsity football players by sobbing and shrieking like a bunch of horny howler monkeys. YEAAAAAAAAA!

ALSO, there are speeches and cheers and chants and dance routines and marching band maneuvers . . . WHEEEEEEEEEEEE!

AND VERY IMPORTANT: This is where the candidates for homecoming queen give their final speeches—a very important indicator of who will win. And a good speech can make or break you. So this is A VERY BIG DEAL TODAY.

First up on the program: The March of Champions!

WOOT! WOOT! WOOT! WOOT!

One by one, each Manatee walks the length of the auditorium to the frenzied, hunk-drunk cries of the student body. The varsity cheerleaders tumble about the auditorium and lead the crowd in the familiar school chants and cheers. They flip and twirl and spin around the boys, doing cartwheels and backflips, giving them all their due.

Each player is introduced over the loudspeaker as he walks onto the stage and takes his seat.

"Bib Oberman . . . Bernie Balch . . . Flip Kelly . . . ," and so on.

And each boy is given an automatic standing ovation. (Well, of course. It's just the way things are.)

But get this: When Bo-Bo Peterson's name was called, he pulled out his Scarlet *F* and walked the length of the stage with it held up high over his head, causing an unprecedented reaction. Some audience members actually booed! YES! BOOED! Which was UNHEARD OF! A MANATEE—BOOED? *That we should live in such extraordinary times!*

And what's more: booed because of ME! I was horrified and thrilled!

Then came the speeches by Principal Onnigan calling for good sportsmanship and honorable behavior at the game and afterward, at the dance, BLAH BLAH BLAH . . . Coach Carter screamed that this was the best team he's ever had the pleasure to coach, YEAH! YEAH! YEAH! And finally, Bib Oberman, the captain of the football team, summed it all up by simply chanting "MAN-A-TEES! MAN-A-TEES!" over and over, until everybody had chanted themselves into a sweat-soaked frenzy of Man-on-Manatee love.

Then there were MORE cheers and MORE pom-pom routines, and these seemed to last for seven or eight hours, AT LEAST. Finally, after all the cheers had been exhausted and we were sufficiently full of pep, it was time for the homecoming queens to give their speeches.

Henny and Alma were introduced and allowed to sit on the stage platform, but because they were merely write-in candidates, they weren't allowed to actually make speeches.

So it was just Lynnette and me.

Me and Lynnette.

Good vs. Evil.

The devil and Miss Bloom.

Lynnette was introduced first. She came out to medium-level applause.

She looked even grimmer than usual. Her jaw was clenched; her eyes were slits; and a large purple vein throbbed, furiously, on her temple.

She cleared her throat and shuffled her notes: "Um . . . number one: I can't believe I have to remind you guys of the most basic reason to vote for me, but I guess I do: Homecoming queens are GIRLS, y'all. Quarterbacks are BOYS. That's the way it is. That's the way God made it. You can't decide what's right and wrong based on the cast of *The Real World*. And you can't just change your values just because you think 'times have changed.'

"Boys are made for some things, and girls are made for others. I mean, what if I wanted to be the boys' locker room attendant?"

(There were many excited "hell, yeahs" from the audience.)

"Or what if Flip Kelly decided he wanted to be a Hooters Girl?"

(There was an eruption of "Hoot! Hoot!")

"What then?

"Okay, second reason to vote for me: My rival—I'm not even going to insult my lips by saying his name— is a newcomer to our school. That alone should disqualify him. Homecoming is about celebrating traditions and memories. So far, our only memory of him is the sickening way he's tried to turn our school into a gay bar.

"It's a fact: Gays are going to hell. I say, if he wants to be queen so bad, LET HIM BE THE QUEEN OF HELL!"

Lynnette broke into a series of inappropriate cartwheels, bouncing across the stage, letting her legs stay spread open perhaps a beat too long, and exposing her cheerleader's underwear, which elicited a few catcalls from the boys.

"YEA!" she screamed. "I've got spirit, y'all! OKAY, GUYS, LET ME HEAR YOU: I'VE GOT WHAT? (*clap clap*) SPIRIT! YEA! GIVE ME AN S!"

"S!"

"GIVE ME A P!"

"P!"

"GIVE ME AN *I*!"

"*I*!"

"GIVE ME AN *R*!"

"*R*!"

"GIVE ME AN *I*!"

"*I*!"

"GIVE ME A *T*!"

"*T*!"

"WHAT DOES IT SPELL?"

"*SPIRIT!*"

"So in conclusion: I deserve to be homecoming queen because I love the school, I respect tradition, and plus, if you vote for the transvestite, we're going to have coed bathrooms. God's truth, y'all."

"YEA!"

And she bounced off the stage to slightly less-than-moderate enthusiasm.

XXXV

Then the principal introduced me to the crowd.

There was a gasp of surprise as I strolled onto the stage in my new Prada pin-striped men's suit (that Dad was ALL TOO HAPPY to buy me). My hair was scraped back into a prim and respectable bun. How's that for a change? Why, I was positively demure! Like somebody's secretary!

AND LOOK! NO MAKEUP! NONE! Well, a little base. And some bronzer. And blush. And lip pencil. And light eyeliner—but that's all STAGE MAKEUP.

The look was TOTAL anti-drag!

I was solemn as soap.

Composed? You bet!

Mary Jane made the right call. She knew that being normal was the most shocking thing I could do. ("Always keep your enemy guessing! Never become predictable!"—from *The 48 Laws of Power*.)

I approached the podium brimming with poise and self-confidence, and stood for a moment, drinking in the attention of my beloved subjects.

SMILE, BILLY!

"Gosh, how to follow THAT?" I said, and applauded as Lynnette left the stage. "Thank you, Lynnette, for that gracious set-up. 'Queen of Hell,' indeed! HEY: with FRANZ like these, who needs ENEMIES, right?"

(Nothing. Crickets.)

(Tough crowd. Okay. Can the corn and move on.)

"Now, my appearance today might come to many of you as a shock, I know. I look positively respectable, eh? And what's THAT all about, right? Sure, I COULD have worn a real showstopper of an outfit and made a big, ugly scene *which is what I'm sure you were all expecting.*

"But no, no, no. Not today. . . .

"And I could stand here and talk smack about Lynnette and tell you why she IS SO WRONG FOR THE POSITION, that rewarding ignorance with prestige is a slippery slope that can only end with the dreaded phrase: 'Academy Award winner Paris Hilton.' But that's unsportsmanlike. And Billy don't swing like that.

"Why, I even had another whole speech prepared where I went for the hard sell, saying: VOTE FOR ME, I'M AN EXPERIENCED TIARA-WEARER, ha-ha-ha, and tried to pass myself off as the spunky underdog with the heart of gold. I could have even played the guilt card by reminding you all that you DID try and kill me, AHEM, so maybe you OWE me this vote to clear your conscience—

"BUT I'M NOT MENTIONING ANY OF THAT.

"Instead, I stand before you today, barefaced and unadorned, stripped of all the usual homo-signifiers you've come to expect. No glitter, no gloss. No lipstick or lashes. Just a fresh-scrubbed face to show you that underneath the artifice, I am perhaps not so different from you.

"You call me a freak.

"You say that I'm 'different' and that I 'don't belong.'

"Well, okay. I accept that.

"But I'm here today to say that deep down, we are all freaks. Yes! Alone in our rooms at night, we are all weirdos and outcasts and losers. That is what being a teenager is all about! Whether you admit it or not, you are all worried that the others won't accept you, that if they knew the real you, they would recoil in horror. Each of us carries with us a secret shame that we think is somehow unique.

"Maybe somewhere out there sits a beauty queen in adult diapers. (And here, LittleAnne Swafford looked guiltily at the ground.) Or perhaps there is a debutante who is addicted to suppositories. (And here, Baba Deschler started to say something, then thought better of it and looked at the ground.) Or maybe there's a young 'cutter' out there who cuts herself in the name of her lord. Or a popular student council member who is secretly manorexic.

"Maybe some of you have a secret double life. Maybe you spent time in juvie for shoplifting a Jones New York blazer, and hope to God nobody ever finds out. . . ."

(And by now, everyone was looking wildly indignant, and terribly guilty—but nobody moved, and nobody dared speak up.)

I paused for a moment to let my words sink in. Then I continued, in a bright and sunny tone: "I mean, can you imagine what it would be like to have any of those problems?

"WELL, WELCOME TO HIGH SCHOOL, PEOPLE!

"We are freaks, because we're teenagers! We are, by nature, oily, throbbing, mutating, misshapen space aliens. We have zits the size of matzo balls and strange patches of fur sprouting daily. Yes, yes, WE ARE ALL FREAKS! IT'S WHO WE ARE! IT'S WHAT WE DO!

"Some of you just pull it off better than others.

"You call me a freak. And it's true.

"I'm asking you all to look inside yourselves—look into that secret place—confront your own inner freak. Don't turn away in shame. Stare it down, really examine it, inside and out, and then maybe you'll believe me when I say to you again that I am not so different from you.

"Yes, yes—gay, bulimic, chronic masturbator, beauty queen with smelly feet, debutante strung out on Ex-Lax . . . It's all the same.

"Now, I don't want you all to think that the meaning of homecoming is lost on me. It's about school tradition and honoring the school's legacy.

"I know I haven't been here long enough to have been a part of your traditions yet, but this is my home now. And they say when you move into a new home, you should start a new tradition.

"Might I suggest a new tradition of tolerance, of inclusion.

"You call me a freak, and I accept that. But I say that I am not so different from you. And if we are, each of us, freaks—then can't we accept what's different in each other and move on?

"Accept me.

"Accept yourself.

"Accept the Universal Freak Show in us all.

"Thank you! Thank you!" I said.

One by one, the shadow students stood and applauded. Others joined in, slowly at first, but quickly, gathering momentum.

Onstage, Bo-Bo Peterson held his Scarlet *F* up high, prompting several shadow students in the bleachers to hold up theirs.

I shot Bib a look and touched my right shoulder with my left hand (his cue).

And he reluctantly held his *F* in the air.

All applause stopped abruptly. Shocked short.

Yes, Bib held his *F* high, but his head hung low.

Everybody looked around and whispered: "What the hell is going on?"

Is this OPPOSITE DAY? Have we fallen into an anti-universe? Is it snowing in hell, perchance?

"WHY WOULD BIB . . . ?" "DOESN'T HE REALIZE WHAT THAT . . . ?" "WHAT'S HE THINKING . . . ?"

Flip shot me a look of complete and utter dismay. OUR FIRST EYE CONTACT SINCE THAT NIGHT!

I walked to the edge of the stage and bowed deeply to the crowd, like a magician who had just pulled off his greatest trick. I gestured to Bib, still obediently holding his *F* of support, as if to say: "Behold the power of BILLY BEYONDO!"

"WELL, IF BIB OBERMAN SUPPORTS HIM!" "I DIDN'T KNOW THAT BIB LIKES HIM NOW. . . ." "CAN'T BE AS BAD AS LYN-NETTE CLAIMS. . . ."

And suddenly, everybody leaped to their feet and began applauding wildly.

There were hoots and hollers and stomps and whistles.

"FREAK! FREAK! FREAK!" they chanted.

So, YEA, BILLY!

GO, BILLY!

It was another major victory on my part, and I was SKY-HIGH! YES! OVER THE MOON! SKIPPING THROUGH STAR CLUSTERS! SURFING ON A COMET'S TAIL!

WATCH ME GO! *WHEEEEEEEEEEEEE!*

XXXVI

ROLLING, ROLLING, ROLLING

Four days left until the election, and it was a cakewalk to the crown.

Yes, yes, I was on a winning streak of legendary proportions!

All my lights were green!

All my oysters had pearls!

And every outfit I tried on looked absolutely adorable!

And it was all thanks to my boy Bib (bless his heart).

He was the tipping point, see.

He was the abracadabra that opened the sesame.

The minute he held up that Scarlet *F*, a watershed wave of approval crashed down on me. There was an immediate and radical shift in the way people responded to me.

Such is the power of the alpha male.

HERE'S LOOKIN' AT YOU, BIB!

Since then, I've been riding the crest of sudden approval.

Now, at school, wherever I go, people stop and smile. They are suddenly interested in my campaign and what I have to say. They ask questions, they open dialogues and initiate actual conversations. They actually want to know me! As you can imagine, it's rather exhilarating. Better than getting donkey-punched in the kidney!

And the timing couldn't be better!

The race is in its final stage now. We are down to the last hours of the last days.

The speeches have all been made; the signs have all been hung. The buttons and balloons and cupcakes and flyers have all been passed out.

The fight has already been fought. It's all over but for the shouting and the floats.

And what a fight it's been, eh?

Let's quickly review:

TOTAL NUMBER OF PRINT INTERVIEWS: thirty-seven, including the *Miami Herald*, the Fort Lauderdale *Sun-Sentinel*, *The Shiny Sheet* in Palm Beach, *The Star* (which claimed that Dame Edna was planning to adopt me and mentor me on tour), plus national exposure in all the gay magazines—XY *Magazine*, *HX*, *Out*, *The Advocate*, and *Genre*.

TOTAL NUMBER OF TELEVISED INTERVIEWS: ten formal sit-downs and any number of passing sound-bites (although lord knows if I'll ever see most of them).

CELEBRITY ENDORSEMENTS: Clancy Duckett, a lesser Queer Eye, openly gay congressman Bill Mendoza, and a postcard from Dennis Rodman.

MOST MEMORABLE FAN LETTERS: I received e-mails from another drag queen still in high school, and right here in South Florida! Yes! A fifteen-year-old Cuban pre-op transsexual in Boca Raton who—get this—hasn't told her parents yet about her hormone injections AND HAS TO TAPE DOWN HER QUICKLY EXPANDING CHEST every morning before breakfast! She wanted advice from other queens going through the same thing. Unfortunately, I didn't have a clue. I mean, that's WAY too hard core for me!

MOST DISTURBING FAN LETTER: The continuing letters and e-mails from my creepiest fan, which are BEYOND pornographic. I just hope he doesn't REALLY attend Eisenhower, and if he does, that I never meet up with him in a dark and empty hallway.

And finally, I can't help but wonder: What about Flip?

It's his big night, too, tomorrow night, remember?

His big chance to shine.

The night he's been working toward his whole high school career. The night he's been dreaming of his whole life.

Scouts from every major Southern university are coming to see the boy prince in action.

Was he nervous?

I wonder . . .

XXXVII

Walking, walking.

The coldest day of the year.

A cold brown drizzle fell down over the city.

I was dressed as the Morton Salt girl, marching through the puddles in the garden, thinking of nothing, nothing at all—when all of a sudden, he was there by my side.

I didn't recognize him at first; he was all bundled up. Then I saw those gooey green eyes and that great ski-slope nose, and I felt my soul being ripped out of my body.

Flip fell into step with me, and it seemed he had never left my side.

"Hi."

"Hi."

We walked a while in silence. There didn't seem to be anything to say. Seeing him again, here, made my head hurt. The sound of rain and the sound of our footsteps seemed oddly amplified.

"Flossie said you might be out here."

"Oh. Yeah. Well."

More silence.

Then he said, "So, tomorrow is the big election."

And I said, "So, tomorrow is the big game."

And we both laughed, both said, "Yeah" and "Good luck."

"Hey, Flip," I asked, "you haven't, by any chance, been sending me anonymous e-mails, have you?"

"Nah," he said. "Why?"

"No reason. No reason." (Hmmmm . . .)

And we didn't say anything else for a while, just walked in step with each other.

He was the first to break the silence. "You should probably know, I'm taking Sesame Blixon to the dance tomorrow night."

"Sesame Blixon!" I groaned. "Oh, Flip!" and I couldn't help but add: "They're fake, you know."

"Tell me about it."

And we laughed uneasily.

"Is it serious?" I tried to act casual.

"Nah, she was just all on my jock one night, you know, so I tapped it, just to shut her up. . . ." But then his words trailed off as he realized what he was saying, and to whom.

I masochistically jumped into a mud puddle, to see if I could possibly be a little more miserable. It was ice-cold, and little lightning bolts of pain shot up through my legs into my heart.

But no . . .

Still wasn't any worse.

I stood in that puddle for what seemed like an hour and watched the water drip off his face. Funny, I'd never seen him wet before. It made him look sweet and vulnerable, like a sad little dog.

I thought for a moment how nice it would be to be a raindrop stuck in one of his lashes.

He stood in a puddle of his own and stared back at me. He looked like he wanted to say something. Like maybe he was drowning, too, and that soon the rain would wash him down the drain, as well, and this might be his last chance to tell me. . . .

"I miss hanging out with you," he finally said, instead.

"Me too."

Then: "I'm sorry, Billy," he said quietly, and I believe he was.

"Me too," I said, and I know I was.

Now, if I were Audrey Hepburn and he were George Peppard, and life were *Breakfast at Tiffany's,* this would be the part where he tells me that people really DO belong together, that I belong to HIM, then we'd find our kitty cat in the garbage can and all kiss happily ever after.

But you know what? Despite the superficial resemblance, I'm not really like Audrey Hepburn at all. And he's no George Peppard, I'll tell you THAT.

There was another extended pause, but I felt like the moment was just about over.

Maybe he just needed an epilogue. Maybe he just needed to see me one last time to solidify something inside of him. Harden his heart against me. Make sure it was really over.

Whatever.

"Well, see ya . . . ," I said, and turned to go back inside. I didn't want him to see how heart-smashing it was to see him again.

He grabbed me. Stopped me. Pulled me back. Held on tight.

He had things to say. Things that had been building up for a long time.

"Billy, wait!" he cried. "I'm sorry . . . about everything. . . . I didn't want to hurt you. I . . . I wasn't tryin' to lead you on. I wish things were different. I wish I could tell you . . . what I . . . how I . . . the truth about . . ."

He let go and looked at the ground. "I'm so miserable," he choked, followed by an even more surprising statement, and in an even more strangled voice: "I wish I was more like you."

It was a stunning thing to hear. And if he'd only said it a few weeks ago, a few months ago, it might have changed everything. That Flip Kelly wished he were more like me! That he admired me!

But no.

Too late.

"You're just so strong, you know," he continued. "The strongest person I ever met. You just don't care. You're you, you know, and that's all there is. Jesus, if I had your balls, maybe then I could tell everybody to go to hell. . . . Maybe then, you know, we, you and me . . ."

Too late, too late, too late.

"Oh, Flip," I sighed. "Look, I'm sorry it all came down like it did, too. I wish things were different. I wish YOU were different. But life goes on. The dogs bark, and the caravan passes. I'm in a different place now, too. I feel sorry for you, Flip. You have a long road ahead of you. There's a lot you need to come to terms with. And that's YOUR journey, not mine. You're right: I know who I am. I know what I want. I've been through all that already. And I hope someday you find out who you really are, too. But until then, you're just always going to be trapped under everyone's expectations. Who knows, though. Maybe someday you'll find someone or something you want badly enough to finally give it all up for. Maybe that's what it will take to give you back your life."

There. It was over. Finally over.

Turns out, it was ME who needed the epilogue. ME whose heart needed to solidify. ME who needed an ending.

I started to walk away. And as I did, the camera pulled back, way back, until I was just a tiny speck walking in the rain. It was dark and cold, and I felt very alone. My eyes were full of rain. I started crying, and some-where in Outer Slobovia (where my life is the top-rated nighttime soap opera), the audience cried with me.

I really loved him, you know.

XXXVIII

THE PREGAME SHOW

It's here!

It's finally here!

The big parade! It's time for my float!

WHEEEEEEEEEE!

And, oh! I DO love a parade!

Seventy-six trombones, and all that!

Look around!

The majorettes in their kicky little tap suits—who DOESN'T want to be one? They are absolute FASHION ICONS, I tell you. The glittery, unsung goddesses of the Astroturf!

And the baton twirlers! SQUEEEEAL! Such skill! Such fun! And so thrilling!

Then there are the marching bands! And the flag-wavers! (The color guard?)

And, oh, the music and the bright stadium lights and the cheers from the people in the bleachers, AND THE CONFETTI! AND THE POM-POMS!

OH! It's almost TOO MUCH!

I could go on. I won't.

But now! to actually BE A PART OF IT!

I'm blessed. Truly blessed.

Why, I feel just like the pope in the popemobile, but pretty, you know, and about 173 years younger. And not evil.

So, maybe not.

Or Jackie Kennedy in her pretty pink suit, waving from the backseat of her convertible, with her husband by her side and . . . oh. Um. Yeah. That didn't end well.

I know! Of course! I'm Cinderella in her horse-drawn carriage! Yes, of course! The spitting image! They say the resemblance is amazing! And WAIT until you see my gown! But . . . hmmm . . . come to think of it, the whole carriage thing didn't end well for Cinderella, either.

Oh, dear. Do these things EVER work out right?

NO, NO, DON'T WORRY. I'm not foreshadowing or anything! I really don't know! I was just asking!

It's about to start.
BOOM-BOOM-BOOM!
DUM-DIDDY-DUM!
HERE WE GO!

First comes the marching band, all rip-roaring and rum-pum-pum, you know, then the color guard, with their flags waving, and the majorettes, all majorly being majoretty, et cetera, et cetera, and it's all JUST GLORI-OUS, of course. Rousing and really rah-rah. AND BLAH BLAH BLAH.

Then:

"Ladies and gentlemen," boomed the voice of Principal Onnigan. "Welcome to the Dwight D. Eisenhower Academy homecoming game preshow! I know how excited everyone is, so without further ado, I present the parade of floats, made by your homecoming queen candidates. First up, we have candidate number one: Miss Henny Nickerson . . ."

Henny's float was on a hay trailer, and pulled by a golf cart.

On the flatbed of the trailer, Henny had constructed a miniature racetrack—*oh, what a surprise*—"the Eisenhower Derby," she called it. The horses were labeled KNOWLEDGE, SPORTSMANSHIP, SOCIAL SKILLS, SCHOOL SPIRIT, MORAL CHARACTER, and FAITH. The finish line was GRADUATION, and the prize was a laurel of HAPPY MEMORIES TO LAST A LIFETIME!

Her motto was BETTING ON YOUR FUTURE!

Which made everyone absolutely HURL over the side of the bleachers. Now do you see why nobody likes her?

"Next up, we have candidate number two, Miss Alma Doty!"

There was polite applause as Alma rounded the gate.

Alma, poor dear, had obviously *really* struggled with her float. And obviously struggled all by herself.

On her undecorated flatbed she had arranged her entire Beanie Baby collection—all 1,375 of them—into the shape of a heart. And her motto FRIENDSHIP NEVER ENDS was written in Magic Marker on shelf paper and taped to the side.

Oh, if only she'd consulted me! I would have told her, straight up, yo, that quoting the Spice Girls is so last century! Rival or not, I would have helped her. Nobody should have to endure the chilly reception her float received.

I don't know why she just didn't ask her fellow shadow kids to help out.

Lynnette's float was next.

"Ladies and gentlemen," Principal Onnigan announced over the loudspeaker, "our number three float and third contestant for homecoming queen—Miss Lynnette Franz!"

There was a burst of expectant applause that quickly sputtered to a lukewarm half-clap once her float actually came through the gate and rolled into view.

Yes, that initial "Ahhh!" was demoted to an "Uhhh" once folks got a good look at it.

"Oh . . . well . . ."

"Um . . . wow . . . okay . . ."

"It's . . . not terrible. . . ."

"No, no . . . the colors are really . . . matching. . . ."

"And SHE looks beautiful!"

"Oh, yeah!"

"She's a pretty girl, no doubt about it. . . ."

"NO SIREE, no doubt about it. . . . And the float . . . it's . . . GOT FLOWERS!"

Let's see:

Lynnette's float consisted of a flatbed platform decorated with swaths of white satin fabric draped like a garland around the sides, some twisted crepe-paper streamers (in red, white, and blue), a carpet of store-bought floral sheeting, and dozens of droopy, partially deflated balloons bobbing behind. . . .

The banner read, simply: TRADITION.

There was a small elevated platform on the flatbed, where Lynnette stood, surrounded by her coterie of loyal, royal attendants—the court of Tiff, Sissy, Baba, Betsy, and Violet, all dressed identically in taffeta gowns of the deepest mulberry, with baby's breath in their hair.

Lynnette waved regally to all the little people and continued to smile prettily, even as she became increasingly annoyed by the lack of thundering ovation that greeted her float's appearance. THIS WASN'T HOW HER FANTASY WENT, Y'ALL.

But here's the thing:.

This float is meant to be your legacy. It should be the ultimate expression of WHO YOU ARE, and the culmination of all your hopes and dreams and heartfelt artistic yearnings! Yes!

In short, it should be "you," but A BIGGER YOU! A BETTER YOU! YOU BEYOND YOU!

So, BY GOD, it ought to be memorable!

So that's why there was such a peevish reaction from the crowd to that rickety little rickshaw she trotted out.

These folks expect a SHOW! They want to be WOWED!

I mean, DEAR LORD, she's only been planning this since SEVENTH GRADE! Is it too much to ask for a little effort?

And if they can't be dazzled by her creativity or moved by her passion, at least they should be amused by some little in-joke or clever cultural reference.

AT THE VERY LEAST, it should include a passing reference to the Manatees, DON'T YOU THINK?

But this . . . THIS? THIS! THIS was beyond boring!

It was pitiful.

AND LAZY TO THE POINT OF LAUGHABLE.

She obviously didn't try very hard. She had obviously used all her "float time" to gossip about who would be wearing what and taking whom to the big dance.

Or maybe she just had such a high opinion of herself, or thought she was such a shoo-in, that she imagined her mere presence in a pretty new dress was enough to win the popular vote.

But now, as her float rolled ominously past the crowd, Lynnette dropped the smile and wave and, instead, scowled hatefully to friends and longtime supporters. They responded with a few hollow "Hey girl!"s and "Lookin' hot!"s. But this halfhearted show of enthusiasm wasn't enough to negate what was already going down in academy history as a social disaster of unparalleled proportions, and one that Lynnette Franz couldn't possibly recover from.

Her float totally Britney'ed, y'all.

"I knooooooow. Can you imagine? She must've just wanted to diiiiiiiiiie!"

XXXIX

The crowd didn't have too long to dwell on it, though.

Because . . .

TOOT! TOOT!

Rumble, rumble.

There was a commotion at the gates.

The stadium lights went down.

There was a crackle on the P.A. system, followed by a sharp squelch.

In the bleachers everybody turned and strained to see what was going on. Some people stood. Others took out their binoculars. "Here comes the drag queen," they whispered to one another. "Now THIS is going to be a show!"

"Ladies and gentlemen . . . ," Principal Onnigan began in his slowest drawl—and the crowd began clapping slowly, rhythmically . . .

Clap . . . clap . . . clap . . . clap . . .

"I now present candidate number four. . . ."

Clap . . . clap . . . (a little bit faster now).

Now add foot stomps, too.

"Riding in float number four . . . ," he said, his voice rising, too.

Here, Principal Onnigan paused to let the clapping grow faster, faster.

Louder, louder.

Clap! Clap! Clap!

"HERE COMES BILLY BLOOM!"

CLAPCLAPCLAPCLAPSTOMPSTOMPSTOMP!

The crowd went ballistic. COMPLETELY AND UTTERLY BALLIS-
TIC! People cheered. Flashbulbs pop-popped. News cameras began
rolling.

For me!

FOR ME!

I can't tell you.

(CHOKE.)

I can't tell you what it meant. . . .

I looked out from behind the banner and saw what looked to be
hundreds of Scarlet *F*s waving in anticipation of my arrival. Like a
bright field of Jujubes.

I saw the faces, I felt the love, and I was finally, finally accepted.

And for that moment, for the first time in forever, I was happy as a
fly in a pie. Yes, I was.

HONK! HONK! HERE I COME!

I came crashing through a giant paper banner that read INVASION
OF THE SUPERFREAKS! in ten-foot letters.

The audience gasped when they realized I was driving a giant purple platform shoe! YES!—13 feet 6 inches tall! A tricked-out lawn tractor, built up with chicken wire, smoothed over with papier mâché, and
covered with glittering paillettes, how about that?

I stood at the front of the shoe, with the steering wheel in the middle, smiling and waving as I zipped toward the crowd at a consider-
able speed. LOOK AT ME! Dressed in my Superfreak costume, my
purple sequin suit, with its red wig and yellow cape fluttering in the
wind behind me. I was every inch the conquering hero!

WHEEE! HONK! HONK!

But wait!

There's more!

Behind me, spilling out into a V formation, were DOZENS OF MINI-ME'S! (Yes! I'm not hallucinating or making this up!) in SMALLER PURPLE PUMPS, made from shopping carts instead of lawn mowers but built up the same way! They knelt in the carts while being pushed by EVEN MORE MINI-ME'S!

Yes! I KNOW! IT'S NUTS! IT'S INSANE!

They were shadow students—all of them dressed in re-creations of the various outfits I'd made infamous: New Wave pirates, swamp zombies, Zelda Fitzgeralds, She-Hulks, and bloody prom queens, their identities suitably obscured.

SO IT WAS A SORT OF COSTUME RETROSPECTIVE! YES! . . . "THE BEST OF BILLY!"

Some carried signs: ALL HAIL QUEEN B!! LET BILLY BLOOM! and SUPPORT YOUR LOCAL FREAK SHOW!

Almost all wore Scarlet *F*s.

Now, just imagine the sheer fabulosity of the scene, so far . . . the spectacle of almost two dozen stiletto-driving Billy Blooms that have all but run amok on the football field . . .

Oh, and on the Jumbotron: EXCELSIOR, O LUSUS NATURAE! or "EVER UPWARD, O FREAK OF NATURE!"

As if in a dream . . .

I circled the track one last time in my purple pump-mobile—

Smiling and waving for my victory lap. . . .

Yes, yes, look at me: dressed proudly in my Superfreak costume . . . with the best of my other outfits trailing behind me in a V . . . listening to the magical applause from the crowd.

Truly, I had reached nirvana. This was heaven on earth.

All in all, I'd say things were looking up for me.

XL

The game. WELL.

The game. HMMMM.

Uh . . . yeah . . . well, ABOUT THAT . . .

You're probably expecting me to tell you what happened, huh?

YEAH.

That's not going to happen.

And I'll tell you why.

I don't know what happened.

In case you haven't noticed, I'm a bit of a sissy. It's true.

I know football like a frog knows bedsheets.

In other words: I'm no FRANK GIFFORD. Hell, I'm not even Kathie Lee.

I mean, I'd love to be able to tell you that *in the third quarter, on the fourth down, at the fifty-yard line, Bib did a dropkick and Flip drove it past the line of scrimmage to the end zone to complete the pass and win the game.*

Or whatever.

But no. I can't. I'm sorry: I don't speak heterosexual.

And don't forget: I had just scored a major social coup. I was delirious. So happy, in fact, that my spirit had left the planet altogether and was tumbling through constellations. I had absolutely no intention of ever coming back to earth, let alone coming back to watch a football game! So my eyes were on the game, sure, but my brain was off swimming through the star clouds of Alpha Centauri!

And if it were up to ME, I'd just end the story back at the float competition. Go out on a high note, you know? THANK YOU AND GOOD NIGHT! Why take chances when you're as happy as that? That was just the HIGH POINT OF MY LIFE back there. Nothing, ever again, can come as close. So why even try?

But (*sigh*) that isn't an option, is it? Life did not just come to a happy halt after my moment in the sun.

No, no, it kept marching right along. And now there's still the big game, still the dance, then the coronation and the happily-ever-after to get to.

So, okay, damnit.

Let me see.

Let me try.

Okay, I'll do my ding-dong Billy-best to relay to you the events of the big game.

Because it's sort of important.

Well, it's actually PIVOTAL to our story.

So let me close my eyes.

And go back . . . back . . .

REALLY CONCENTRATE. . . .

What do I see?

Tight ends.

MMMMMMMM.

Tight ends in a big huddle.

I see the Okeechobee Beefsteaks—like battering rams. Like charging bulls.

I see the Beefsteaks ALL OVER our boys. Taking them down.

Tackling. Toppling.

On top of Flip. ON TOP OF FLIP?

I see worried faces . . .

. . . frantic cheerleaders . . . .

I hear the groans from the fans growing louder, more desperate. . . .

I see Dottie Babcock and the God Squad on their knees in the bleachers; I hear them singing "Onward Christian Soldiers" and praying to Jesus to "please protect our boys and give the evil Beefsteaks a pox, a plague of boils, preferably by the next quarter, and please let Flip be Your humble servant and, through him, guide the Manatees to a victory, in Your name. Amen."

And here's where I wish most of all that I could tell you exactly what happened.

Because there were only a few seconds left on the clock.

Fifteen seconds (that lasted twenty minutes, but don't get me started . . .).

We were behind by three points.

In the bleachers everybody was standing. Leaning forward. Mouths open.

Tense. Tenser. Tensest.

Hoping . . .

For what?

A miracle?

Something that could save the game?

Hup! Hup! Here we go!

Manatees and Beefsteaks took their places near the finish line.

Heads down, asses UP.

Flip and Bib exchanged serious, knowing looks.

Bib touched his nose and right cheek. Flip nodded.

The referee guy waved his arms and blew his whistle.

And the clock started counting down again . . .

And . . .

KABLOOM!

Something happened.

A BIG something.

A complete and utter Manatee massacre, that's what happened.

My God, it looked like a Civil War battlefield out there. All our guys were down. Buried.

The Beefsteaks pulled off a collective stomp-down on their sorry, pretty-boy asses.

WHUMP!

And every single one of our boys disappeared under an avalanche of beefcake. Beefsteak. Whatever.

I couldn't see Flip. I couldn't see Bib.

Gone. Gone. They were all gone.

There was a hush.

Thirteen . . . twelve . . .

Nothing. Not a sound.

Not a whisper of a whimper.

Not a hint of sniffle.

Time slowed down, of course, to the melancholy drip, drip, drip that exists between two spaces when all hope has been lost. . . .

I wish I could tell you about that moment, that eternal moment when there's no good reason to continue on.

I wish I could explain to you how it happened; why it happened; what we all felt.

But even if I COULD tell you the details of that once-upon-a-time between thirteen and twelve seconds . . .

And even if it was a full-on, balls-to-the-wall, moment-to-moment, play-by-play account of what went down . . .

Well . . .

It wouldn't really matter.
Because I could NEVER—
NO, NEVER—
NEVER, EVER! . . . *POSSIBLY* . . .
Tell you about what happened NEXT!

I could NEVER do justice to this part of the story. If SHAKESPEARE, himself, came down from heaven with HOWARD COSELL at his side . . . and TOGETHER, they entered my body and took control of my mouth to tell the rest of the story . . . well, it still wouldn't do it justice.

You could never know the thrill that was felt when at twelve seconds . . .

There was a GRUNT!

And great movement from the bottom of a Beefsteak pile . . .

UP! CAME! FLIP!

WHAT?

YES!

He's UP and OUT, and SOARING toward heaven!

And we are now at ten seconds. . . .

See how bad I am?

Because here I've forgotten to mention that the ball was STILL IN THE AIR, still in play. Like a UFO or genie's head, it seemed to be hovering in place, hanging in a state of suspension. . . . Huh? I know . . . I know. . . . So clumsy. . . .

I'm not worthy.

My tongue isn't worthy of your noble ears.

But yes, the ball is still in the air, still soaring.

Still in play . . .

Nine seconds . . .

Nine . . .

Eight and a half . . .

And Flip leaps, lightning quick, UP from the pile, OUT from under. He reaches UP, UP, and grabs for the ball . . .

THE BALL OF DESTINY . . .

That has been waiting for him, waiting for him to recapture after all these years. . . .

And here is where Time did a nutty little twist on itself. It circled 'round and doubled back, and . . .

SUDDENLY, we were back to that *first* moment of Flip's *first* glory.

We were there and we were here.

It was all rolled up together.

We were existing outside the laws of reason. . . .

Flip was, once again and forever, a hero, our hero. 'Twas ever thus. He's always been there saving the day, and now so are we. He did it then, and he's doing it now.

Now and then and again.

One Flip. Forever and ever.

Amen.

Look at him soar! See the light in his eyes!

The flame of greatness burns so brightly in him!

He's soaring into the air again, OUR HERO!

Eight seconds.

YES. He reaches for the ball.

GO ON! GO ON!

HE REACHES OUT TO GRAB THE BALL.

YES!

AND HE ALMOST HAS IT! YES!

BUT!

BUT!

I can't tell you.

    I can't say it.

    No, and this time I really mean it.

    Oh. Oh. Oh, dear. Oh no. Oh my, oh my.

The horror! The shock!

    See here! See now!

    Flip trips, flops, and drops back to the ground.

Yes. That's right: Flip flopped.

    Jesus wept.

Flip fell to the ground.

    HARD.

    He hit the field, and there was the very loud CRACK! of something important being broken. Was that the shattering of a kneecap? The snapping of a femur? The hobbling of a foot? Whatever. He hit the ground, and his whole life burst into a million little pieces.

Funny, how life will do that.

    Funny, that it did that to Flip. Of all people.

    And us.

    Now. Just when we needed him most.

OH! OH! BUT NOW!

    RIGHT NOW!

    THERE'S MORE!

    We were all so focused on Flip, poor Flip and his doomed leap for the ball . . .

    We never even noticed that BIB . . .

    BIB! . . .

    Bib, TOO, had come up out of his own pile of Beefsteaks, just a few steps away.

And maybe it was because we failed Plane Geometry or were too intent on making Flip our hero once again, but it seems perfectly obvious NOW that the ball's trajectory was always out of Flip's reach, that he never even had a chance. BUT if you actually followed the ball's arc and did all the proper calculations, you would see that it WAS about to fall DIRECTLY INTO BIB'S HANDS!

Yes!

It's true!

And nobody noticed this!

Not one person!

Even as it was happening!

Why, even BIB looked at the ball that SUDDENLY, MAGICALLY, landed in his hands with all the shock of a man suddenly brought back to life.

Which he was?

He was.

He was given another chance.

Another shot.

And CRACK!

With six and a half seconds left—

He didn't think, he didn't plan.

He just reacted.

And he was OFF!

Yes!

Six seconds left! Just six seconds!

He was like a flood, a flash flood, racing, crashing, pushing forward.

Sweeping faster and faster across the field.

Unstoppable.

A force of nature.

Half running, half tumbling, half leaping, leaping . . .

Five . . . four . . . three . . .

Leaping, flying . . .

Two . . .

And as he slid into . . .

One . . .

The crowd went NUTS!

HE WAS SAFE!

The ball was in the zone, or behind the line, or past the marker, or he had slid into home plate, OR WHATEVER!

Apparently, he did it! He made it! He SAVED THE GAME!

And lo, there were great WHOOPS of joy, and savage WOOT WOOTs, and thrilling ULULATIONS that rang through the night air.

The dam burst. The crowd surged from the bleachers onto the field, past Flip, poor Flip, hobbled and humbled, alone and in need of emergency care—they ran onto the field and lifted Bib up and carried him on their shoulders.

Once again God had seen fit to bestow upon our school another miracle.

And now?

Now?

Bib was up. Flip was flat.

Sure, sure.

So, tell me: For a sissy-faggot who wasn't paying attention, how'd I do? Do I have a career in sportscasting?

XLI

And I watched all of this from the stands. Bib's victory wasn't mine to celebrate. No matter how joyous his mood, I deeply doubted that he would want me holding his butt in the air.

Besides . . . I have a dance to get ready for! And a victory of my own, hopefully, very soon!

I stood up, stomped twice to get my feet circulating again, and wondered if I should go offer my services to Flip. But then I saw an ambulance had arrived, and that the paramedics were already checking him out. And . . . hmmm . . . they appeared to be frowning at his foot. Which can't be good. So, no. Leave it alone.

I took a final glance at Bib, happily held aloft, receiving the glory he's certainly due, fending off the groupies, and suddenly finding himself the object of much interest to the dozen or so college football scouts who had come to check out Flip but decided that he was, in fact, the better catch.

Oh, poor Flip.

Poor little lamb . . .

Those scouts! This game! It meant EVERYTHING to him!

It was his WHOLE WORLD! The Twenty-Year Plan!

Why, he just lost EVERYTHING tonight! His WHOLE HOUSE OF CARDS came tumbling down on him!

I felt his horror.

I was gripped with sympathy panic.

His whole future had been unceremoniously ripped from him. . . .

WHAT WOULD HE DO?

WHERE WOULD HE GO?

WHAT WOULD BECOME OF HIM NOW?

I wanted to run over there. Help him through this. But no.

No.

He probably wants some time alone to process everything. He doesn't need me around right now. Poor little thing . . .

I looked over at him.

Then looked again.

What was *that*?

That *look*?

There?

That strange look on his face?

Was that . . . ? Was he . . . ?

HAPPY?

What? What?

Why, that's CRAZY TALK.

Why would he be . . . ?

But THERE IT WAS!

LOOK! LOOK!

A slight smile played upon his lips—yes!—even as he was lifted onto the stretcher. . . .

That was the look of happiness. Yes!

But why would he be happy? Had he lost his mind? Flipped his lid?

Or was it something else . . . ?

Look at him. That expression. There was something else. . . .

Something mixed in with that happiness. . . .

A slumping satisfaction, a loosening of tension . . .

RELIEF!

He was RELIEVED!

But why would he . . . ?

WHY, YES! OF COURSE! He was relieved because THE PRESSURE WAS OFF! HE CAN BE WHATEVER HE WANTS TO BE!

Then it all came pouring down on me.

Wait, Billy . . .

If that was true . . .

Think . . .

Think hard . . .
If he felt that way . . .
You think that he . . . ?
NAH.
He couldn't have . . .
He WOULDN'T HAVE . . .

Did he lose the ball on purpose?

Did Flip take a fall to free himself from that all-devouring future of his?

He looked over at me from across the field, and I looked wonderingly back at him. Before the doors of the ambulance closed, our eyes locked. He smiled. We connected. And I knew—yes, I just KNEW—that's exactly what had happened.

XLII

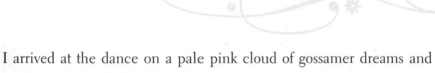

I arrived at the dance on a pale pink cloud of gossamer dreams and enchanted moonlight.

And my, but the gymnasium looked LOVELY! Just LOVELY!

I took a moment to soak up the decorations—the balloons and streamers and bubbles and disco balls—and thought, *DOESN'T IT ALL JUST SEEM MAGICAL?*

As I floated across the gymnasium floor I caught a glimpse of myself in the mirror, and had to remind myself to breathe, I WAS THAT GORGEOUS! Why, you've never seen such a vision of perfect beauty! I was the very essence of froth and fizz—YES!

I wore a sparkly, petal pink ball gown made of spun sugar and fairy's breath, simply too divine. My hair was artfully arranged in a fire fall of blazing red curls—and on top rested a crown of diamonds that reached to the moon! That's right! THE MOON!

I was a shimmering mirage, a glittering fancy. . . .

Glinda the Good Witch can EAT MY DUST!

I swept grandly into the middle of the room so as to make a proper first impression.

The press had been awaiting my arrival, and they were not disappointed. I delivered all the tinsel and glamour they'd come to expect. I struck a regal pose, and the gymnasium erupted in a sea of flashes.

There was Clancy! "Oh, hello!"

And Medea! "How do you do?"

All the other local and statewide media. "Hey there! Hi there! Thanks for your support!"

The students all smiled and waved, and wished me luck.

I spoke warmly with fellow candidate Alma Doty, who wore a pretty olive green gown and nervously wished the night were over already.

I spied Lynnette and her royal posse of douche bag duchesses in the back corner, where they spent most of the night hissing and clawing and making everybody uncomfortable.

But for me the evening passed in a heavenly haze of "Good luck's" and "Go Billy's."

As the great moment grew closer, the crowd began to buzz with excitement.

At ten minutes to midnight, the four nominees were both brought onstage amidst a great swooshing of gowns.

Principal Onnigan walked to the microphone holding the name of the winning candidate in his hand.

A hush fell over the crowd.

"GO, BILLY!" someone shouted from the shadows, and a warm ripple of applause went through the crowd, setting off a fresh strobe of camera flashes. I smiled sweetly, while Lynnette's sweet, sweet smile momentarily flipped upside down.

"People, please," the principal shushed. "We'll all know in just a few minutes who the winner is, but first let me congratulate BLAH BLAH BLAH . . . the varsity football team . . . BLAH BLAH BLAH . . . Coach Carter for his unbelievable dedication BLAH BLAH BLAH . . . the decorating committee who did such a fantastic job . . . BLAH BLAH BLAH . . .

OH MY GOD, WILL HE EVER SHUT UP? . . . the chaperones . . . AND ON AND ON AND ON . . . the floor wax company . . .

WILL YOU JUST GET ON WITH IT?

". . . and what will surely go down in the academy's history as the most . . . colorful . . . homecoming race ever. . . . But now, the votes have been tabulated and you have all made your feelings abundantly clear. . . ."

I bounced up and down with anticipation.

"The winner is . . ."

I gave a big, fake I'm-so-worried smile and held my crossed fingers in the air.

". . . LYNNETTE FRANZ!"

And I squealed, and started my royal run toward the microphone to . . .

Um . . . HUH?

"HERE SHE IS, LADIES AND GENTLEMEN: LYNNETTE FRANZ, YOUR NEW HOMECOMING QUEEN!"

Lynnette gave me a solid push as she breezed past me, grabbing her tiara with a "Harrumph!" and nudging the principal out of her spotlight and away from her microphone.

The crowd, the hateful, fickle crowd, who just moments ago were MY friends, were on MY side, now applauded wildly for HER as confetti and balloons rained down from the ceiling.

And the press, who had seemed so pro-Billy, now all surged toward Lynnette, and gushed excitedly, and congratulated her on her win as they snapped pictures and got their quotes.

WELL, this was a surprise.

This wasn't how it was supposed to play out!

No, not at all.

"OHTHANKYOUTHANKYOUTHANKYOU!" Lynnette gushed, and suddenly the stage was infested with her royal court, shrieking and weeping and jiggling for joy.

I stayed glued to my spot, mouth hanging open wide, like a halibut. A big, twinkling halibut.

"What are you still doing onstage, Freak Show?" Tiff Tarbell hissed, and stomped on my foot with her heel. "You lost. It's over. Get down. Go away."

Oh.

Right. Sure. Of course.

Get down. Go away.

You bet. Sure thing.

I was shocked. Confused.

XLIII

I shuffled offstage, unnoticed, and slipped out the back door just as Lynnette began yammering on about what a clear message her victory sent.

I walked for a while in the pale moonlight—the loser fairy queen—and shimmered sadly, all by myself.

La la la.

SNIFF!

Right about now, I thought, Lynnette was probably dancing her first dance with her new king—and they were the happiest couple there, of course, of course.

The press was probably packing up. Movin' on! Story over! And with it goes my fifteen minutes of fame. Can you believe, after all that, not one of them even asked for my reaction? Not one picture was taken. I was yesterday's news. Literally. Even Clancy had deserted me in the end.

I was once again, quite suddenly, nobody.

I was, once again, out in the cold.

"SIC TRANSIT GLORIA! GLORY FADES!" I shout.

And: "THE CHEESE STANDS ALONE."

Funny how quickly it can all turn. One minute you're IT! The name on everybody's lips! You're a big to-do!

Then the next, it's "Billy WHO?"

Fame is a fickle bitch, that's for sure. You see it all the time. Doesn't matter who you are or how great your talent. The famous and the infamous. The great and the merely adequate. Bigger stars than you. And then?

Dust in the wind.

"Billy WHO?"

And for what? What's it get you?

So you make a big noise. Scramble to the top of the heap. You get your fifteen glorious minutes; you're a big wheel at the cracker factory. People worship you.

Vanity! Vanity! All is Vanity!

Where does it get you?

Sic transit gloria, my friend.

Look at me now: I feel completely destroyed—chewed up, digested, and then vomited back up again.

I don't know if I can just go back to the old Billy. I don't remember how to act in that world anymore. I've seen too many things, you understand. Like Icarus, I've flown too close to the sun. At seventeen

I've seen it all. I've been there, done that. Climbed the highest peaks. Scaled the loftiest heights. I'm like Eva Perón. (At least, the Madonna version.) I've seen the best and worst of humanity. I can't just start all over again, back at square one again!

I wandered farther from campus, deeper into the swamp.

XLIV

Now, I'm as plucky as the next girl . . .
And I WILL survive . . .
I know we all must cross the desert of our days, BLAH BLAH BLAH . . .
And "let each man skin his own skunk" and all . . .
YEAH YEAH YEAH . . .
And I TRY not to complain . . .

But sometimes . . .
Sometimes . . .
(SHAKES FIST AT GOD!)
(CRIES TO THE WIND!)
(FALLS TO KNEES IN ABJECT DESPAIR!)
Sometimes, I swear to God, it's like herding kittens—you know what I mean? I just can't keep it together. I can't hold on to it. The joy keeps slipping away.

And how DID Lynnette end up winning, anyway? Her float was just awful. Her speech sucked out loud. Half the student body hated her. The other half was scared to death of her.
And everybody SEEMED to be on my side.

I drove a shoe, for Christ's sake!

I wore a cape!

So what's up with her big win?

I guess no matter how much they came around, and how much everybody ended up liking me, it was still too much for them to vote for a
drag queen to represent their school. It was just too big of a leap.

I see that.

Well, of course they weren't ready for it!

It was a miracle that I'd gotten as far as I did! How could I have ever
even imagined I had a chance?

Lynnette SHOULD have been queen. She really did represent them.

I stopped for a moment to smell the night-blooming swamp roses before
spinning across a field of sighs.

As for me, it was never about actually BEING the queen.

It was about winning them over. Showing I was WORTHY of being
their queen.

And I did.

I got my support. My point was made. I won their respect. The sea
of Scarlet *F*s and the crowd's response during the parade were real. I
don't need a crown to be QUEEN OF THEIR HEARTS! And you
know what? I might not have won, but I broke down some barriers and
blazed a trail for the NEXT drag queen that comes along, so that she
can go farther and climb higher. . . .

And jumpin' Jesus—Lynnette has been on the campaign trail since
seventh grade. She wanted it so bad. So . . .

(*BIG SIGH.*)

She'll probably make a good queen.

Yes, yes, the voters probably sensed that it meant more to Lynnette,
and voted with their gut instincts.

I'm just going to vote for Lynnette, they all thought. *It's the right thing to do.*

And I'm cool with that.

Really.

⁓

I sat down to rest for a moment on a stump at the edge of a dark, wooded area.

And all of this would be just fine and dandy, and I could happily concede defeat in a well-fought battle and be completely dignified in my defeat, and then we could all have a big *7th Heaven* ending, if only . . .

If only . . .

If only Sissy and Violet hadn't snarled at me the way they did, and Lynnette hadn't snatched the crown with such an irritated snarl like she did, and Tiff hadn't stomped on my foot the way she did, and Clancy hadn't so completely abandoned me the way she did. They all just twisted the knife, didn't they, like a goddamn corkscrew.

Why do they all STILL have to be so nasty? Even in victory? They're just incapable of change, aren't they?

It just shows you, you NEVER know. . . .

It's like I said before—one minute, you think you've got it all fig-ured out, and things are going great, then in an instant everything can turn. . . .

Crackle, crackle.

What was that?

Is anybody there?

Anyway. As I was saying, things can just turn on a dime.

Rustle, rustle.
  Crackle, rustle.

There, again! I totally heard something.
  Was there something in the bushes?

Crackle, crackle.
  Shuffle, shuffle.

Louder. Closer.
  Hello?
  Someone there?
  I pushed aside some brush and leaned in to take a look.
  Nothing but the moon. . . .
  No, wait!
  That's not the . . .
  There was a loud WHOOSH! and THUD! as something FLEW
OUT OF THE SHRUBS and tackled me, and quickly pushed me to
the ground, and then this something, or someone, clocked me on the
head—With what? A rock?—before dragging me into the dark under-
brush.
  It all happened so fast, in the beat of a black heart. . . .

It seems the blow to my head knocked all thoughts out my ear.
  My head was still cloudy.
  My vision was wavy.
  I couldn't tell what was happening.
  Everything was muddled, like I was buried in pudding.
  Was it a bear?
  A mountain lion?
  Oh my God—a GATOR ATTACK?
  What was on top of me!
  What? What?

And then it was ANOTHER few minutes before my eyes adjusted to the dark and I could see the face of my attacker. . . .

CREEPIN' JESUS!

WHAT THE HELL!

Bernie Balch! Yes! Drunk as a lemur! Straddling my chest, and pinning my arms above my head. Muttering darkly in my ear. His rancid, whiskey breath making me gag. Practically lying on top of me, trapping me completely.

Well, it was the very LAST thing I expected.

"WHAT ARE YOU DOING?" I screamed. "GET OFF ME!"

That's when he BIT ME. Yes, BIT MY NECK, which I thought was an odd method of keeping me in line. In fact, everything about this was weirdly off-kilter. From the way he had me pinned, and the way he was breathing so heavily on me. Then there was the way he was looking at me. Well, I was confused, as well as scared. VERY WEIRD.

I've been fag-bashed before, and, sir, this was no fag-bashing.

I looked up at his perfectly round, perfectly flat face, like a bad moon rising, and wondered what the hell was going on.

What was HE doing in the middle of the Everglades at one in the morning?

I listened as he continued to whisper hoarsely in my ear. He muttered vile, dirty, and disgusting things that I'm much too much of a lady to reprint here. Suffice to say, he was laboring under the delusion that I found him attractive. *BLECH!*

I hocked up a loogie and spit it at him.

Which only seemed to excite him more.

He leaned into my face, closer, closer . . .

He shut his eyes . . . and opened his lips, slightly. . . .

EW . . . HE'S NOT! . . . OH MY GOD!

He KISSED me.

Yes, on the lips.

With a groan.

He jammed his hard, dry little tongue into my mouth, and I gagged. I gagged. I almost threw up in his mouth.

I tried to scream, but my mouth was lost under his great, gaping brute-hole.

I'd rather suck on a bedsore than have his tongue in my mouth! *ECH!*

That's when it came into focus.

The big picture!

What was really going on here!

The things he was saying to me . . . What he wanted to do to me . . .

It was familiar; I'd heard it before. . . .

YES!

MY GOD!

It was Bernie! Bernie who was sending those creepy, anonymous e-mails! Bernie, who detailed the twisted and perverse things he wanted to do to me! It was Bernie, Bernie, Bernie, all this time, who hated me, not because I was gay, but because HE WAS! It was BERNIE, the latent homosexual who took out his self-loathing on me in biology, when ALL ALONG, THIS WAS WHAT HE REALLY WANTED!

All this time!

All that pain!

And it was never even about me?

My God! My whole world!

All that hate!

All that disgust and contempt!

And it had nothing to do with me!

Oh my God. I'm going to be sick.

What a waste!

What a wicked, wicked waste!

It can't be real. This can't be happening.

If kittens in catsuits started voguing on the flat surface of his face, I could sooner believe THAT was real.

Anything would be easier to comprehend.

Anything except this atrocity.

This monstrous miscarriage of humanity.

This man, this moon, this evil in the round.

This abominable piecrust. This leering, foul-mouthed "happy face."

And yet!

It is!

It is happening!

All the while, the vile mutterings continued. Things like: "You like this, don't you?" and "You want me!"

Lies. Vile, vulgar, horrific lies. All of it.

XLV

Teetering on the crack of doom.

World dripping red.

Red: like the fires of Mordor.

Like the dying sun of Krypton.

Suddenly I thought: *NO!*

Suddenly I decided: *NO MORE!*

Blood and fire and hate and rage . . .

Streaming through my veins.

There! My voice: "GET OFF ME!"

Now louder: "I SAID GET OFF, YOU FLAT-FACED SICKO!"
Adrenaline. Sweet, hot adrenaline.

I am angry now, oh so angry. . . .
She-Hulk angry.
SUPERFREAK angry!
And then I remembered!
I don't have to take this!
I HAVE THE POWER!
And then . . . oh yes . . . OH YES! . . .
HERE HE COMES!
HERE COMES SUPERFREAK!
Yes, I am Superfreak. I am here and I am mighty. I am all-powerful.
I am the rainbow flag made flesh. I am dignity and strength when all
is gone.
And you'd be wise to watch out, Bernie Balch, because I AM
PISSED.

I suddenly had the strength of A HUNDRED DRAG QUEENS.

"YO, DEEP-DISH!" I yelled, and kneed him in the gut. When he
doubled over, I gave him an uppercut to the jaw and leaped to my feet.
"WELCOME TO THE FREAK SHOW, BITCH!
"YOU HUMP! YOU SWEAT STAIN!" I cried as I kicked him.
"YOU DISGUST ME! How dare you push yourself on me! I may be
gay, but I have standards. And you are a freak! A hobgoblin! A runty,
splayfooted hillbilly!
"You shouldn't have picked on me, you feeble maggot. How dare
you rip my costume, violate my person, and pollute my soul. You've
made a powerful enemy. For I am Superfreak, and I will not rest until I
avenge your trespasses!"
And I let him have it. I showed him the power of my fury.

When I was done, and my anger had been sated, I ripped some fabric from my already shredded gown (another one!) and bound his hands and feet together, leaving him hog-tied in the mud. I then made a gag for his mouth.

"Well, you're going to stay here in the mud until I feel like calling the police and telling them where you are. And that might not be for a few days. But when they do untie you, I guarantee that will be THE LAST good thing that's gonna happen to you FOR A LONG TIME. Oh, I AM filing a police report this time. Attempted rape, battery, attempted murder. . . . I'm sure I'll think of more. You shouldn't have messed with Superfreak, faggot!"

And I stumbled through the underbrush . . .

   . . . out of the darkness . . .

   . . . and into the pale, trembling moonlight . . .

                                             ∽

Running, running.

   Always running.

   One step. Two step. Three step. Four.

   "Yes. Sir! Yes, sir! Please, sir! More!"

What's the rush?

   Why the hurry?

   Bernie isn't going anywhere.

   You're safe.

Isn't it obvious?

   Don't you hear it?

   That voice!

   That horrible little voice!

   That one! There!

In the back of my head!
I can't escape it!

Growing louder. More insistent.
Then louder, louder still.
It's horrible, horrible.

And what's it saying?
It's telling you the truth, Billy! The terrible, awful, no-good truth!
Are you ready for it? Can you possibly face the stark, staring reality of
who you are and why this keeps happening?
Listen!
This is what it says:

Don't you get it? Don't you see? The chaos. The violence. It just keeps
coming. It never stops. The panic. The pain. It's all around you. It's
always all around you.
It's always out there. Somewhere out there.
Looming. Lurking. Ready to pounce.
You can't escape it. You never will. No matter where you run, where
you hide. It's who you are. It's what you do.

It's you, Billy! It's because of you!
You are a drag queen! It's your nature! You provoke. You expose. You
arouse and inspire.
You open wounds and push buttons and rattle cages.
You are a fire starter. A witch!
You unleash demons. You do! You do! You waken slumbering tigers.
You know you do!
It's the path you've chosen. The life you desire. It's in your designer
genes. Of course, few will understand. Few will follow. It isn't easy. You've
known that all along. That's the price you pay.

But the pain!

My God!

The pain you bring to yourself!

Is it worth it? Really, Billy? Look at where you are. Look at what it's gotten you. Do you enjoy it? Do you get off on it? You must. You must. On some level. My God, you invite it in. You court it. Like a lover. You feed off it. Because it's always there. Always all around you.

Martyr! Masochist! Fret-monkey! Pain-monger!

Wound-gatherer!

Yes!

You hoard it. You take it in. Like you deserve it. Like you feel you have it coming. Why is that, I wonder?

And so it goes. On and on. For the rest of your life.

Stop.

Drop.

Hit the ground.

It was all true.

There was no use fighting it anymore.

There would be no more moving on.

No more forward motion.

Not until I faced this one last enormous truth:

It's never going to get easier for you, Billy. The world is going to keep on throwing things at you. These moments are going to keep coming, and it's how you react to them that define you.

You can be a martyr to a moment.

You can be a hero because of it.

You can become a prisoner to one that defined you.

Or a victim of it.
The choice is yours.

So there it was.
    There I stood.
    What to do? What to do?

XLVI

I sometimes dream that I can fly, that I am pushed off the ground like a cork in the water and I bob in midair. But if I think about it, if I concentrate on how I got there or what the feeling is, then it's gone and I fall back down. It becomes a game of not concentrating, of not paying attention. I can't allow myself to think about where I am or how I got there. Only when my mind is free can I soar again.

And so it was this time.
    I let it all go and was pushed up off the ground, propelled forward, set in motion. I was able to continue on as long as I kept my mind blank.

Free from myself.
    Free from my thoughts.
    My movements are automatic — left foot, right foot.
    Now stop. Now go.
    I moved forward, yes forward, always forward, and let my mind attach itself to each passing object.
    One car, red.
    Two cars, blue.

A store window. A street corner.

A man, just one man, with no connection to me, a man with no anger, nothing to inflict on me.

On the wall someone had spray-painted: "I love to hog space," and what could that even mean?

On the street a newspaper headline reads MAN AMPUTATES ARM TO GET HANDICAPPED PARKING SPACE, and I simply don't get it.

Keep moving. Keep on going.

You're almost there, now, Billy. Don't give up.

Go, Billy, go!

It's just up ahead. Past that light. The realization you've been searching for. The truth is right there in front of you now.

You're home, now, Billy. There it is. HOME.

Yes, in the door, down the hall, up the back staircase.

Then I crawled into my cupboard, my lovely old cupboard, and let the inky, black darkness cover me.

XLVII

ENDGAME

I was alone, walking through a beautiful garden that smelled like sleep. And an angel appeared in the garden—at least I think it was an angel. He was seven feet tall, covered in light, and moved in waves. He had glorious flaxen hair, liquid green eyes, and a sweet, sweet smile. He pulled me close and kissed me softly, just once, and then he was gone. . . . And after that I was falling, free-falling into nothing, without a center, without weight, down and down for such a long time, until suddenly

there were hands, hundreds of them, covering me, caressing me, lower-
ing me softly to the ground. I found myself in a place I had known once
before, but had somehow forgotten. Then a voice spoke to me; as gentle
as the rustling of leaves, it spoke in the language of the wind. And this is
what it said:

"Once upon a time, in the southern region of a dying civilization, there
lived an unhappy little drag queen who made his home amongst the
ruins and danced in the shadow of the night.
  "And it came to pass the end of a millennium. The stars decreed that
a freak should lead mankind into the light of a new age. That freak is
you, Billy Bloom."

And God said:

There is no right or wrong, Billy.
  I made it all up.
  No good or evil, either.
  It was all a joke.
  Mankind looked to me with such eager young hearts,
  And such eager young minds,
  How could I resist.
  I didn't even create this world.
  I just happened upon it one day
  While wandering through the universe.

Morality is your own invention.
  It's up to you.
  You must find your own path,
  And live with your own decisions.

There is no meaning.
  No purpose.

Definitions are useless.

Each moment arrives without form. Without reason.

It's up to you. Each of you. All of you.

To look at each new moment. Examine it. Fill it with reason. Give it a purpose. Give it meaning. Choose its path. Then let it go. Set it free . . .

"But God," I asked, trembling, "how do I bring reason to the anger and chaos, when its reasons are hidden from me?"

And God said: "You forgive."

And here's where I started to get on God's nerves: "But, begging your pardon, your Lordliness, but how can I forgive what I can't understand, and how can I understand what is hidden? I'm talking about Bernie here. And Muv. And Flip."

"Persistent little human, knowledge is overrated. Don't concern yourself with understanding the motives of others. You will never, ever succeed. It's not in your biology. And as for forgiving others . . ."

Here he paused to laugh. A mighty roll of thunder echoed throughout the garden.

"It's not up to you.

It's not even up to me.

There IS no forgiveness of others.

There is only forgiveness of self.

'EGOMET MIHI IGNOSCO.'

That's Latin, human: 'I myself pardon myself.'

Horace said it two thousand of your years ago, and it still holds true.

So, Billy, stop worrying about what others think.

Stop giving them power over your life.

Then, forgive yourself.

Stop straining to be something you're not.

Just relax and let you be you.

You are a magnificent experiment.
A whole new creation.
What's inside you is still entirely untested.
Go fly; see what you're made of. . . ."

Epilogue

I heard a knock on the cupboard door and awoke with a start. It was Flossie.

"I figured you might be in here," she said.

I climbed clumsily out and rubbed my eyes. *What was I just dreaming about?*

Oh well.

"I don't know what all happened last night, but you sure got everybody all worried. The phone has been ringing off the hook. The Plantation police called, your principal called, Clancy Duckett called, Mary Jane called fourteen times. Apparently, she's the one who found Bernie when she went out looking for you. She figured out what happened and called the police. He's in custody now. . . . Then there are messages here from someone named Bib. Someone named Bo-Bo. And here's Payton Mannes's. . . .

"And your father is just UP A STUMP, he's so frantic. He's been looking for you all night. He tried to find you after the parade, at the game . . ."

"Wait: DAD was THERE? At the parade?"

"Yes, and he was very proud of you."

I couldn't believe it! He drove out to see ME? KNOWING I would be appearing in public in drag? And he was STILL proud?

What a TRULY INSANE night it had been. All around. On every possible level. Literally, the best of times, the worst of times.

Flossie made some hot chocolate, and after I called Mary Jane and the detective back, I sat down and told her what had happened. I cleaned it up a bit, though, leaving out all the graphic details and any mention of Superfreak. I assured her I did NOT need to go to the hospital; I was fine, just a little sore.

"So . . . ?" Flossie asked as the conversation wound down. "That's the last of the Eisenhower Academy, I take it? Will you be homeschooled from now on, God help us all?"

I didn't even have to think about it.

"Oh, I'm going back," I said. "I'm not backing down now. Believe THAT. I'm going to finish out the school year, by God. Mary Jane and I are planning to meet with Principal Onnigan on Monday to set up a Gay-Straight Alliance. We set up the meeting last week, and I have a feeling that after tonight, we won't have any problems. I still have so much to do. I feel like the shadow kids need someone to guide them, and show them how to rebel for real. And I'm not going to rest until I'm sure that Bernie is held accountable for his actions. So, no, no, I'm making too much headway to give it all up now. I'll make my mark there, yet, by God."

"What about Flip?" she asked.

"Oh, I have a feeling it's not the end of THAT story, either. . . ."

"No. I mean, what do you want me to tell him? He's walking up the driveway right now."

FLIP?

HERE? NOW?

Oh my God, I look a fright! I've got twigs in my hair, mud in my drawers, and a thistle up my nose! There are rotting leaves in every crack and crevice on my body. And I'm still covered head to toe with the stink of Bernie Balch.

Looked frantically for beauty products.

Nothing!

Lord help me! I needed inspiration, QUICK!

I quickly scooped up some Crisco and used it as hair product, then dusted on some flour to powder my face. A little nutmeg as blush, some olive oil as lip gloss, and finally, I spritzed myself with lemon fresh Pledge.

Flossie watched, slack-jawed. "Oh, yeah, that's MUCH better," she said when I was done.

We both laughed.

NO TIME, NO TIME!

I ran and opened the door, and there he was! My old friend! My old hero! And just the sight these sore eyes wanted to see!

He, too, was battered and bruised, bless him, and was leaning on a crutch for support. But his eyes were clear and bright, and he was smiling, smiling at me, and the attention was overwhelming.

"You shouldn't be here," I said to him, and he said to me, at exactly the same time.

"No, you need to go to the hospital," we both said.

And "I heard what happened" and "I saw what happened" and "I'm so sorry" and "I can't believe it," at pretty much the same time, but pretty soon we were both laughing at our seriously traumatic, life-changing nights, and I was helping him up the stairs, practically carrying him.

"You poor thing," I said, and fluttered around him, making a big, embarrassing fuss over him. Should that foot be elevated? Did he need some water? Aspirin? And where was that footstool?

"Billy! Billy! Stop!"

He made me sit and tell him what happened in the swamp last night.

So I told him about Bernie, and not the sanitized version, either. I spared nothing. Not one detail. And Flip got so mad and so upset and punched the air and wiped away tears and swore a blue streak and promised me a hundred times that Bernie would pay for this, by God, and how much he wished he had been there to stop him and help me. And you should have seen how proud he was of me for fighting back, yes, and even more so for kicking his goddamn ass.

Then, finally, when we had finished with all that . . .

He looked tenderly into my eyes and told me he had another reason for coming here, today.

"I had to see you. . . . I need to tell you . . .

He grabbed my hand and held it tight.

I held my breath and tried not to fly up to heaven, or burst into flames, or dissolve into a puddle of goo.

No, now was not the time to have an aneurysm or spontaneously combust.

He looked deep into my eyes and told me that he HAD thrown the game, just as I suspected. He said that he lost the ball on purpose, and it was the best thing he'd ever done.

"I did it for you," he said, and my head began to swim.

The air began to sparkle.

What? Why?

I couldn't . . .

quite . . .

breathe. . . .

He couldn't stop thinking about what I said the other day, about someday finding someone important enough to give it all up for. . . .

"You were right," he said. "And I did it for you, Billy."

"What are you talking about?"

"It's you. It's you. You're the one."

And he pulled me into a kiss.

Happy, happy, finally happy.

And there were fireworks and rainbows and a hail of "hip, hip, hooray's" as church bells rang and the whole world cheered and danced in the streets. Yes, there was peace on earth when love saved the day and Flip and I lived FABULOUSLY ever after.

Well, of course!